BRENDÁN

BY MORGAN LLYWELYN FROM TOM DOHERTY ASSOCIATES

Bard
Brendán
Brian Boru
The Elementals
Etruscans (with Michael Scott)
Finn Mac Cool
Grania
The Horse Goddess
The Last Prince of Ireland
Lion of Ireland
Pride of Lions
Strongbow

THE NOVELS OF THE IRISH CENTURY

1916: A Novel of the Irish Rebellion
1921: A Novel of the Irish Civil War
1949: A Novel of the Irish Free State
1972: A Novel of Ireland's Unfinished Revolution
1999: A Novel of the Celtic Tiger and the Search for Peace

BRENDÁN

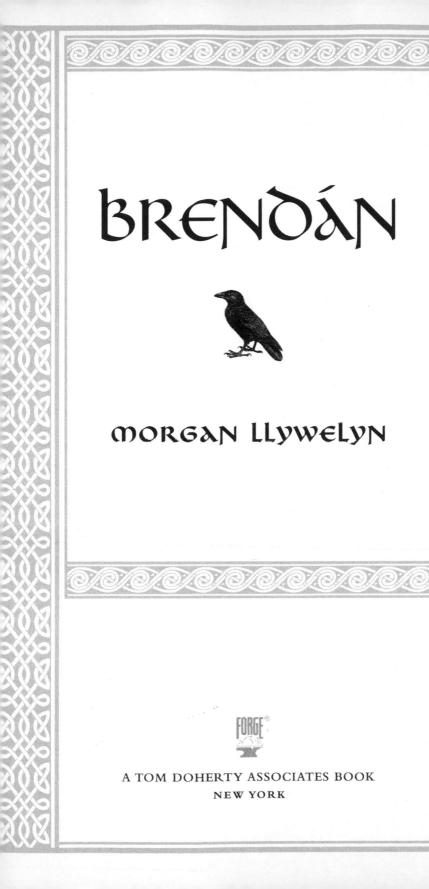

MORGAN LLYWELYN

A TOM DOHERTY ASSOCIATES BOOK
NEW YORK

This is a work of fiction. All of the characters, organizations, and events portrayed in this novel are either products of the author's imagination or are used fictitiously.

BRENDÁN

A Forge Book
Published by Tom Doherty Associates, LLC
175 Fifth Avenue
New York, NY 10010

www.tor-forge.com

ISBN 978-0-312-86099-8

First Edition: February 2010

Printed in the United States of America

0 9 8 7 6 5 4 3 2 1

For Seán,
Ruth Knott Hapgood,
and,
always and forever,
for Charlie

BRENDÁN

PROLOGUE

I had prayed long and deep. Bare bony knees on cold stone floor; tonsured head bent over folded hands. Day and night and day again.

At last I arose, rather stiffly I confess, and summoned fourteen members of our community: Gowrán, Colmán, Tarlách, Moenniu, Dianách, Liber, Sechnall, Anfudán, Eber, Cerball, Aedgal, Crosán, Machutus, and Fursu. When they had joined me in my private oratory I closed the heavy oaken door. Locking a vision inside.

"Brothers," I said, "I speak to you as the Abbot of Clonfert, but also as your friend. We know each other well and I trust you completely. For now, what I am about to say must be for your ears only. It could amount to nothing or it could be something wonderful. Either way, we should go a little farther along the path before we say anything to the rest of the monastery."

The fourteen nodded solemnly.

I continued. "My kinsman Fionn-barr has told me of a discovery made by his son Mernoc, who is the steward of Christ's poor in Altraighe-Caille. While Mernoc was fishing in the Western Sea to feed his charges he . . ." I paused; said a silent prayer. Plunged ahead. "Mernoc says he has found the road to Heaven."

The assembled monks men looked startled, thrilled, or disbelieving. Each according to his nature.

Remaining calm myself—but only because I had taken considerable time to pray over this first—I went on. "Mernoc came upon a small group of islands which he is convinced mark the gateway to Paradise. He returned to Ard Fert and told his father, and Fionn-barr hurried here to inform me."

"That is ridiculous," Brother Tarlách said scornfully. "Did either of them offer any tangible proof?"

This was exactly the response I had expected of Tarlách. "Fionn-barr brought Mernoc's cloak to show to me," I replied. "In spite of the journey from Ard Fert to Clon Fert, the cloak is still permeated with the fragrance of those islands: a mingling of flowers and fruit and the very essence of spring which could only be the perfume of Paradise. I shall pass it among you so you can smell it for yourselves.

"Brothers, do you recall the ancient tales of the Isles of the Blest? I think they are more than legend, and Paradise lies somewhere in the Western Sea. I have my own reasons for believing this, private reasons. But I do believe. That is why I have sent for you."

The serene quiet of the oratory was replaced by the

tense hush of expectancy. The monks—even Tarlách—leaned forward to hear my next words.

"From you who are dear to me and have shared the good fight with me, I now seek advice. If it is God's will, I shall go in search of Paradise. What say you? What advice would you give?"

"Go forth, Brother Abbot!" they cried with one voice.

"And will you go with me?"

Thirteen replied without hesitation. "Brother Abbot, we have left our clans and given up our inheritances to follow you. Our future is in your hands. We shall go with you to death or to life, asking nothing but to obey the will of God."

Only Sechnall demurred. "I am the oldest monk at Clon Fert," he pointed out, "and such a voyage would be beyond my strength. I beseech you to take my nephew instead. Solám is sturdy and devout, a better man than me."

"There is no better man than you," I told him. "However I respect your wisdom. We will take Solám instead. A family should be guided by its elders, and we at Clon Fert are a family."

"A family of brothers about to embark on a great adventure!" cried Fursu, unable to contain himself any longer.

"And you will be our captain," Colmán added. The eyes of the erstwhile warrior met mine. Such clear eyes. So fearless.

I allowed myself a slight smile. "I believe 'navigator' is the more appropriate term," I said.

CHAPTER 1

Within a vault of bone the Navigator was thinking.

Not much else to do in your head when your eyes are closed.

He could hear, of course: the manic clamour of seagulls wheeling over the waves. Smell, most certainly: the pungent odour of seaweed rotting on the strand. Feel the unyielding boulder beneath his buttocks and the unstable sand beneath his feet.

Mostly, he was thinking.

Yesterday a god spoke to me on the mountain.

No.

Yesterday the god spoke to me on the mountain.

No.

Yesterday God spoke to me on the mountain.

Brendán gave a bemused shake of his head. *Begin at the beginning, old fool,* he admonished himself.

The boulder on which he sat was one of many littering the beach, detritus left by the receding ice nine thousand years earlier. The glaciers were long gone but the sea continued to arrive. With every tide it stole more of the land, gnawing a wide circle of limestone out of the bay of *Tra Lí*. "Tralee" referred to the shore of a small river which ran into the sea at that point. A sparkling, laughing river, hurrying home.

Brendán rarely thought of himself as old; hardly thought of himself at all. He was unaware that his thick black hair had long since turned white. His leathery face was spiderwebbed with lines, but the muscular forearms resting on his sturdy thighs would have done credit to a much younger man. Within their frame of black lashes his eyes were still the blue of deep ocean.

Today those eyes were looking inwards. Brendán was preparing to write a journal—*iris* in the Irish language—a word which also could mean faith or belief. Over the years a number of people had urged him to make a record of his extraordinary adventures. He had always declined. Until yesterday. When the project became a compulsion.

The Will of God, that's what Íta would call it. Íta. He smiled to himself. *She is with me still, safe in my memory. Strolling beside a moss-embroidered stream, teaching a small boy the names of the birds and flowers.*

"Sister Íta, why is a rainbow?"

"Because God is laughing, dear heart."

My memory is a jackdaw's nest of trivia and treasures. Breathtaking adventures and the first drink of foaming milk still warm from the cow; awesome discoveries and the song of a bird on an ice-spangled morning; beauty and horror, grief and ecstasy. Ah yes, the ecstasy that seizes a man and lifts him like a hare in the talons of an eagle.

A large bird angled down from the sky, passing so close to

Brendán's head that he felt the turbulence of wings in the air. *There you are!* he thought with joy.

He opened his eyes.

And slumped in disappointment.

A cormorant had landed on a nearby boulder. The large seabird was standing upright with wings outstretched, balancing on stone as it had balanced on air. After a leisurely survey of its surroundings—and judging the man to be an object of no consequence—the cormorant settled down and began preening its dark feathers. Arranging each quill according to a precise pattern.

It's not you, of course. I should have known better. Brendán began arranging his thoughts into a pattern, which he then spoke aloud. "Life is a voyage from launching to beaching," he declaimed. His voice was hoarse from years of shouting into the wind.

The cormorant raised its head, revealing the cruel downward hook of its beak. Glittering eyes fixed on the man.

Brendán stood up slowly to avoid frightening the bird. "Our immortal souls are deposited in frail vessels of flesh that carry them for an indefinite amount of time. We passengers have no choice in the matter. We are taken wherever the unseen Commander sends us until we are forced to disembark."

The cormorant made a clucking noise.

I agree with you, bird. The whole thing does seem rather arbitrary. "Mine is that branch of the Celtic race known as the Gael. I was born in Kerry, the kingdom of Ciar, where the many of the Gael still held to the old faith. However my parents had been converted to Christianity. At my christening I was given the name *Braon-finn*, which means 'bright drop.'

Íta always called me "Braon-finn."

"My father was a grandson of Alta, of the kingly line of Fergus Mac Roy. I stress this for a reason. My calling demands humility, but anyone can make an earthworm abase itself. Great effort is required to persuade an eagle to acknowledge a higher authority."

Abruptly lifting his arms towards Heaven, Brendán exulted, "I have been persuaded! I have seen things few men have ever seen and learned that the limits of being are not what we thought they were!"

The cormorant gave a raucous screech and flew away.

Brendán sank back onto his boulder. *Was that a bad omen?* He could smell rain on the wind. And he was tired. His whole body ached, bone and muscle.

Don't give in to superstition or it will swallow you. Who said that? I'm not sure; time passes and faces blur into other faces and only the words remain.

In the beginning there was the Word . . .

"In infancy I was put out to fosterage," he said aloud, even though he had lost his audience. "My parents sent me to Íta, a devout Christian and the favourite daughter of a chieftain of the Déisi tribe. Íta had founded a small nunnery on the Meadow of Deep Soil and established a school for boys. In time the nunnery grew into an abbey of renown, but it is still known as *Cill Íde*—Íta's Church.

"One of my earliest memories is of the clear voices of women singing the praises of God in his house. The tiny chapel of the nunnery was built with smooth oak planks tightly fitted together and roofed with shingles of yew wood. The wood absorbed the music, resonating with it long afterwards." *Whenever I entered the chapel I could hear the walls singing.*

"Cill Íde was an island of stability in a sea of waving grass. Five round, timber-and-wattle huts were grouped around the chapel, like chicks around a hen. Íta and three more nuns slept in the largest hut; we boys occupied the others. Nearby was a rectangular structure that served both as our refectory and a guesting house for travellers. Food was prepared in a lean-to some distance from the chapel, and the clay ovens were even farther away, in case of fire." *I shall never forget the fragrance of baking bread.*

"A drystone wall protected the precincts of the nunnery from roaming cattle. The grassland beyond the wall was watered by countless streams which sought the River Shannon—'As our souls seek God,' according to Sister Fithir. South of the meadow, the knees of the distant mountains were blanketed with oak forest. When we were naughty Sister Fithir would point to those mountains and warn, 'God watches you from his high seat.'

"God so permeated the atmosphere of Cill Íde that I never thought to question his existence, but I was curious about everything else. While she was mending my sandals I once asked Sister Muirne, 'What is the sky?'

"Sister Muirne had long, graceful fingers. In the refectory she played the harp, music to make us feel hungry. She could also play music to put us to sleep. Hers was a wonderful gift. When rowdy boys listened to the voice of the harp they forgot their quarrels.

"In answer to my question Sister Muirne said, 'The sky is the roof God spreads over the world.'

"After pondering this from Terce to Sext, I sought out Sister Lerben, whom I found sweeping the earthen floor in God's house. Sister Lerben's red-knuckled hands were never idle. If there was no one to talk to she talked to herself in a rambling monotone.

" 'When will the sun and moon fall on us?' I asked the nun.

" 'They can't fall on us,' she assured me, without interrupting her sweeping. 'They'll be up there forever.'

"At Nones I approached Sister Íta, whom I considered the final authority on everything. In my earliest years I thought God must look like Sister Íta. She had square, competent hands, very clean in spite of all the work she did. I loved to watch those hands.

" 'The thatch roofing on the huts is full of insects that fall down on us,' I said. 'Sister Muirne told me the sky is the roof of the world, so is the sun a bee? Is the moon a beetle? Sister Lerben says they can't fall on us, but why not?'

"Laughter bubbled up in Sister Íta. 'Dear heart! What amazing notions you have. The sun and moon aren't insects, they're your Father's jewels.'

"'My Father?'

"'God,' she replied. Still laughing, she scooped me into her arms and hugged me tight."

I was pressed against a full bosom and softly yielding body. A heart overflowing with love beat close to my cheek, sharing the rhythm of life.

I assumed everyone was like Íta.

"In this happy nursery I grew from babe to boy, together with ten or twelve other lads of the warrior class. I did not know I was Sister Íta's foster child; I simply assumed she was my mother. Small children do not question the circumstances of their life, they accept them. Theirs is the earliest and purest faith.

Purity was important to Sister Íta; it was one of the virtues she urged us to cultivate. She did not explain what purity was, not to a crowd of scruffy little boys no higher than her hip. But if she loved purity, so did I.

I was not the best-behaved boy at Cill Íde, however. Should I mention that? Perhaps not. My tendency to act on intuition instead of obeying instructions will become apparent later.

"No wine would ever taste as sweet as the water from the nunnery's well. We ate chewy black bread and soft cheese made by the nuns' own hands, and imbibed their faith in a gentle Christ, the Lamb of God, along with our buttermilk. Before every meal we prayed to Our Father as Christ had taught. After every meal Sister Íta reminded us, 'God most loves a pure heart, a simple life, and open-handed charity.'

"Secure amidst all three, we fell asleep on pallets stuffed with fragrant grasses and awoke in the morning to the song of the lark. Looms humming and cattle lowing. Dust motes dancing in slanting sunlight. Order and calm and continuity.

I assumed the rest of the world was the same.

Fool that I was.

"The nuns, who referred to themselves as Brides of Christ, were all young women, and for a good reason. Establishing a nunnery demanded physical strength as well as moral conviction.

Íta was a true daughter of warriors, a strong, courageous woman. And a wise one. The older boys teased me about the dark until I developed a terror of it. Sister Íta told me, "There is nothing in the dark that isn't there in the light," and gave me a candle to put beside my bed. We lit it together from one of the candles in the chapel. "When you are ready, you can blow this out," Íta said. Not 'if,' but 'when.'

To justify her faith in me, one night I blew out my candle. Afterward I got up and felt my way around the hut, stumbling over my sleeping comrades. I found nothing that wasn't there in the light.

I never asked for the candle again.

"A local chieftain had been so impressed by Íta that he offered her a vast amount of land to use as she willed. She had accepted only enough for a vegetable garden and a field of grain. The nuns maintained their community without any outside help. They made the clothes and raised the food, ploughing the earth with a blind ox Sister Fithir had rescued from slaughter. On the open meadow they grazed a few cows for milk, and a flock of sheep. If the nuns were not at prayer or busy with the school they were collecting firewood or churning butter or spinning wool." *I learned to count by numbering the strands that made a bindle.*

Far out to sea the cormorant changed direction, circled back. Rode the wind until it hovered above the stony beach where the Navigator was composing aloud.

"The boys at Cill Íde were like the sons of privilege everywhere, bold by nature and unruly by preference. Sister Íta tamed us with gentleness. 'Always be courteous,' she insisted. 'Courtesy is the fat that flavours the meat of life.'

"The older lads were expected to learn Latin, the language of the Church; a discipline they resisted at first. But Sister Íta convinced them. 'Learning is the game we play for pleasure,' she said with a wink as if divulging a secret.

"Another of her sayings was: 'Jesus is the lord we follow for joy.' We boys exemplified the precept. Our days were spent running and laughing, hiding and seeking, pummelling one another indiscriminately, falling asleep on the grass, jumping up to start a new game. And I always in the heart of the pack. *Or was I? Even then, did I not tend to go my own way and think my own thoughts?*

"Herding mice in a meadow would have been easier than controlling us. The nuns did not interfere unless our rough-and-tumble antics turned serious. Then it was always Sister Íta who came at the run to wipe a bloody nose or dry furious tears. She never apportioned blame, but distracted us with a song or story until the quarrel was forgotten. Thus we were defended from one another. And from ourselves. Never again have I felt as safe as I did on the Meadow of Deep Soil.

"To each boy Sister Íta imparted the conviction that no matter his faults, he was loved deeply, permanently, and without qualification, by herself and God. She gave us a rock to stand on. My feet are planted there yet."

Brendán closed his eyes for a moment. *Alas, one cannot remain a child any more than the blackbird can remain in the egg.*

"In high summer men from Sister Íta's clan came galloping over the grassland to make any necessary repairs to the structure of the nunnery. Some were mounted on small horses whose tails had been dyed bright red or vivid blue. Those of higher rank drove wickerwork chariots decorated with plumes. *A good chariot was worth twelve cows.*

"The men's hair either streamed to their shoulders or was plaited into complex patterns and dyed like their horses' tails. Faces were clean shaven except for flowing moustaches, the emblem of the warrior class. Beneath their sleeveless coats they wore knee-length linen tunics dyed with saffron. Gold brooches fastened the mantles on their shoulders. More gold adorned their necks and arms, fingers and ears, until they gleamed like the sun. Gorgeous and gaudy and proud; warriors of the Gael.

"By contrast the nuns clothed themselves in grey wool, finely woven but absolutely plain. Their gowns hung straight from neck to feet. They possessed no gold or treasure of any kind. The priest who visited us to say Mass in the chapel even brought his own chalice and paten. Cill Íde was simplicity itself. Nothing in excess. The nuns spoke in low voices. In the presence of men they spoke more softly still.

"The other boys admired the warriors and followed them everywhere, imitating their bold swagger and brandishing spears made from branches. I was more intrigued by the foreign traders who occasionally visited Cill Íde. Ireland was the last port of call for men who plied the world's trade routes. They described the Irish as 'World Enders,' because there was nothing beyond us but the Great Abyss: the Western Sea that ran to the edge of the world and beyond. When the traders brought their exotic merchandise to our gates I was always wildly excited.

Sharp eyed, oily tongued men with wide smiles and extravagant gestures, they spoke with enviable familiarity of sunblessed Egypt and subtle Persia. I listened to them with my mouth hanging open like a gate.

"The traders exchanged worked iron and woven flax for the nuns' herbal medicaments and fine wool. They displayed jewels of jet and amber and malachite, and tiny sheets of gold leaf as thin as fish skin, but the nuns were not tempted. 'Desire only what you need,' was the rule at Cill Íde.

It's still a good rule.

"When she was with the traders Sister Íta's demeanour changed. She became the warrior she might have been; standing taller, shoulders back and chin lifted. She spoke in a firm voice and drove a hard bargain. The traders admired her for it. They called her 'The White Sun.'

At twilight other visitors—either three or five in number—occasionally approached the nunnery. Yet they never came as far as the wall. They stood off at a distance, silent within hooded robes. We boys could never get a close look at them. If we tried they melted away into the trees. When I asked Sister Íta about them she replied with a single word: 'Druids.'

The cormorant dropped like a spear from the sky, seized a hapless fish in its beak and flapped away.

A shudder ran up Brendán's spine. *When overtaken by its fate, did the fish feel terror?*

Chapter 2

Sitting at his table in the scriptorium at Clon Fert amidst half a dozen other monks painstakingly copying manuscripts, Brendán wrote, 'In my youth as now, Ireland was divided into five provinces. Each comprises a separate kingdom: Ulster in the north, Connacht in the west, Leinster in the east, and Munster in the south. Central to these like the hub of a wheel is the Royal Kingdom of Meath.' He paused to dip his feathered quill into the little pot of sticky ink. His eyes were smarting. The oil was smoking in his lamp, but it was hard to stop writing. The narrative had him in its grip and there was so much to tell. To explain.

Can any of it be explained?

'Gaelic nobility extends downward from kings and princes to the warrior aristocracy. The noble classes are bound by laws of reciprocal obligation. Tribal chieftains, who are lesser kings, are loyal to their provincial king and supply him with warriors on demand. In turn, the provincial kings pay tribute to a high king who rules at Tara, in Meath. Tara is the heart of Ireland, where five royal roads meet.

'Roads are of vital importance because they provide a network for trade through impenetrable forest and across dangerous bog. Provincial kings go to great trouble to maintain them; their personal honour is at stake. Honour is the foundation of Gaelic society and prestige is the mortar that holds our society together. Dispensing lavish hospitality is essential to maintaining prestige, so the kings build the most splendid hostels they can afford for travellers passing along their roads.'

Brother Tarlách leaned across Brendán's shoulder to squint at the words scribed on the vellum. His breath smelled of smoked herring. He was the only monk at Clon Fert who genuinely preferred fish to meat. "Is that going to be a spiritual apologia like Patrick's *'Confessio'*?"

Brendán laid down his quill. "I would not presume to emulate Blessed Patrick," he said gently. "This is merely an iris, a humble recounting of my experiences."

"You've been busy with it ever since we came home from Ard Fert."

"I have," Brendán agreed, hoping a terse reply would discourage further conversation. Tarlách could be a test of patience.

Undeterred, the monk went on talking. "Did I ever tell you that my father was a famous hosteller in Ulster? Every traveller in the north of Ireland took shelter under his roof at one time or another. You can ask me anything you like about hostel keeping; anything at all. Did you know that Brehon Law obliged us to keep three vats of drink filled and ready at all times? One with wine, one with ale, and one with buttermilk."

Suddenly Brendán's eyes twinkled. "Which one did you steal a drink from when no one was looking?"

"That's not very Christian of you," Tarlách muttered. He wiped his perpetually dripping nose on his sleeve.

Giving him a smile of childlike innocence, Brendán said, "I was only teasing you, Brother. I remember what it was like to be a young man. In fact many memories are coming back to me now and I'm eager to capture them, so if you'll forgive me . . . ?" He lifted his quill.

Tarlách continued to hover over him. "If you want my opinion, you should begin by describing the incident with Judas Iscariot. That was a lot more interesting than what you've written there."

Brendán put down his quill for a second time. "In a journal, Brother Tarlách, events are placed in chronological order."

"But aren't you telling what you remember?"

"I am."

"Then you can begin wherever you like. Memory skips around, you know."

"Perhaps you should write your own journal," Brendán suggested with what sounded like— but was not—infinite patience.

Tarlách straightened up. "I have enough work to do," he said indignantly. "You assigned it to me."

"Just so," replied the abbot of Clon Fert. Only two words, softly spoken. Yet this time Brendán put the invisible weight of his office behind them.

Tarlách returned to his own writing table. The Navigator went back to his journal.

When a monastic scribe copied any part of Holy Scripture he had to be mindful that it was the word of God. No monk would dare to correct God. But Brendán could correct his own work until it said what he wanted it to say. He relished the freedom such writing afforded, and accepted the discipline it imposed. Knowing he needed both.

Words . . .

On the walls of the scriptorium book satchels made of wood and leather, elaborately carved and ornamented with gilding, were hung from pegs to protect the precious sheets of vellum from damp. The air was redolent with timber and calfskin and inks. Old manuscripts and new. Sacred words and informative words. Words.

Words.

Brendán's fingers caressed the shaft of the quill before he wrote: 'Nunneries and monasteries also offer hospitality to those who seek shelter.' *From such chance visitors the boys at Cill Íde heard of flamboyant warrior kings who led huge cattle raids and stole other men's wives. Sadly for us, in deference to the sensibilities of the nuns, their guests never related any of the details. The only stories the nuns told us were about Christ and his disciples. When I pleaded to hear more about the warrior kings, Sister Lerben said briskly, "Christ is the King of Kings—that's all you need to know."*

Or did she say that? It sounds more like Bishop Erc.

A great yawn rose up in Brendán and forced his jaws open. He sprinkled sand on the written words to dry them and carefully cleaned his quill on a scrap of silk. Easing his tired body from the high stool, he made his way to bed.

Erc's memory followed him down the passageway like a shadow. A long narrow shadow that carried one shoulder higher than the other.

Tarlách's right about the way we remember things. It seems like only yesterday . . .

Erc, son of Daig and bishop of Altraighe-Caille, was a determined man. Being resolute was necessary for any disciple of Christ in a land that danced to a wilder music. For Erc it was imperative.

His father was a chieftain. Erc's greatest wish had been to be a warrior in his father's service, but a childhood accident left him unable to bear arms. He would never win glory on the battlefield. He could never be a hero in a land that celebrated heroes.

Although Erc was bitterly disappointed, there was another route to prestige. He possessed gifts of the mind sufficient to gain admittance to the order of Druids, the intellectual class of Celtic society. Members of the order were not practitioners of a specific religion, nor were they priests in the Christian sense of the word. The Greeks were more nearly correct by describing Druids as poet-philosophers.

A physical disability was no bar to Druidry. Erc could have become a teacher or historian or musician or satirist or student of the stars: all highly respected offices. But the innermost circle of Druidry was closed to him.

Chief Druids were those who, from childhood, had demonstrated an intimate awareness of the Otherworld. Its mysteries were not mysteries to them; its patterns were carved in their bones. They could move in and out of the realm of spirit, seeing that to which others were blind.

Erc lived only in the tangible world. He had to face the fact that he could never be a chief Druid, the equal of kings.

He did the next best thing, undertaking the arduous twelve-year course of study necessary to become a brehon, a judge and interpreter of the law. Brehons held the second-highest rank in Druidry. Erc's tribe had celebrated his achievement with a great feast. Warriors carried him on their shoulders. With more years of work he could gain the title of *ollamh*, the ultimate degree of learning. He was on the verge of a spectacular success.

When something unexpected had intervened.

Morning light streamed through the windows of the scriptorium, buttering the flagstones of the floor. Brendán wrote, 'In my fifth year at Cill Íde, Sister Íta told me I must go on a journey.'

In my excitement I tugged at her robe, the wool so soft to the touch. "Where? Where am I going?"

"To be with your people in Kerry."

"But you are my people."

When Íta smiled she had dimples in her cheeks. "We are all God's people, dear heart."

"Then why . . ."

The smile slipped from her lips and fell away. She looked stricken; I thought maybe it had fallen into the neck of her gown. "Because . . ." She folded her hands—the strong hands I loved—and said nothing else. She could not bear to hurt me.

Her reluctance conveyed itself to me. I took a step backwards—the first time I ever backed away from Íta, though it would not be the last. "I don't want to go anywhere else."

"You have to, Braon-finn. We must accept the Will of God."

"What's that?"

"The greatest of all the Mysteries," she replied.

I did not understand. I still don't. Faith must fill the gap of knowledge.

'My transport was a brightly painted wooden cart pulled by a shaggy pony with plumes in his mane. Three armed warriors acted as my escort. One stationed himself on either side of the cart while the third led the pony.

I was certain I could drive the pony myself if they would give me the reins. They refused. From their accents I could tell the men were not Déisi. They spoke as if they had stones in their mouths.

'My escorts kept the pony at a trot most of the time while they ran effortlessly alongside. When we made camp for the night I was put to bed in the cart under a leather cover.

The warriors lay down beside the fire and were warmer than I was.

"We were on our way again at dawn, jolting along steep trails where the cart threatened to overturn, or following causeways across bogs where heron fished."

My escorts warned that a hostile tribe might try to take me hostage, which sounded exciting, but didn't happen. Nothing happened. We saw only grassland and forest and mountain. And once, some great red deer who came to the edge of the trees to stare at us. Kings in their own kingdom.

'My enthusiasm for the adventure gave way to boredom. Time doubled back on itself; I slept in the daylight and did not know I slept, the condition being scarcely different in my child's mind from wakefulness. Dreams and reality flowed into one another with no demarcation.

The journey became a penance; distress inflicted without apparent reason on a little lad who previously had known only kindness.

But if not for that first journey, where would life have taken me at all?

Putting down his quill, Brendán narrowed his eyes and peered into the past. Trying to see Erc's face again for the first time.

When the cart disappeared from sight Íta returned to the nunnery. Feet dragging, shoulders slumped. Until that day she had considered herself the most fortunate of women. She had been a well-loved, high-spirited child who could ride a horse or hurl a spear as well as any of her brothers. When she was thirteen her parents had converted to Christianity. Three years later Íta had taken a private vow to remain a virgin in honour of Christ's mother, and persuaded her father to let her found a nunnery.

Her vocation allowed her to concentrate on the love of God, while the school satisfied any maternal instincts she might have.

And yet . . .

Braon-finn. The sturdy little fellow with the beaming smile had embedded himself her heart. His wide-eyed, candid gaze revealed an exceptional innocence, even for one so young. She longed to shield him from every blow life might offer. Yet there was nothing weak about him. He played with inexhaustible energy, concocted pranks that outsmarted boys older than himself, and prayed as earnestly as if Christ stood at his elbow.

The boy brimmed with promise like the largest honey tree in the forest.

While still a toddler he had approached Íta and held out a chubby hand. A tiny object lay on the moist palm. "Flower," he had announced.

"No, Braon-finn, that's a seed."

Closing his fingers over the seed, he had stood with his head cocked as if listening. After a moment or two he gave the nun a sidelong glance through his dark eyelashes. "Flower's asleep," he whispered. "In the seed."

Íta had hoped to keep him with her until his fifteenth year, the age at which a boy became a man. Under her influence he would have chosen peaceful pursuits instead of the ubiquitous tribal warfare; he could have survived in a land where warriors lived short lives and died hard.

Now he was taken from her. Everything had happened so quickly; there had been no mention of his return. The cart rattled over the meadowland and was swallowed up by the trees.

Gone.

Who else would appreciate how deep the child's soul was? Who else would give him the exact combination of strength and tenderness he needed?

The nun stepped through the doorway into the chapel.

The answer filled her like water pouring into a cup.

> **A child needs many things. Some will be beautiful and kind, some will be painful and cruel. All will shape him as I decree.**

A rebel spark flared in the woman's breast. Flared wildly and flamed high; swept through her and created another woman with another life entirely; flamed and dwindled and died.

Íta fell prone on the earth and extended her arms in the shape of a cross.

* * *

When the leather cover was lifted from the cart the little boy blinked at the sudden light. He had been asleep again, unaware the wheels had stopped rumbling. A dark silhouette peered down at him. "We expected you yesterday," said a male voice.

The child gaped wordlessly.

The man caught him under the armpits, grunted as if with pain, and then lifted him out of the cart. "Yesterday," the man repeated. He set the little boy down and dismissed the warrior escort with a flick of his hand. "Close your mouth and come along, child." His was a voice of exceptional sweetness. Yet he spoke quickly, as if he could not wait to get one word out of his mouth before reaching for the next.

Lifting the staff he had propped against the side of the cart, the man walked away. When he realised the little boy was not behind him he stopped and looked back. "Do you understand? You must follow me."

Beneath the stranger's robes his body looked misshapen. To the child this explained his need for a walking stick, though not its form. The wooden staff had a rounded hook at the top and came to a point at the bottom.

It might be some sort of weapon.

The little boy spread his feet wide apart and stood his ground. "What are you?" he challenged with as much belligerence as he could muster. "Are you taking me hostage?"

Erc's lips twitched with amusement. He retraced his steps until the shadow of his crooked shoulder fell across the boy. "I am bishop to the Altraighe, which is your tribe. I have been watching over you since you were born. I know everything about you."

In a world turned upside down, all the child was sure of was himself. He resented this stranger making claim to his sovereign territory. "You can't know everything about me," he stated flatly. "You. Can. Not."

"Of course I do."

The little boy narrowed his eyes to slits. This gave him a surprisingly cunning expression. "I can hear the sun singing. You didn't know that, did you?"

Bishop Erc was disconcerted. "The sun . . . singing!?"

"The sun. Singing. I've heard it lots of times."

"Ah . . . that is a pagan. . . . Sister Íta should have . . . come along now," the bishop said brusquely, "there is fish soup waiting for you. You are hungry, surely? Children are always hungry." He extended a hand. After a moment's hesitation, the child reached up to take it.

They began to walk together. Tall and small. One leaned on his staff. The other dragged his feet with weariness.

The land was strangely luminous. From somewhere nearby came a constant low roar, like that of a dangerous animal.

The child tugged on the man's hand. "What's that sound?"

Erc listened for a moment. "Ah, you hear the belling of the silver-horned stags." His rapid voice slowed; became a melodic chant. "It is the voice of the sea, little lad. The eternal symbol of God's power lies beyond the strand."

The boy stared up at him. "What strand?"

He gestured towards a distant ribbon of sand dunes studded with coarse grasses. "The beach at the edge of the sea. Down there."

The sea.

Down there.

They came to a high earthen bank, passed through an unguarded gateway, entered a space delineated by roof and walls and peopled with shadows. When they spoke to the child their words bounced off his ears. After a few bites of food he could not taste he was put to bed.

The sun dropped towards the sea. As he fell asleep he heard it singing.

Many years later Brendán wrote: 'I was taken to Kerry and

delivered to Bishop Erc, a lanky man with a great bald dome of forehead. In childhood he had fallen from a tree and shattered his shoulder. The injury healed badly, leaving him misshapen. Erc called his disfigurement a gift from God and claimed it made him a better person.'

The child awoke suddenly and totally. He was in a small chamber partitioned from a larger space by a screen made of rushes. The walls were constructed from hard-packed earth. His bed was a pallet of reeds laid on the floor. The only light came through one miniscule window that framed a dawn sky.

The air smelled of salt. Tangy. Exotic.

He sat up, knuckling his eyes. "Hoigh?" he called tentatively.

Bishop Erc came around the screen, followed by a grey-haired woman carrying a tunic over her arm and a basin of water in her hands. The boy greeted them with a tumble of questions. "What is this place? Why am I here? Who are you again? Why did you say the Altraighe was my tribe? My mother belongs to the Déisi, doesn't that make me Déisi? Or do I get to choose? Can people choose their tribe?"

Obviously there was confusion that must be corrected. While the woman washed the boy and helped him put on his clothes, Bishop Erc made the effort. "The holy man known as Patrick sent me to this territory years ago," he explained, "to convert the Altraighe to Christianity. In addition to being their spiritual leader I help with their temporal problems, which are many. Mere survival can be a challenge here. In addition, their small tribe is at risk of being subsumed by the much larger tribe of the Ciarrí Luachra."

"Subsumed?" queried a muffled voice.

"Absorbed, let us say. If the Altraighe are absorbed into the Ciarrí Luachra they will lose their *propria natura*, their unique identity. Hoping to avoid this form of extinction, your father . . ."

The little boy's head popped out of the neck of the tunic. His thick black curls were tousled, his dark blue eyes enormous. "God Our Father?"

"*Your* father, who died several weeks ago in a fishing accident. Surely Íta informed you?"

The child stared at the bishop in horror.

Oblivious to the effect his words were having, Erc went on, "As I was saying, your father felt the Altraighe could be strengthened by establishing connections with a tribe equally as powerful as the Ciarrí Luachra. When you were born I helped him to arrange a Déisi foster-mother for you. Fosterage is practiced among most classes but especially by chieftainly families, because it can provide useful alliances in case of war. The ties of affection are often very strong and. . . ." Erc stopped talking. Took a close look at the white face staring up at him. "Do you understand what I am saying?"

"Our Father is dead," the little boy whispered. He began to shiver uncontrollably. "God is dead."

Chapter 3

The bishop's plans for the day unravelled while he and his wife—she of the tunic and basin—struggled to cope with a distraught child who kept insisting, "I want to go home. This isn't my place. Please, I want to go home. Why can't I go home?"

Erc's wife said reassuringly, "You *are* home, little man—you were born only a brisk walk from here." Although Eithne had a mouth made for smiling, there were brackets of discontent between her eyes. She had never borne the bishop a son to follow him in the priesthood. Daughters, yes; any number of them, though only two had survived to maturity. But no sons. Privately Eithne suspected the Druids had cursed her.

She never mentioned this to her husband.

"You have a good home among your own people," the bishop told the child. "Your clanhold is known as *Annagh*—the Marshy Place—but Finnlugh wisely chose a firm strip of land known as *Fenit* for. . . ."

"Fenit?"

"The Wild Place."

"And Finnlugh?"

"Your father. The chief of your clan. The house he built for Cara at Fenit is. . . ."

The boy was shocked. "God is Our Father! His house is at Cill Íde!"

"God is Father to us all, of course," Erc agreed, "but Finnlugh and Cara were your parents and their house is at Fenit. I shall take you to your mother as soon as. . . ."

"Sister Íta is my mother." Once again the little boy regarded the bishop through slitted eyes. "Are you saying I have two mothers? And two fathers? Or no fathers? Because didn't you say God died?" This last accusingly.

"I never said any such thing. I meant your father was dead."

"God is My Father!" shouted the child, turning crimson. "Sister Íta told me so!"

Eithne had rarely seen her husband at a loss for words. Women, she told herself, are much better at times like this. "I'm sure Sister Íta also explained what it means to be a Christian," she interjected. "Surely you would you be willing to help a poor woman who needs you very much?"

The boy blinked. "Me? Help?"

"Your mother's grief at the death of her husband is destroying her. She eats nothing, hardly ever sleeps, keens all day, and walks the seashore by night, clawing her skin and tearing her hair. We hope that restoring you to her will restore poor Cara to herself. Surely no woman could resist her last-born son."

From this the child gleaned only one fact: "Last-born son? I have brothers?"

"You had three," said Erc. "The oldest two died in battle. Faitleac, who studied with me, has joined the monastic order at the abbey of Clon Tuaiscirt. Your parents also had a daughter who was born only a year before you. She is young but sensible, so I have given her the task of caring for your mother until such time as the poor woman regains her senses."

"Who gave you permission to bring me away from Cill Íde ?"

"I did not need permission. I am your bishop, which gives me the authority to. . . ."

"You're not my father."

"No, I am acting in his place. I am your father in God, as it were."

"God is my Father," asserted the boy. "Even if he's dead." He folded his arms across his chest and glared at Erc, daring the man to contradict him.

The bishop tried to be patient with me but I must have tried him sorely. He explained what he knew to be true; I insisted upon what I believed to be true. Each of us was convinced he was right.

It was my first experience of confronting disparate truths.

One of the first souls Erc had claimed for Christ was a clan chieftain called Finnlugh, who was related to the legendary warlord, Niall of the Nine Hostages: Niall the Sea Raider, who once had kidnapped a sixteen-year-old Briton called Patricius and sold him into slavery in Ireland.

Years later Erc had been converted, and then elevated to the bishopric, by that same Patricius—the Christian missionary now revered among the Irish as Patrick. It was Patrick who had sent Erc to the Altraighe.

Lives woven into a Celtic knot.

Erc believed it was his destiny to transform Finnlugh's kin into Christians. The task had proved more difficult than he anticipated.

If any part of Ireland could be described as inherently pagan, that place was Kerry. Men and women in the southwest corner of Ireland were large bodied and long limbed, with handsome features and thick black hair. Both sexes had strong voices from shouting above the prevailing wind. Emotions were slow, deep, often inarticulate, but strongly felt. Passions like primordial ooze heaved beneath the surface.

The Altraighe were stubborn people who had to be won soul by soul and did not always remain converted. A man might be a good Christian until he drank too much ale one night and beat another man to a pulp. A woman in childbed was likely to call upon deities other than Christ.

The human eye could not be trusted in Kerry. Jagged purple peaks brooded on the skyline like mythic kings, flinging forth armies of swirling cloud to seize the folded hillsides and deep valleys, then dissolve into polychrome air bannered with rainbows. Dangerous forces lurked amid the broken terrain, concealed by roseate heather and golden furze. Even more dangerous was the sea. Encroaching on Kerry with clawing fingers, using a bounty of hake and cod and ling to lure men into its wild pagan heart.

In such a setting life was precarious. To placate the ancient gods the natives participated in complex, mysterious rituals. Rituals conducted by Druids.

But change was on the way.

In his journal Brendán wrote: 'Insular Ireland had avoided the iron fist of Imperial Rome, but would not escape the softer hand of Christianity.

'Patrick had not been the first missionary to visit these shores. Obeying the adjuration to go forth and spread the Good News, Christian missionaries were among the most widely travelled men of their time. Within three centuries of Christ's death they had begun visiting Ireland from Britain and Gaul.

'In 431 Pope Celestine, the bishop of Rome, sent a bishop named Palladius to "care for the Irish." Although he succeeded in baptising a few of the natives, Bishop Palladius did not gain general acceptance and soon returned to Rome. Celestine had then assigned a recently ordained bishop named Patricius to take his place.

'Patricius had been born on the northern frontier of Roman Britain, where Roman troops regularly confronted warlike Scottish Picts, Anglo-Saxon smugglers seeking to avoid Roman taxation, and sea raiders from Ireland. Patricius was "freeborn according to the flesh" in his own words. His father, Calpornius, who owned a large country estate west of Luguvalium, was a Christian deacon as well as a decurion. When the armies of Rome pulled out in order to defend their homeland against the barbarians and Britain descended into chaos, Calpornius struggled to maintain Roman order in his territory. This background prepared Patricius for the mission he would one day undertake in Ireland."

A devout Christian raised with Roman discipline and organization; what a shock Patrick must have been to the wild Gael!

'Patrick approached the native Irish with a weapon against which they had no defence: understanding. In his youth he had lived among them as a slave, and he understood they were pagan in body and soul. For more than a thousand years their beliefs had shaped every aspect of Gaelic life. A wise man, Patrick realised that a force which has existed for so long cannot easily be killed.

'Instead of trying to convert the Irish at sword's point, he grafted Christian images onto aspects of the elder faith. Year by patient year, in ways large and small, Patrick convinced the Irish that accepting Christianity would not eradicate the sacral, but enlarge it. Pagan sacred ground, pagan healing wells, and pagan festivals were gently redesignated as Christian sites and wells and festivals.

'To help explain the tripartite nature of the Christian deity—Father, Son, and Holy Spirit—Patrick used both the three-leafed clover and certain goddesses of the Gael. Badbh the Crow, Nemhain the Frenzy, and the Morrigan, Queen of Battle, were the three faces of War.

'The choice Patrick offered the Irish was between a god of love and one of destruction. By the time of his death he had won large swathes of Ireland for Christ.

I wish I had known him. At least I knew Erc, who had.

'Almost from the beginning the Church in Ireland was organized along the lines of Roman civil administration. Bishops filled the role of provincial governors. The territory a bishop governed was known as his diocese, and was subdivided into parishes headed by priests.

'To aid in administration of his diocese Bishop Erc took over a large earthen rampart, or *lios*, near the Bay of Tra Lí. Once it had been the fortress of chieftains. Within its high walls Erc established an ecclesiastical center which he called *Tearmónn Eirc*—Erc's Sanctuary—and organized according to plans laid down by Patrick himself.

'At its heart Erc erected a rectangular sod-walled church, facing the rising sun. The bishop's house was built into the rampart beside a small scriptorium. Opposite them were lean-tos for storage and a reed-thatched refectory that doubled as a classroom. The remaining space was given over to tiny beehive-shaped huts, or *clocháns,* of unmortared stone. Their only furnishings were a reed mat for sleeping, a reed stool for sitting, and a sheepskin for a blanket. The roofs were corbeled; the only doorway was so low a man had to crouch to enter. An adult could not stand erect inside. The clocháns were an exercise in humility.

'Novices studying with Erc in preparation for the priesthood lived in those cells. During my years at Tearmónn Eirc, so did I.

Every detail is scribed on my soul. The cells smelled of earth and stone dust. The rough stones were tightly fitted together at the top so that no rain entered, but during the day a small amount of illumination filtered through tiny chinks in the walls. In this grainy twilight one relied on touch as well as sight. My nimble fingers soon discovered little niches in which to store my belongings. Over the years those niches would be crammed with oddments I collected: colourful stones and seabirds' feathers and even a twisted silver buckle dug out of the sand.

When daylight faded the cell became a different place. Black lay on my flesh like fabric, with weight and substance. I thought I could hear it breathing. A great hungry animal in the cell with me. And I with no candle.

The presence of the Dark became analogous in my mind—in all our minds, because we discussed this—with the Devil. Christ within us was the only light.

'Aside from the stone clocháns, most construction was of hard-packed earth. Trees would not grow around the bay, so the little timber we had timber was obtained through trade with the Ciarrí Luachra. The altar in the church was carved from a single massive oak and plenished with a solid gold chalice and paten. These had been commissioned from a northern goldsmith called Assicus. *Erc lavished upon his church the luxuries the Gaelic nobility lavished upon themselves.*

'Nestled against the outside wall of the lios were workshops for thc artisans who made bells and crosses and every form of adornment for the church. The bishop believed creativity identified a person as being spiritually alive. "What they create is not as important as the fact that they do create," he said. "With the work of his hands Assicus praised God."

'In addition to earning a livelihood for themselves and their families, the men of the parish were kept busy with the ongoing maintenance of the ecclesiastical center. Repairing walls, mending roofs, sluicing out the cesspit that emptied through a drain under the rampart, tanning leather for sandals and book satchels, filling large, shallow pans with seawater to evaporate for salt, smelting ore to make bells and buckets and door hinges—the tasks were endless.

'Then as now, land ownership was not vested in any one individual but held in common by the tribe, which was composed of clans descended from a common ancestor. The Altraighe consisted of but a few clans. Because their territory contained little arable land they harvested the sea. Cod, haddock, plaice, flounder, sea trout, pollock, wrasse." *No matter how devout the fishermen were, when a big shoal of herring was running only the women attended Mass.*

'Members of the Altraighe sought the bishop's support, both physical and spiritual, in every aspect of their lives.' *Erc was not a young man but he gave endlessly of himself. Tearmónn Eirc was a hive of activity from dawn to sunset; a splendid education for a boy eager to learn.*

I am writing as if I were important but I am no one; an individual of modest abilities who was taught about humility by a fish and about forgiveness by a monster. A number of monks could tell this story in better Latin and with greater clarity. But this is my story; the memories are mine to recapture as I can.

I shall narrate the events of my final voyage in the order in which they emerge from my memory, though not always the order in which they transpired.

Three monks whom I had not chosen for the mission came scrambling down the steep hillside and splashed through the shallows. As the boat was being launched they tried to climb into it. Colmán lifted an oar to push them away, but I stayed his hand.

"We have neither space nor supplies for them," said Liber, who had been put in charge of provisioning our vessel.

Tarlách added, "They didn't even help build the boat."

The interlopers fell to their knees in the water and extended imploring hands towards me. "We want to be pilgrims for the rest of our days. Allow us to go wherever you go, Brother Abbot, or we shall remain in this place until we die."

I said, "You are likely to die sooner if you come with us. We are venturing out onto the Western Sea and only God himself knows what lies ahead of us. We might sail off the end of the world and fall into the abyss."

"If you are willing to take the chance, why can't we?"

"I have taken care to select only those men who are stoutest of body and spirit for my companions," I explained. "We have fasted for three days of every week in order to cleanse our bodies, and prayed for forty days to prepare our souls for this voyage. My failure to include you is not a criticism but a kindness. I spare you from trials you are not equipped to face."

The three insisted I was mistaken. Each of them claimed special abilities which would more than qualify him to make the voyage. While my crew grumbled among themselves and our boat skittered like a restive horse, I stood with folded arms, listening until the last argument had been uttered and the last plea made. Then I said, "I have explained my reasons, yet still you demand to come with us. Very well. But I tell you this much. One of you has performed a deed of great merit and God will reward him in due course. For the other two a dreadful judgement awaits."

Each man assumed he was the one who would be rewarded. All three climbed into the boat.

I had warned them. They could never claim I failed to warn them.

CHAPTER 4

On the morning following my arrival in Tearmónn Eirc I attended Mass,' Brendán wrote in his journal, 'together with other members of the Altraighe. *My tribe. Strangers to me. Each acknowledged me with a nod or a smile, but I was too befuddled to respond. Thank God they were Christians and forgave me.*

After Mass the little boy said to the bishop, "Your church is very dry, but how can it be God's house when God's house is at Cill Íde ? No one can have two houses. Are there two Gods?"

Erc frowned. "Only one God," he said firmly. "One God, who is not dead. One God who is All. You will understand in time."

"I want to understand now."

Erc busied himself gathering up his cloak and staff. When the boy glanced dubiously at the staff, Erc said, "This is called a crosier, the symbol of Christ the Good Shepherd and emblem of my office. Think of me as a shepherd who will take care of you."

The child was looking at him as if he spoke in another language entirely.

Brendán wrote, 'After Mass the bishop took me for a long walk to the Wild Place, and my mother." *Wild Place indeed. There was nothing gentle about Fenit. No tree, no flower; only a little rough grass clinging to the earth with fierce intensity. My birthplace was on the north shore of the bay of Tra Lí, with the great empty sky brooding overhead like the eye of God.*

I thought it more beautiful than the bishop's church.

Meeting Cara was an unsettling experience. She was nothing like Íta. The woman was as thin and brittle as a dead twig. Her face was scored with long red weals where she had clawed her own flesh. She looked at me once, emitted a piercing shriek, then closed her eyes and never looked at me again. She would not let me touch her—nor did I want to. Cara smelled of rot and decay, of pernicious grief.

The only life in the house was her daughter, Brige, a thin little girl with slightly pointed ears. She held out her arms the moment she saw me. "My brother!" she exclaimed. Her enthusiastic hug warmed me to my toes. The scent of her pale skin reminded me of ferns and moss, but her little hands were chapped and red.

We chattered happily together while the bishop tried to have an intelligent conversation with Cara.

With no success at all.

Erc waited until he and the boy were out of earshot of the house—and of Brige waving from the doorway—before saying, "I trust you understand why I could not leave you in that house. The poor child has all she can do to take care of her mother."

"And you say Cara's my mother too? How do you know that?"

"You ask too many questions."

"But how *do* you know?"

"I was present when you were born."

The boy stopped walking and looked up at the man. "You were?"

"Indeed I was. I shall never forget it." Erc's swift voice slowed once again, altered its rhythm. Became music. "You entered this world at high tide during a full moon. While your mother laboured to give you birth, a surge greater than any in living memory roared out of the ocean. Infants are born bloody, yet when you emerged from her womb clear water streamed off your flesh. You appeared to have been lifted straight from the sea. The watery portents surrounding your birth could not be ignored, so I christened you Braon-finn."

"You christened me?"

"The authority came to me through Patrick from Jesus Christ himself," the bishop chanted. "You were born four hundred and eighty-four years after the birth of Christ. Four hundred and eighty-four years after you die Christ will still be remembered."

The chant ceased. Erc blinked, cleared his throat. "Contrary to our hopes," he said in his normal speaking voice, "your presence has not ameliorated your mother's grief. Seeing you may even have made it worse. You do look uncommonly like Finnlugh."

"What will become of her?"

"We shall pray for her."

"How will that make her better?"

Erc had learned that he could not dismiss this child with facile answers, so he worded his reply carefully. "By helping Cara to be whatever God wants her to be."

"You mean God *is* still alive?"

"Of course."

The little boy heaved a sigh of relief. "All my fathers aren't dead, then."

Erc was not an emotional man, yet for a moment he rested his hand on the child's curls. "Come along now, boy," he said. "We have a long way to go before dark."

"And you will send me home tomorrow?"

"By 'home,' you mean Cill Íde?"

"Yes."

"In all good conscience, I cannot. I would be remiss in my responsibility to your family if I did not keep you here and tutor you myself."

"But you have to send me back to Cill Íde! Sister Lerben's going to teach me the Latin alphabet." The little boy's voice wavered at the very end. Not tears, but almost.

"A commendable beginning," said the bishop, "but only a beginning. Men who are called to the priesthood come to me for an education. You too are going to have that privilege. I shall teach you to read and write in Latin, and also in a phoneticised version of the Irish language. In addition you will study mathematics, geography, and canon law. Our scriptorium contains books from Rome and Alexandria. The world is about to open up to you, my lad." He paused to clear his throat. "Perhaps we should begin by calling you Brendán. That is how Braon-finn would be pronounced in Rome."

"You can't change my name!"

"Of course I can. I named you in the first place."

The boy had not known the meaning of the word 'subsume,' but he recognised the sound of inevitability.

He squared his small shoulders and rolled the name across his tongue. "Brendán," he said aloud. Trying out the sound.

'So began the second phase of my life," he wrote in his journal. 'The bishop installed a sense of discipline which I sorely lacked. In the beginning, one-third of my day was allotted for prayer and one-third for study. The remainder of my time was for those things which the bishop deemed necessary to life; eating and sleeping, but also contemplation.

Not 'play,' however.

To step from sunlight into shadow. To feel the world shift as things change and change again, and realise nothing will ever be the same.

Different is not necessarily worse.

When Erc returned home to Eithne with the newly named Brendán he did not offer an explanation for the change, nor did she ask. She knew he would tell her eventually. The bishop's wife was his unacknowledged confessor.

In their bed at night Erc said, "I suspect Íta and her nuns are imparting a one-sided vision of Christianity to the boys in their charge."

"Is that so?" Eithne tried to sound surprised. She knew where this was going. Having made the decision, her husband needed to justify it.

"Íta can afford to prattle of lambs and good shepherds," the bishop said. "That is all she knows of life. As her father's favourite daughter she finds no rocks in her path—she has only to ask, and whatever she wants is given to her. It has never been like that for me."

"Never," Eithne echoed. She was well trained in responses.

"I have worked hard for everything I have. You know how difficult it is to get the smallest amount of funding out of Rome. Even Patrick had trouble."

"I know," said Eithne.

"It was time to take the boy away from Íta," the bishop went on. "Bringing Christian enlightenment to the Irish depends upon opening their minds to new ways of thinking. And that requires education. Unfortunately, the Church of Rome is preoccupied with the barbarians who are destroying civilisation. Goths, Visigoths, Vandals, Huns . . ." Eithne felt her husband shudder. "We need an army of dedicated Christians here," he stressed, "to defeat the forces of paganism and superstition on this island. Ours is a new sort of warfare, Eithne, and no one is better suited for it than Finnlugh's last son. Having spent some time with him now, I know him to be a child of uncommon strength and will. But if he is going to join the struggle he must be properly educated."

"And is he?"

"Is he what?"

"Going to join the struggle?"

"Of course he is," Erc said briskly. "The boy was consecrated to the task at birth. The sea claimed Finnlugh—but Christ claimed Finnlugh's last son. It is my obligation to prepare him for his special life."

Erc understood the requirements of a special life. His own noble blood had not protected him from pain and disappointment, but everything he had endured was worth it. Ultimately his sacrifices had taken him to Tara and the court of the high king, and then to the Hill of Slane on a cold spring morning . . .

Brendán laid the quill aside. The real work of writing took place in the head.

Loneliness weighed hard on me at first. The bishop did not want for words; he spoke to me frequently but discouraged my asking questions. Any conversation with him was inevitably one sided. I could talk to Eithne, of course, but she wasn't interested in the things that interested me.

I sorely missed the boys who had been my brothers, my playmates, my friends. The other residents of Tearmónn Eirc were adults. Their conversations took place in the air above my head.

The novice priests, all of whom were much older than I, conversed almost exclusively in priest language. "Icky icky icky, ooyus ooyus ooyus." I was jealous and fascinated—every boy loves a secret language. Recognizing a few of the words I had heard at Mass, I tried to join in. My first efforts were awkward. The others laughed. Ninnidh, a relative of the bishop, accused me of being slow-witted.

On that day I resolved to master the language of Rome.

Brendán resumed writing. 'Time was measured in canonical hours announced by the ringing of bells adjuring us to pray. Matins, Prime, Terce, Sext, Nones, Vespers, and Compline. All of life's other activities were fitted into the spaces between. The bishop did not share Íta's philosophy of gentle simplicity. He preached the value of bare subsistence for focussing thoughts on God. My bed was a mat of reeds laid on hard earth, and I was given just enough food to take the edge off my hunger without ever satisfying me. We all were.

Only later did I realise that Erc's austerity had a practical reason behind it. Altraighe-Caille, embracing the bay of Tra Lí, was not fertile farmland.

'My clothing consisted of a thin woollen coat with a hood attached, worn over a plain tunic that fell almost to my ankles. The same leather sandals served me summer and winter. The only difference between my attire and that of the novice priests was the heavy cloak, or *brat*, which I had brought with me. Eithne insisted I be allowed to keep it, but the bishop would not let me wear it except in the most extreme weather.

'The bishop explained that Christianity recognised three degrees of martyrdom: green, white, and red. White meant giving up everything one loved for the sake of God; red meant giving up life itself in his name. I was to undertake green martyrdom, which involved fasting and labor to free oneself of evil desires.

At my age I did not know what evil desires were. Sister Íta had never mentioned them. Yet the bishop arbitrarily attributed them to me.

Am I being objective in my depiction of Erc? Are my remarks coloured by knowing too much about him, or not enough?

To give him credit, the bishop was as strict with himself as he was with others. He ate sparingly and wore the same clothes summer and winter, varied only by the vestments he put on for divine service. Eithne had made a great shaggy cloak for him, but I never saw him wear it.

Erc commanded respect by using the formal language of a brehon, even in casual conversation. On one drawing of breath he could employ more long words than I had heard in my short lifetime. There were moments when the poetry inherent in the Gael shone through—that was his gift. The beauty of his voice on those occasions drew people to him, and through him to Christ.

Among the Irish it is well known: whatever a person might say in the ordinary way, when he speaks poetry he speaks truth. That's why I believed in the silver-horned stags. The bishop spoke of them in his poetic voice.

One summer's day when no one was watching, I ran all the way to the strand to search for them.

The sea. Right here.

I never thought there would be so much of it.

The little boy had stared in awe at the dark blue water, the living water, glimmering all the way to the horizon. Fearful and fascinated, he watched it advance with a rushing hiss and a skirt of foam, fall back, advance again. Coming ever closer. Swallowing the pebbled sand and carrying it away; leaving different pebbles in trade.

When he shaded his eyes with his hand he could see as far as Fenit. Between himself and Fenit he noticed a strip of high ground jutting out from the land; a disintegrating promontory being eaten away by erosion. The great bay in front of him was freckled with fishermen in little boats, casting their nets.

Water was access. By sea one could circumnavigate Ireland. Rivers made travel within the interior possible. Large rivers were navigated in sturdy dugout canoes carved from immense oak trees. Bowl-shaped vessels called coracles were useful in shallow water. The most common type of boat was the currach, a wickerwork frame covered with oxhides that had been tanned with oak bark and stitched together with leather thongs. Currachs were propelled by spoon-shaped oars, though it was possible to rig a mast and sail.

Currachs were built in different sizes and readily portable. A strong man could carry one, a dozen men could fish from one, or even transport a cow and her calf to an offshore island for grazing. The currach was indispensable in the territory of Altraighe-Caille.

Brendán shaded his eyes with his hand so he could watch the men fishing, but they were too far away for him to see any details. Nor did he hear the belling of the stags, or glimpse their silvery horns on the crests of waves. There were plenty of other things to interest him, however. He sat down to strip off his sandals and tie the thongs together. Then he slung them over his shoulder and set out to explore the beach.

The tide line was littered with exotic stones he had never seen before, with gelatinous growths dissolving back into ooze, with fragments of tiny skeletons hinting at miniature monsters. Treasure trove for a small boy. He ran from one to another with shouts of glee. If only Sister Íta were here! She would know the name of this, and that. She would marvel at the numerous seashells and call them jewels. She would . . .

Brendán stubbed his bare toe and yelped with pain.

Crouching down to rub saliva on the toe, he discovered the culprit. It was a stub of wood. Sister Íta had taught him about trees and plants, so he knew that white ash had no business growing on a beach. The boy scrabbled in the sand . . .

. . . and uncovered part of a skeleton shaped by the hand of man.

A flexible wooden lath to which a fragment of oxhide, slimy from long immersion in water, was laced by disintegrating strips of leather.

Brendán tightened his fingers around the wood. Cocked his head as if listening. A play of emotions ran across his face like the shadows of clouds on water.

He stood up and gazed towards the distant boats, then began walking along the beach. When he came to the eroded promontory, he scrambled up the side and buried the fragment of wreckage on the top. From a nearby tumble of rocks he took enough stones to erect a small cairn over the grave. White quartz stones, glittering in the sun.

The task completed, he stood beside the cairn and turned his eyes towards the sea. Not thinking much of anything. Letting his eyes follow the movement of the waves. Listening to the cries of the gulls.

Gradually he became aware of himself and the ground on which he stood as existing *apart*, in an Other Place.

The world was outside. In this Other Place he felt intensely alive, yet deeply at peace.

Brendán told no one about his adventure: the first totally private thing in his life. He returned whenever he could to the promontory. Over a matter of months he was troubled to observe that the strip of headland was shrinking. Would the Other Place vanish with it?

The seasons passed. A year and then another. Brendán was kept busy studying and working and praying, trying to please the bishop and trying to grow into an individual in his own right. Erc was unremitting in his criticism of his godson.

"Why are you staring at that bird when I am talking?" he would challenge abruptly, awaking the boy from reverie.

"I was studying the structure of its wing," Brendán explained. "Don't you think it's a miracle the way it works?"

"The creature is nothing but an ordinary seagull; a scavenger. You waste your time with such nonsense, Brendán. You are here to learn from books; from the wisdom of those wiser than you."

One autumn afternoon Brendán fled to the promontory in search of respite. There had been severe storms during the summer and the finger of land was appreciably smaller. The climb to the top was less steep. Once again he stood beside the cairn—was it smaller too?—and looked out over the bay.

The immense sea heaved as if alive. Beneath its restless surface countless living creatures were also in motion: fish and crabs and lobsters and sea monsters too, or so the fishermen claimed.

Squinting against the glare off the water, Brendán tried to imagine a sea monster. Concentrated so hard he lost any sense of self.

The voice came to him then, like the muted roar of the sea in a shell held to the ear.

Observe the direction of your life. Outward. Always outward.

In Tearmónn, Eirc the bishop's wife was never still. She took tireless care of the bishop; cooking his meals—with meager ingredients because there was nothing else—making and mending his garments and sandals, maintaining his house and church, entertaining his visitors, lifting his spirits when they were down, and listening to his problems when they seemed about to overwhelm him.

She also cared for anyone in the community who was ill and prepared the food for the refectory. The meal provided once a day for the novices and Brendán—except on fast days—consisted of coarse bread, a portion of boiled legumes and sea vegetables, and a cup of thin beer. A gannet's egg was a rare treat. The bread was gritty and tough. The grain was acquired through barter with the Ciarrí Luachra, who kept the best for themselves.

When Brendán failed to appear for his daily meal Eithne was worried. The boy had a voracious appetite; it was not like him to forget his food. She decided not to tell the bishop—not yet. She did not want to get the child in trouble, so she went looking for him herself. At twilight she finally came upon Brendán returning. His eyes were filled with stars.

"Where were you all this time?" she demanded to know.

"Looking at the sea. It's where I go to contemplate."

Eithne laughed. The word was bigger than the boy. "Do you even know what 'contemplate' means, Brendán?"

"I do know, it's from the Latin. *Contemplor* means to consider carefully. I consider the sea."

That night in their bed Eithne told her husband, "Brendán has his father's blood in him. The sea's calling him."

"He is going to be a fisher of men like Christ's apostles from the Sea of Galilee."

"That may not be what he wants."

"What he *wants*?!" The bishop sat bolt upright in bed. "What are you saying, woman? Childish fancies are irrelevant. Brendán has a hungry mind, he soaks up learning the way blotting sand soaks up ink. He will walk in the footsteps of blessed Patrick himself; he will become a star in Christ's crown and do us all honour. You have a way with the boy, Eithne; you must help him appreciate his good fortune. I rely on you."

Eithne rolled over and closed her eyes. She knew what would happen. Erc would claim Brendán's successes. His failings would be hers.

The following day the bishop told Brendán, "You are not to go near the sea again. It would be a great pity if you were to repeat your father's mishap. You are meant for better things."

"But . . ."

"I expect obedience from you, young man."

"I understand." The boy dropped his eyes. But he made no promises.

Winter was hard in Altraighe territory. The wind off the sea was savage. The ice along the shore dug in its claws and held on hard. Boats were beached; fishermen set about repairing their battered gear. Fires were fed with sods of turf or dried cowpats that smouldered sullenly on the hearth. In late winter families were forced to gather furze in the mountains for fuel. Dead, brittle stems and tough roots quickly burned away to nothing, but gave off great heat while they lasted.

The bishop excused his students from their studies to assist the tribe. Festooned with baskets and bags, Brendán and the novices were sent south to the lower reaches of *Sliabh Mis*, the Mountain of Phantoms. Aside from a bristly carpet of greyish-brown furze, the landscape was barren. Slides of rock and shale waited to trap the unwary, to twist a knee or snap an ankle. Relentless wind scoured and burned any exposed skin. Dark cliffs loomed menacingly over the searchers, guarding an abandoned fort built into the living rock by a former king of Munster. A pagan king whose spirit, people claimed, had never left the mountain.

The novices signed the Cross on their breasts before they set to work gathering furze.

I meant to do my share but my thoughts kept wandering; trying to envision the people who once lived in the fort. I longed to see their faces. Hear their voices. Were they like me or very different? What caused them to abandon their stronghold? What manner of spirit had they left behind?

Bishop Erc said I had too much imagination. He frequently admonished me for daydreaming when I should be concentrating on practical matters, but it was hard to think about feeding a hearth fire when I was in the presence of mountains. Mountains sacred to our ancestors long before Christ was born.

Anchored by Sliabh Mis on the landward side, a broken chain of mountains swept along the peninsula of *Corca Dhuibhne*, south of the bay of Tra Lí, and culminated with *Sliabh Diadche*. Solitary Sliabh Diadche was said to be the second highest mountain in Ireland. Local people believed "Diadche" referred to its divinity. Bishop Erc insisted it only meant the backside: the end. As with many Irish words, the definition was open to interpretation.

Many years later Brendán wrote: 'Adapting our native tongue to Christian usage was not easy. Some of the novices at Tearmónn Eirc had grey beards but no allowances were made for age. Young and old alike were expected to make the adjustment.

'Studying Latin helped. The languages of Rome and the Gael were not compatible; one could not subsume the other, but moving back and forth between them made our minds more agile.

By the time I was ten years old my mind was very agile indeed. I appreciated that Latin, for all its precision, lacked the subtlety and vivacity of my native tongue. The Irish language was a rainbow. Latin was a rock.

'Bishop Erc provided what he described as the basic education for men aspiring to the priesthood. In addition to Latin we were thoroughly instructed in Holy Scripture and the Canons of the Church. The bishop also taught us as much as he thought we needed to know of the world beyond our shores. *We listened, both horrified and fascinated, as he told of the barbarians who had plundered Athens and sacked Rome. When he said "pagans" he grimaced as a man in pain. By his own admission Erc had never been out of Ireland, yet the images he painted with words were so vivid we could smell the blood of the slain and hear the screams of the mutilated.*

'By daylight we examined maps drawn by long-dead geographers, showing our humble, almost negligible, place in the world. On clear nights we lay on our backs while the bishop explained the map of the stars. *For astronomy alone I owe Erc a debt I can never repay. Only years later did I realise he must have studied the skies as a Druid.*

He tutored us in another esoteric subject which must have come from the same source: the secret language of ogham. Angular lines carved on stone to give directions or convey necessary information. Ogham was not a complete language in any sense, could not even be called "writing," but under certain circumstances it was useful. As I would discover.

'Mathematics was my least favourite subject. I found it hard to submit to the tyranny of numbers, but the bishop insisted. He explained that coins, not barter, were the rate of exchange in the civilised world. *By "the civilised world" he meant the Roman Empire. Doubtless Erc had acquired his admiration of all things Roman from Patrick.*

'The bishop told us, "In Ireland Patrick undertook to convert the chieftains first. Because of the intense loyalty of the Gael to their chieftains, he knew they would follow their leaders into the new religion. At the beginning Patrick had no following himself, however. Without attendants a man lacked prestige, and without prestige Patrick could not gain an audience with the chieftains. He wisely dispensed gold coins to their sons, and in this way built a sizeable retinue of followers."

If Patrick was clever and pragmatic, Jesus Christ, as described by the bishop, was exceptionally robust. No weakling could have commanded the devotion of the rugged fishermen of Galilee.

"Strong men will only follow other strong men," Erc told us. "Consider the conversion of Aenghus, who reigned as king of Munster from a stronghold on the Rock of Cashel. Aenghus had a mighty reputation as a warrior. It was said of him that even the hair of his head would not bend.

"When the king's wife embraced the new religion, her husband was scornful. Aenghus declared that Christianity was nothing more than a refuge for the feeble and insipid. Night after night his wife urged the king to at least meet Patrick and hear what he had to say. 'What harm can a few words do to your ear?' she asked. For the sake of peace in his household—the only place where he ever knew peace—at last Aenghus agreed.

"On the summer solstice Patrick made his way up the steep path to the top of the Rock of Cashel. His climbing stick, which had a crook at the top and a pointed end, was actually a shepherd's staff." At this point the bishop had held up his own crosier by way of demonstration.

"Aenghus kept his promise and granted the missionary an audience. While Patrick talked about the meek inheriting the earth, the king gazed out over the rich grasslands of Munster and planned his next cattle raid. At last even Patrick's patience failed. Raising his staff, he drove it into the ground with both hands to gain the king's attention.

"Aenghus gave a great cry.

"Looking down, Patrick was dismayed to see that he had driven his staff clear through the king's foot. He unwittingly had pinned the unfortunate man to the soil of Cashel."

Brendán chuckled to himself, remembering.

Even the bishop had smiled as he continued, "Patrick was horrified, but Aenghus was mightily impressed. He assumed the gesture was part of Christian ritual, and then and there re-thought his view of Christianity. Obviously it was no religion for weaklings, but a muscular faith worthy of a muscular king. Aenghus was baptized that same day. He became one of Patrick's most devoted followers, bringing many along with him."

In his journal Brendán wrote, 'Bishop Erc believed that Christianity must be practical as well as idealistic, participatory as well as observational. When I first arrived at Tearmónn Eirc I was assigned to trim candles. Within weeks I was filling lamps and transporting books to and from the scriptorium. Eventually Erc's craftsmen taught me to prepare wax tablets for temporary writing. Next I learned how to fashion quill pens and ink horns, and make repairs to book satchels.

I was very careful about even the smallest detail. The tiniest stitch, the slightest drop of glue had to be exact. Creation was a form of prayer; anything shoddy or carelessly made was a sin.

'As I grew older I assisted with the forging of bells and other heavy tasks. *I had not expected it to be such hard work, being a Christian.*

'If God permeated Cill Íde, Erc's Christianity filled Tearmónn Eirc to overflowing. The literacy lessons given to laymen were for no other reason than to enable them to study Holy Scripture. In the rare moments when he was not praying or teaching, Erc was likely to seize upon some hapless person occupied with his own business and lecture him on the Gospels. Yet it was tremendously exciting. Even a child could recognize that something extraordinary was happening. A warrior culture that had lived by the sword for a millennium was being conquered by ideas.'

Smiling, the nun had approached the little boy and held out her hand. "I have a piece of honeycomb for you, Braon-finn."

The child saw angry red bee stings on the nun's hands. "But you're hurt!"

Sister Íta had kept smiling. "There is no gift without cost," she replied.

We made our first landfall on an unfamiliar strand, hoping to take more water aboard. Our search was unsuccessful. The three latecomers seemed the least disappointed; they were still assuming the self-conscious affability of uninvited guests.

When we returned to the boat a figure walked towards us. The finely modelled features could have belonged either to a girl or a young man. When the person spoke the voice did not solve the mystery; it was sweet and pure, without gender.

Holding up a basket heaped with bread and a large water jug, the stranger said, "Receive this blessing from the hand of your servant. A long journey lies ahead of you, but neither bread nor water will fail you from this day until the first day of Eastertide."

"Our eyes look upon an angel," murmured Brother Gowrán. I concurred. We all knelt and prayed. When we arose the stranger had vanished. Marvelling, we launched our boat.

And sailed on.

Chapter 5

When Patrick was a slave herding sheep on Slemish Mountain,' Brendán wrote, 'God spoke to him in a dream, urging him to escape and flee Ireland. With God's help he did. Many years later a crowd of the Gael began appearing to Patrick in visions. They pleaded with him to return and convert their people to Christianity. With God's help he did that too.

Children accept. Theirs is the earliest and purest faith, and by the grace of God I have never lost mine. By opening myself to the possibility of miracles I welcome them into my world. As the years pass no hard shell has formed around my soul, making me deaf and blind. I can still hear the sun singing.

Whenever he could steal time for himself from the busy schedule Erc assigned, Brendán sneaked down to the strand. And the sea. His disobedience weighed but lightly on his soul. Sometimes he simply stared at the expanse of water, awed by its elemental force.

"What is . . . ?" Brendán would whisper. "Why is . . . ?"

No wonder the pagans worshipped the sea. Confronted by the Great Inexplicable, theirs was a natural response.

Brendán was instructed by the nature around him. He was interested in everything that lived, but particularly birds. In caves and crevices along the western seaboard of Ireland the fastidious yet much-maligned chough, a member of the crow family, made its nest. He enjoyed watching them riding the updrafts of wind, their glossy black feathers highlighted with blue and green, their beaks and legs an intense red.

God must love beauty very much, I told myself, because he created it in so many forms. Was that an odd thought for one so young? God made me thoughtful just as he made me curious. Such gifts are given for a reason; not carelessly dispensed to agitate a man's days.

The fishermen grew accustomed to seeing the boy alone on the strand. They knew who he was and who his father had been. Brendán helped them spread their nets to dry on the beach while they answered his questions about boats and fish and tides and clouds and winds and water. Their wives fed him, their children played with him.

One bright spring afternoon Dubán, a wiry man in his middle years, was carrying his currach to the water with the help of his friend Gaeth. They noticed Brendán watching them. Dubán called out, "It's a fine day to be on the water. Join us."

"I don't know how to fish," said the boy.

"We won't be fishing anyway. I've resealed the seams of this boat, and I need to test them. Come on."

Tingling with excitement, Brendán clambered into the currach and crouched in the center. Dubán sat in the prow, holding an oar. Gaeth pushed the boat into the water, then jumped in and lifted the other oar.

Outwards!

A few oar strokes carried them beyond the shallows. A gentle swell lifted the boat. When the currach rose with the water, Brendán's heart rose too. He grinned with delight.

The next swell took them, and the next; each one larger than the one before.

The boat's rocking motion steadily increased.

The boy's grin began to fade.

"It's quiet now because the tide's still going out," Dubán remarked, "but once we put Ard Fert behind us you'll get a real sense of the sea."

Brendán opened his eyes wide. "Ard Fert? The High Grave?"

"The strip of headland over there." Dubán nodded towards the eroded promontory.

"A Milesian fortress stood on it once," said Gaeth. "Now all that remains are the ruins of an ancient tomb."

Curiosity overcame Brendán's discomfort. "Who were the Milesians?"

"The first of the Gael: the invaders who defeated the Tuatha de Danann, the peoples of the goddess Danu. When the sons of Milesios arrived in Ireland some of their ships beached not far from here. I could show you the actual place."

"The bishop never told us about any Milesians."

Above the boy's head the two men exchanged glances. "Leave it," Dubán warned Gaeth.

"I won't leave it! He should have access to a bard. The bishop knows perfectly well that history didn't begin when Patrick arrived, but. . . ."

Brendán interrupted, "What does a bard do?"

"Bards remember for us," said Gaeth. "They memorise and recite poems that tell the history of entire tribes, going back for countless generations. The bards know who we *are*."

"Gaeth's brother was a bard," Dubán added. "He died years ago."

"He was *killed* years ago," muttered the other man.

"Did you bury him in the High Grave?"

The boy's innocent question shocked Gaeth. "Of course not!"

"Time and weather have it almost destroyed by now," Dubán said. "When we were children we went up there sometimes, but we never touched the tomb. The Druids said we would be cursed forever if we disturbed it."

Brendán started to ask about the Druids. Stopped. Sat very still.

The boat rose and fell. Swooped and swung.

Brendán's stomach swooped and swung.

When the first of the great ocean rollers struck the currach he turned a delicate shade of green.

"I said," Dubán repeated, "would you like to have a try with the oars?"

"Not quite yet," murmured the boy.

"If you change your mind . . ."

"That's all right," said Brendán. Even more faintly.

While the two men discussed tides and currents for his benefit, he huddled in misery in the bottom of the currach. Time passed. Nothing improved.

Without looking over his shoulder, Dubán said, "Always make the sea work for you, Brendán. We'll go out far enough to ride back on the incoming tide. You understand?" When there was no response he turned around; looked down. "Are you all right, lad?"

Brendán gave up the struggle. Shame-faced, he clambered to his feet to spew the contents of his stomach over the side.

At that moment the sea heaved upward like some huge beast coming out of hibernation.

The currach stood on end.

I flew.

For years afterward I relived that moment in my dreams. Caught so briefly between sky and sea that I had no consciousness of either, I was aware of something extraordinary. A spangled rainbow radiance enveloped my entire being. It lasted no more than the blink of an eye and ended when I struck the water. But it was real.

What are dreams, Sister Íta?"

"Dreams are one of the ways in which God talks to us, Braon-Finn."

Rain was falling again: a heavy rain that bled the light from the sky. The scriptorium filled with shadows. Brendán lit a lamp so he could continue writing.

Remembering.

Down down down into salt water that flooded into my throat and nose. Burning them, choking me. I had been watching the sea for months yet understood nothing about it until that day. The sea was harder than a fist and colder than cruelty. No prayer for mercy could touch its icy heart.

The light was not suddenly gone, it was as if there had never been any light. As if no eyes had formed in my eye sockets. All I had was the memory of an incredible radiance on the other side of the dark.

A hand closed on his hair. His last conscious thought before the terrible darkness overwhelmed him was of Sister Íta. Rescuing him.

Like most of their fellow fishermen, Dubán and Gaeth could not swim. A man who could swim was tempting fate, daring it to toss him into the sea and leave him struggling for agonising hours before succumbing to exhaustion. Better to die at once and have it over with.

But they would never be forgiven if they allowed the godson of Bishop Erc to drown from their boat.

One man frantically plunged into the water, hoping to catch the boy before he sank too deep to reach or was swept away by the current. The other was left trying to keep the currach stable in a running sea.

In his journal Brendán wrote, 'On the day we set out on the greatest of all adventures there was a running sea. We launched our boat in quiet water at the mouth of the creek below Diadche. Bending to the oars, we rowed until the sea took hold of us.

Always make the sea work for you.

'The tide carried us far out beyond the ninth wave. Then the sails were raised and the oars shipped.

And we were in the hands of God.

During that first day some of the brothers talked constantly to hide their nervousness, but I was calm. God gives each person a gift. Some are as obvious as Sister Muirne's talent for music. Others appear to be of no benefit. Erc's broken shoulder was one of these, yet it had led him to Christ.

My gift is intuition. A sudden urge that comes from nowhere, yet is irresistible.

Some might call it a flaw in my character.

I was frightened of lightning and bee stings and half a dozen other imagined perils—until I was offered a ride in a boat. Intuition prompted my acceptance. When I was flung into the heart of the sea I discovered what real terror was.

Surviving the worst that could happen endowed me with physical courage. This was the quality above all others which would make my remarkable future possible.

"How could this be?" Erc roared at his wife. "Were you not watching the boy?"

"You mean your student? You never asked me to stand guard over your students."

The student in question lay wrapped in blankets on the stone hearth, as close as possible to the fire. Brendán's lips were blue and he was shivering violently, but he was alive—at least for now.

Two men stood to one side watching him. They were shivering too, though not from the cold. Dubán and Gaeth were not sure how the bishop would react.

"What can be done for him?" Gaeth asked hoarsely.

As everyone in the room knew, the best healer in the territory lived not far away. If a deep-lunged man shouted from atop the wall of the lios, his shout would be heard and passed on to another, in the time-honoured method of communication, until the healer heard it and came running.

The Druid healer.

Eithne rolled her eyes towards her husband.

They had been married too long; Erc knew her thoughts. He replied with the silent jut of his jaw. No Druids. "Brendán is in God's hands now. If God wants him to live, he will. Let us pray."

The four adults knelt on the swept earth and bowed their heads over their folded hands.

Afterward they told me I was ill for a long time. I don't remember; everything ended for me with the dark.

When at last I woke up, a girl was sitting beside me. Her face was only a blur. I thought she might be Íta and called out to her.

She laughed and I slid back into the dark.

The next thing I remember is Eithne trying to spoon a little warm broth into my mouth.

"You gave us a dreadful fright, Brendán."

The boy could not answer. His throat felt as if a furze bush had been shoved down it. When he turned his face away from the spoon he saw the girl again, standing in the shadows. She was not Íta after all.

Eithne said, "In your illness you kept calling for your brothers. I suggested you might be lonely for another child, so the bishop sent for. . . ."

Brige stepped out of the shadows to take the spoon from Eithne's hand. "Taste this for me," she urged.

The light returned with Brige. Not the unearthly radiance I recalled, but a tender glow that lit a lamp in my soul. From the beginning I knew she was not like the rest of us. Brige could sing to the bees and make them swarm, but they never stung her.

At least I was no longer afraid of them.

During Brendán's convalescence Brige fetched water, collected fuel for the fire, sewed and swept and scrubbed—performed all those tasks which had grown difficult for an aging woman. Under Brehon Law Erc could have taken a second wife if his first wife agreed and the second wife would have inherited these tasks, but Brehon Law was pagan law and Erc would have none of it.

As they lay in their bed at night, Eithne casually called the bishop's attention to the improvement in their domestic arrangements with Brige in residence. She did not make suggestions; she merely sowed the seed. In a soft voice, in the night.

After a few such nights Erc told Brige, "I have decided that you will remain in my house. Your brother benefits from your proximity and you are a great help to my wife."

Brendán received an expanded explanation. "Keeping your sister here leaves your mother with no youngsters to raise," Erc pointed out. "Therefore I am sending Cara back to her own clan. They have an obligation to her, and their holding is out of sight and sound of the sea, so she will be spared constant reminders of her husband's tragedy. In time she may even recover her senses. Her house will be given to a family with children."

"But . . ."

"Yes, Brendán?"

"Finnlugh's house. Should it not be mine?"

"When you are old enough you will be ordained as a priest and sent out to convert the pagans. Wherever you go, God will provide such dwelling as you require. Things always work out when we put our trust in him," Erc emphasised.

The bishop said I would be a priest, so I would be a priest. I was still of an age when the certainty of authority was comforting. I pitied fishermen and farmers, all those who must struggle throughout their lives to be worthy of God, while I was marked as God's own from the beginning.

At heart, the bishop was a simple man who looked for simple answers. He did not know, as I was to learn later, that sometimes there are no answers.

As soon as Brendán was strong enough he returned to his cell and his studies. Returned to the little drystone hut he had to stoop to enter. The tranquil silence within the dome and the scent which he recognised as his own settled around the boy like a cloak. In just such a way an animal knows its own burrow and gratefully returns.

The novice priests rejoiced in his recovered health—except for Ninnidh, a sallow man with thin red lips that were always wet, and a veiled gaze that never engaged with Brendán. The boy felt insulted. Ninnidh only acknowledged those he thought were above him in station.

'The years that followed were among the happiest of my life,' Brendán confided to his journal. 'My sister, Brige, was a constant joy. Her bright spirit was the spirit of the rainbow and just as hard to capture. She spent long days working indoors, yet there was always a whiff of field and forest about her. She was like some wild creature who overcame its shyness and lifted its head to be patted.

'The bishop would not allow Brige to attend lessons with me. Under Brehon Law women from noble families could receive an education, but Tearmónn Eirc conformed to the rules of Rome. Bishop Erc said, "Roman law considers the female, the weaker sex, as an adjunct but never a partner. God in his wisdom gave men greater strength and superior intelligence. For this reason, both authority and the education behind it should retained by the male for the protection of the female."

I didn't argue the point. Perhaps I should have. Many years have passed since then, years during which the women in my life have been the comfort of my life. Now I know that a man dying in agony cries out for his mother.

Privately I thought it was unfair to deny my sister that which was freely given to me, so I decided to teach Brige myself. I repeated Sister Íta's adage: Learning is the game we play for pleasure. Brige gladly entered into the game. She mastered numbers more quickly than I had done and was not above boasting about it. I loved her for her faults and not in spite of them. Perhaps God gives us faults so we will know we are not gods.

Late one afternoon Brendán and his sister made their way to a secluded nook behind one of the craftsmen's huts; their favourite classroom, out of sight but sheltered from the prevailing wind. The two children sat down side by side. Brige asked, "Did the bishop tell any good stories today?"

Brendán shook his head. "Not today. He was talking about the monastic movement. You know, nuns and monks. 'Monk' comes from the Greek word *monachos*," the boy elaborated, showing off, "which means 'one who is alone.' "

"What is 'Greek'?"

"The language spoken in the city of Athens; that's somewhere in the east." Brendán vaguely waved his hand in the direction of sunrise. "The Athenians are very intelligent, they study science and philosophy and any number of interesting subjects."

"Science" and "philosophy" were unfamiliar terms to Brige, but she did not ask about them. Her brother was likely to respond with more information than she wanted.

Brendán continued, "The bishop doesn't speak Greek, but he knows a few words. He says it's important to learn something about the east because Christianity consists of an Eastern Church and a Western Church, with one branch at Byzantium and the other at Rome. Monasticism began in the east, in Egypt and Syria, where a few men and women left the overcrowded towns and went to live in the wilderness."

Brige tried to pleat her smooth forehead into a frown of disapproval. "That was very foolish of them."

"It was very wise," her brother contradicted. "The bishop says they chose to be alone with God."

"Alone with God." The girl unexpectedly clasped her hands over her heart. "Oh, how beautiful! So much better than being alone with a madwoman!"

It was the first time she had referred to her existence with Cara. Brendán was startled. With a child's natural self-absorption, he had never thought about the lives being lived out of his sight.

Brige's remark expanded my horizons. Within days I was aware of currents in the bishop's house. Below the surface, unseen yet powerful.

Erc and his wife shared their Sabbath meal with Brige and me; my one escape from the diet of green martyrdom. The collation included a small piece of fish and an even smaller portion of red meat, usually venison. Remembering how I looked forward to the meat still makes my mouth water.

Ninnidh often found an excuse to visit the bishop on Sabbath days. He brought a gift—a little jar of oil or a small basket of fruit, nothing ostentatious—so he would be invited to stay. During the meal he did not speak to us children. He scarcely acknowledged our presence, he was too busy buttering the bishop with flattery. I would have thought Erc too clever to be taken in, but if Ninnidh failed to visit us, Erc was clearly disappointed.

Sister Íta taught that we should love everyone. She didn't know Ninnidh.

To Eithne, any and every guest was welcome. Ours was a poor diocese among poor people and there was hardly anything to share, yet Eithne always managed to produce some small delicacy. Her plain face lit with a kind of beauty when she offered the gift of hospitality. She hummed to herself while she prepared the food. And occasionally she laid a gentle hand on the bishop's shoulder in passing.

* * *

In 325 A.D. the Roman emperor Constantine had convened the first Ecumenical Council of the Church to establish universal doctrine and deal with serious controversies. More than three hundred bishops—the majority from the eastern branch of Christianity—and a number of lower clergy gathered at Bithynian Nicaea, between the Mediterranean and the Black Seas. The often-fraught Council eventually produced an official creed for Christians, and announced that all churches should celebrate Easter on a date to be determined each year by the bishop of Alexandria and promulgated by the bishop of Rome.

Following a long debate about clerical celibacy, the Council also forbade priests to marry. With some reluctance they agreed that men who already were married when ordained would be allowed to cohabit with their wives, but continence was urged even for them.

Ireland was a long way from the Roman province of Bithynia. The Gael, whose Druids taught that spirits are immortal and death merely an interruption in a long life, could accept the Risen Christ. They could accept the redesignation of pagan wells as holy wells, and pagan festivals as holy feast days. They could not accept the idea of an arbitrary date for Easter. They celebrated Christ's resurrection on the day when Patrick first lit the Paschal Fire in Ireland, and that was that.

Likewise, the men and women of the Gael—a passionate people long governed by Brehon Law, which took human nature into consideration—were not willing to accept restrictions to their sexual lives.

In his journal Brendán wrote: 'In the Ireland of my youth, priests often married in order to become more fully a part of the community they served. Most monks and nuns chose to remain celibate so they could devote themselves entirely to God." *Yet humans are sensual beings, and God must have made us so for a reason. After all these years my little apostle still rises to praise Him.*

When the dreams began I didn't understand them, not at first. I was accustomed to the familiar dreams of childhood, reflecting the life I knew.

My new dreams were quite different.

In the Western Sea we encountered a fish that looked like a woman. She swam for almost half a league beside our boat, her pale flesh glimmering up at us through the dark water. Several times she came to the surface as if to breathe. Once she raised what might have been an arm—or a fin—and appeared to wave at us.

"Let's try to catch her in our net," urged Brother Moenniu.

I shook my head. "You don't know what manner of being you might catch." I continued to lean over the gunwale, watching her.

Brother Aedgal said, "She's a woman, a beautiful woman, you can see that for yourself."

"What we see and what is really there may not be the same thing."

"You have a man's eyes and a man's parts as we all do," Brother Colmán asserted. "Surely you won't leave her to die."

"Surely I will not take her out of her element and into this boat," I replied. "We have no right to abuse her. She exists, whatever she is, and that is enough. She is one of God's creatures."

I continued watching her with my hands folded as if in prayer.

The fish . . . the woman . . . came so close to the boat I could almost reach out and touch her. I did not. With the set of my shoulders I warned the other men not to attempt it either.

When I thought she could see me I said, very softly, "Hello."

The woman . . . the fish . . . hung immobile in the water and looked up at me.

I could feel my heart thudding in my breast.

Before the creature submerged for the last time she gave a ringing cry that reverberated across the waves.

We sailed on.

Chapter 6

Erc's many wise judgements as a brehon had brought him to the attention of the high king, Laoghaire—a son of Niall of the Nine Hostages. Subsequently Laoghaire appointed Erc to his inner circle. Thus he had been present on a day which became legend: the day when Laoghaire the pagan confronted Patrick the Christian on the Hill of Slane.

Years later Erc told the novices at Tearmónn Eirc, "In actuality, the royal hill of Tara is a long, low ridge, but on a fine day every major peak in Ireland is visible from there. Tara can be wonderfully bright in summer. The chief poet and his retinue are in residence then, composing poems of praise to the high king or satires to deflate the pomposity of lesser men. The foremost brehons convene to debate the *Senchus Mór*, the Great Law. Music rings through the stronghold during all the waking hours, binding the tribes in harmony. Artisans throng from the farthest reaches of the land to proffer their finest creations.

"Inevitably, winter comes. I recall one bitterly cold, dark winter, rife with dire omens. There was but one grain on the stalk and one acorn on the oak. Children sickened. Cattle died. During the Festival of Imbolc the udders of the ewes were supposed to fill with milk, but they remained dry and their lambs starved. Spring did not appear. The winter dragged on.

"The desperate people pinned their hopes on the rituals of their grandfathers' grandfathers. The Festival of Bealtaine would begin with the kindling of the sacred fire on Tara, and the sacred fire would recall the life-giving heat of the sun.

"On the eve of Bealtaine, every fire in the land was extinguished. Climbing the Hill of Tara to await the ceremony, I made my way towards the royal enclosure like a blind man, following the sound of voices. There was not even a torch to guide me. On punishment of death, no other light was permitted to preempt the sacred flame.

"An immense pile of oak branches which had been interwoven according to an ancient pattern stood in front of the High King's house. By the time I arrived a number of dignitaries had gathered there. They shuffled their feet in the dark and chafed their hands to warm them. Dubthach, the chief poet of Ireland, was murmuring to himself, committing the scene to memory. Meanwhile seven Druids danced in a sunwise circle."

"Exactly what *are* the Druids?" a youthful voice interrupted. "Are they so very evil?"

What the bishop knew empirically and what he chose to believe as a Christian were two different things. A pursing of his lips warned Brendán that interruptions were not acceptable.

Erc resumed his narrative. "Swathed from shoulder to ankle in a dark red cloak lined with wolf fur, King Laoghaire was standing beside the chief Druid, Lucet Mael. The Chief Druid held a tiny stone lamp, shielding its flame with his hand so no ray of light emerged. When the sacred moment arrived Lucet Mael would use this lamp to light a torch soaked in pine resin, then set the giant bonfire alight. The sacred flame would drag the sun up from its cold grave to signal the coming of spring, and the light of the newborn sun touching the face of the High King would re-affirm his kingship."

Erc stared into space with unfocussed eyes. The remembered scene was more vivid than the one before him.

Waiting in the cold, in the dark, while the stars wheeled overhead, he had felt the timeless tug of superstition. From the vortex created by the collision of known and unknown, anything might emerge. The world was hedged with horrors. Only Druid magic—the ability to negotiate with the implacable gods of nature and manipulate natural forces to conform to the needs of man—stood between the Gael and disaster.

Any moment now. Any moment. Only Lucet Mael knew when. The Chief Druid waited as patient as a cat sizing up its prey. Soon now . . . one heartbeat more . . . the chief Druid reached for the torch . . .

A rival fire blazed in the distance! Its golden light shone like a beacon across the plains between the Hill of Tara and the Hill of Slane.

King Laoghaire was outraged. "Who has dared to commit such a crime in my kingdom? What is the explanation of this sacrilege?"

Lucet Mael licked his fingers and held them to the wind, then sniffed them three times. "Eternal life to you, great king," he said in the time-honoured formula, though his voice was unsteady. "This much we can tell you. The fire which was kindled before the fire on Tara must be extinguished this same day. Otherwise it will blaze forever."

The assemblage gave a gasp of horror.

"We go at once to put out the fire and kill the man who lit it!" cried Laoghaire. He ordered twenty-seven chariots and charioteers. Flogging the horses at every stride, the royal party plunged down the slope and out across the valley, racing to meet Fate. In one of the chariots, Erc the brehon hung on with all his strength while the cart bucked and jolted and the cold wind brought tears to his eyes. . . .

With a great effort, the bishop dragged his mind from past to present. He gazed thoughtfully at his audience. Could he ever convey to them the full wonder of what had followed, the singular miracle which had transformed his life?

"When a rival fire blossomed on the Hill of Slane," he said, silently praying for the drumbeat to begin inside him, the gift of oratory, "the High King set off to punish the transgressor. I was among those who accompanied him. Anger carried us with the speed of the wind until we reached *Ferta-fer-Feig*, the Graves of the Men of Feig, from which the hill took its name. There the charioteers drew rein. According to custom at burial sites, they turned the faces of the horses to the left and their own faces to the right.

"Lucet Mael went to summon the violator while the rest of us waited well beyond the light from the usurping fire. It was important to keep the High King safe from its malign influence. We sat down to show the criminal no honour. As the sky began to grow bright—unaided by any fire on Tara—the anger of the Druids increased.

"A sliver of sun gilded the horizon; the Druids hissed through their teeth. Then a sturdy grey-bearded man came towards us from the Hill of Slane. In one hand he carried a shepherd's staff. He walked with purposeful strides like someone who has nothing to fear. Lucet Mael had to trot to keep up with him. As he approached, the stranger called out in a clear voice, 'Some trust in chariots and some in horses, but we go in the name of God!'

"Unaware of what I was doing, I leaped to my feet. Dubthach, the chief poet, also stood up, but the rest of the king's party sat as if carved in stone. Patrick came straight to me and said with a broad smile, 'The eternal God blesses you.' At that moment the power that was in him reached out and took hold of my spirit. It has never let go.

"The High King ordered his personal guards to seize the stranger and kill him on the spot. But each time they approached Patrick the earth shook so violently that they were afraid to touch him.

"King Laoghaire demanded that his Druids question Patrick. They tried every trick they knew to expose flaws in the man, but he turned their words against them and exposed their own flaws instead. Their tempers snapped like dead branches. The man who identified himself as a messenger from Christ remained calm. He said nothing in his own defence, but spoke with great dignity of peace. And love."

As he spoke those words, the gift returned to Erc. The bishop's voice began to ring like a bell. "I myself heard Patrick in that golden dawn. A holy man from the frontiers of Britain was opening a new frontier. The vitiated past was being swept aside. The Creator of All Things was manifesting a new face in Ireland!"

In Ireland, thought Brendán, feeling prickles rise on his arms. *Right here.*

All that was youthful and ardent in the boy responded.

In his journal, the Abbot of Clon Fert wrote, "Laoghaire the High King was never converted, but the seed Patrick planted on that Easter morning has flowered dramatically. Until the coming of Christianity, knowledge had been passed down through the oral tradition for countless generations. The missionaries brought literacy to Ireland. As the monastic movement grew, monks were assigned to make copies of the Gospels. The Gaelic passion for exuberant patterns and vivid colours soon exerted its influence; the manuscripts became works of art.

'Monasteries competed with one another for the most gifted scholars. When Ninnidh completed his novitiate at Tearmónn Eirc he departed for further study at a new monastic school called *Clon Ard*—the High Meadow. The founder of Clon Ard, a former warrior and sea raider called Finnian, was renowned for his knowledge of the Greek language.

Hatred is a sin. Sins, according to the bishop, result from deliberate actions. We can choose not to commit them. The virtues Erc extolled were passive: obedience, humility, submission.

That's why I had so much trouble with them.

I don't remember choosing to hate Ninnidh, but I must have done. His departure came as a great relief to me. He had begun throwing sly looks in my direction as if he knew all about the strange dreams that troubled my nights.

There was something wrong about those dreams and I knew it. Although Brige and I lived in each other's shadow I could not confide in her. Even to myself I could not explain what was happening.

Before the arrival of Christianity prudery had been unknown among the Gael. Poets extolled the white breasts of women and praised the naked legs of young men. Eithne and Brige bathed unabashed in my presence, making no any attempt to hide their bodies. When I recalled that I had never seen a nun naked I wondered why.

That's when my dreams began.

The lanky boy whose tunic strained at his shoulders and whose arms had grown too long for his sleeves complained to the bishop, "You never answer my questions about the Druids. You explain everything else, but not Druids. Exactly what are they?"

"Pagans," Erc replied in a voice rimed with ice.

"A pagan is someone who doesn't believe in our God. Many people don't believe in our God. What makes Druids special?"

The bishop could no longer evade the question. With evident distaste, he said, "The Greeks described the Druids as the intellectual class of the Celtic race. Perhaps that was true once, but no longer. The Druids are evil because they want to keep us trapped in the past, where they control all wisdom and the people are enslaved to superstition.

"Fortunately Christ has brought a new truth and a greater wisdom, Brendán. By his sacrifice he set us free. That is all you need to know."

Someone was always telling me, "That's all you need to know." But I wanted to know everything.

Brige was a growing girl. Her body demanded more than frugal fare, and constant short rations were dimming her bright spirit. On a morning when the gnawings of hunger became unbearable, she confided in her brother.

His reaction was immediate. Before the bells rang for Prime, he had persuaded Dubán to give him the use of a coracle and a paddle. Gaeth provided some lines and a seine, and Brendán took to the sea. Disobeying the bishop was a small sin compared to letting his sister be hungry—though he did obey Dubán's injunction to stay near the shore. "If you lose this boat I'll have to build another," Dubán said, "and that would hardly be fair repayment of my generosity, would it?"

When Brendán caught his first fish he was as proud as a warrior spearing a wild boar. Gaeth's wife boiled the fish and wrapped it in seaweed. Brendán concealed his trophy beneath his cloak and carried it to Tearmónn Eirc in triumph. "Don't tell the bishop I gave you this," he warned his sister.

Brige was indignant. "Do you think I'm stupid?" Before he could reply she added, "Can you catch another one?"

Within weeks Brendán had his own small currach, complete with a triangular sail. He learned to read currents by the colour of the water and to sense dangerous rocks beneath the surface. To determine the direction of the sun on overcast days he peered through a sliver of iolite given to him by Dubán. Gaeth had contributed a small leather pouch containing flint stones and shreds of tinder for kindling a fire, equipment every experienced sailor carried in case he was forced ashore far from home.

"Be sure to fasten that bag around your waist," Gaeth warned. "Never leave it lying in the boat."

The boy began sailing farther westward, paddling his currach into unfamiliar shallows. Observing varieties of fish he had never seen before; marvelling at the grotesque shapes of seaweed which writhed as if with a life of its own.

Giving his imagination free rein.

Diadche held a peculiar fascination for Brendán. The solitary peak stood aloof from the rest of the mountain chain. Cloaked in heather; crowned with clouds.

I imagined the mountain as a giant ogham stone with a message only initiates could decipher.

Wild tales were told about Diadche, stories that Erc dismissed as superstition. Most of the Altraighe who lived on Corca Dhuibhne avoided the mountain. A stone fortress built on the eastern slope had been deserted for generations. Any red deer who reached the wild and scraggy glens on Diadche's flanks were safe from the spears of hunters.

While exploring the coastline below Diadche, Brendán discovered a natural harbour where a little creek flowed into the sea. The landward side was steep, making access by that way difficult. It looked as if no one ever visited the place.

The narrow harbour became Brendán's favourite destination. He beached his boat and kindled a fire to cook a fish, or stretched out on a stone shelf to take a nap. Sometimes he gazed up at the frowning brow of Diadche with a feeling of kinship.

The two of us alone. Out here.

He was discovering a taste for solitude.

The hush of a snowflake on the soul.

I could never have been a warrior. My ears despise the clang of sword and spear; they want the music of birds and the songs of the sea.

* * *

Erc was well aware of his godson's activities. Nothing that happened in the parish of Tearmónn Eirc escaped the bishop's notice for long. But in spite of his original injunction to stay away from the sea, he said nothing about Brendán's disobedience. Over the years, Brendán had reminded Erc what it was to be a boy. In the recesses of the bishop's memory lurked a youngster who was forbidden to climb certain tall trees but climbed anyway, just because it *was* forbidden.

When more fish began to appear in Eithne's iron cooking pot, Erc did not question their source. He merely said, "God provides."

As long as Brendán kept up with his studies, he was tacitly allowed the freedom of the sea. It was only a matter of time until he began going out with the adult fishermen.

He was in his element.

Serious fishing demanded all of a man. The effort of rowing against the tide and the intense concentration of hauling in the nets left no energy for conversation. That only came later, at the end of the day, when the fishermen gathered on the beach to divide the catch and spread their nets to dry. One man would bring a jug of fiery liquid to pass around while others built a fire.

That was the time for talking, and listening, while the wind blew smoke into Brendán's eyes and the sea murmured to itself like a living thing. The time for being, at last, part of the tribe.

As sure as the jug of liquor there was always a *seanchaí*, a storyteller, even if the tribe had no official bard. At the request of his audience the seanchaí might give a vivid description of Hy Brasail, the distant Isles of the Blest: the paradise of the Gael where no one ever grew old.

He spun nets of magic in which he captured the iron-weaponed Milesians and the mysterious Tuatha de Danann and displayed them like a catch of silvery herring. Or, clothing myth with flesh, he brought epic heroes such as Cúchulainn and Fionn Mac Cumhaill to thundering life for the entertainment of his listeners.

Everything was there, in the night. By the sea, under the stars.

Whenever the seanchaí paused for breath, or a drink from the jug, Brendán besieged him with questions. Brendán was intensely curious about those very aspects of the Gaelic world which Bishop Erc sought to suppress. The storyteller recounted the names and qualities of the numerous ancient gods of the Gael: nature gods for the most part, such as Manannán Mac Lir. In spite of Christianity, the Lord of the Sea remained a powerful deity among the fishermen.

Brendán also learned there were a number of Druids among the Altraighe, though they never went near Tearmónn Eirc. Or if they did, they were not wearing the ritual robes which would have identified them.

As far as I could tell, the Druids posed no threat to any Christian. They simply existed; part of the landscape and part of the people. Yet, from the day he arrived in Altraighe-Caille, Erc had waged unrelenting war against them.

The bishop's hatred of Druids puzzled me.

One day the answer came to me when I was thinking of something else entirely. As answers often do.

Erc hated the Druids not because of their philosophy or their threat to our religion, but because he had been a Druid. He had to hate them to justify leaving them.

The seasons became years; flew away like startled birds. Novices were ordained and left Tearmónn Eirc; other men took their places. Not all aspired to the priesthood. An increasing number were preparing for a monastic life, though some of these were barely able to raise a beard.

Ruan was Dubán's youngest son. A few years older than Brendán but no taller; a swarthy boy with brooding, heavy-lidded eyes. The Gael were a garrulous race, talking—or singing—at every opportunity, but Ruan was an exception. He spoke very little and did most of his communicating through gestures. Brendán found the older boy's diffidence a challenge. Slowly, patiently, he had set out to make friends with him. In time he was rewarded with the lifelong loyalty of a steadfast soul.

For such a dark lad Ruan had such a bright smile.

Born and raised in a tribe of fishermen and taken aboard boats as soon as he left his mother's arms, Ruan disliked everything to do with fishing. He detested the flavour of fish, the smell of oxhide boats smeared with rancid fat, the buffeting winds that scoured a man's flesh, the backbreaking labour that made men old before their time.

Most of all Ruan hated the incessant roar of the waves. Unlike the rest of his tribe, he had never learned to ignore the elemental voice which filled his waking hours and underscored his sleep.

The voice Brendán loved: the belling of the silver-horned stags.

Who knows why two people become friends? Perhaps it is shared interest, perhaps shared experience. Perhaps just familiarity.

Or perhaps friendship is a gift from God.

One day Brendán remarked to Ruan on the increasing number of would-be monks at Tearmónn Eirc. "I've never seen a monastery myself," Brendán said, "but I suppose they're rather like Tearmónn Eirc. In places where there's more stone than timber, that's what they use to build them."

"Must be dark inside," Ruan commented.

Brendán laughed. "They must have lamps, or at least candles, for those who are copying manuscripts. Prayer is the main occupation of monks, though, and they don't need much light for that; only peace and quiet."

Ruan raised his heavy eyelids. "Would a monastery be very quiet, then?"

"I suppose so."

Ruan shifted weight from one foot to the other. "How does a man become a monk?"

"He'd have to be a Christian, of course, and I suppose it would help if he could read and write."

In that moment Ruan knew he had found his calling. "I'm a Christian, Bishop Erc baptised me. But I can't read and write. Would the bishop teach me? If you asked him? Remind him that my father helped save your life."

Brendán regarded his friend with astonishment. "Why would you want to be a monk?"

Ruan shrugged. "It's that, or fishing."

The arrangements were soon made. "By the time you leave Tearmónn Eirc you will be welcome in any monastery in Ireland," the bishop assured Ruan. "But you shall have to work very hard, very hard indeed."

Ruan shrugged. "I'm used to hard work."

When Brendán offered to help tutor his friend, the bishop agreed. Ruan learned quickly, like a man grabbing a lifeline. Their work together cut into the time Brendán spent on the bay, but he did not begrudge it. He simply got up earlier and stayed out longer.

How did I manage to cram so much into those days? Was it merely the energy of youth—or was time flexible, expanding to suit my needs?

Is there even such a thing as time? Is it not just a point in eternity? We believe our years march forward through time but do they not, perhaps, circle around it instead?

Brendán could not ask such questions of Brige, whose mind rejected abstractions, or of Ruan, who was fully occupied with the simple task of opening his mind at all. So Brendán phrased his query within his own head and waited for God to answer.

One day when the two friends were in the scriptorium studying a manuscript, Ruan asked, "Why do you want to be a priest, Brendán?"

"I'm destined for the priesthood."

"I was destined to fish. But I'm not going to. That's what I want to do," he said, pointing at the page open before them. Elaborate black letters written on creamy vellum. Swirls of coloured inks entwined like ivy. Gleaming gold leaf. "The bishop says we should devote the work of our hands to God. I have two good hands. God's welcome to use them. I'd rather make something beautiful than gut fish." He flashed his rare, radiant smile.

While young men like Ruan prepared for the monastic regimen that one day would give Ireland an unequalled reputation for scholarship, the barbarian tides continued to roll across Europe.

The last of the food the angel gave us was only a memory by the time Aedgal caught sight of an island on the horizon. A favourable wind promptly filled our sails. Our boat glided over the water as smoothly as milk glides down the side of a pitcher.

I smiled to myself, recognising the hand of God.

When we drew near the island we saw a huge number of fat sheep. They were as large as cattle and covered the ground like drifts of snow. "Where could they have come from?" Brother Molais wondered. "There cannot be enough grass on the whole island to produce such magnificent creatures."

Brother Solám wondered, "Where is their shepherd?"

But they were alone.

As we beached our boat, the sheep turned their faces towards us. Calm, gentle faces, filled with the patience animals know but Man has forgotten. They placidly watched us come ashore. A few lambs even walked forward to greet us, extending their tiny muzzles to sniff our fingers.

"Today is Maundy Thursday, the beginning of Eastertide," I reminded the brothers. "We shall conduct divine service here. As you see, we are being presented with the Spotless Sacrifice."

The sheep watched me with their yellow eyes.

I sent the monks out among the flock to select one. "Bring me the finest animal you can find," I told them. "The sacrifice must be worthy."

Eventually they selected a mighty ram. He offered no protest when they tied a rope around his horns and led him back to me. I placed my hand on the forehead and gently scratched the animal between his great curving horns.

I said Mass while the ram stood quietly beside me.

Afterwards I removed the rope and set him free.

And we sailed on.

CHAPTER 7

In a sun-drenched city on a hot spring morning, two men in heavy clerical robes sat on opposite sides of an olivewood table. The table's surface was lost beneath an avalanche of documents. The older priest, who was plump and red-faced, withdrew a scrap of soggy linen from his sleeve. "Today is even hotter than yesterday," he remarked as he mopped his brow.

His newly-assigned secretary was quite young, yet habitually wore the expression of an old warhorse during a bad day on the battlefield. "If you were not so fat the heat would not bother you," he said cruelly. Although the secretary resented any suggestion that he had obtained his position through family connections, he was oblivious to offending others. "Here, can you explain this?" He handed a thin sheaf of documents across the table.

The older priest gave it a cursory glance. "These are changes of appointment. What do you not understand?"

"The last item on the second page."

"Ah yes. *Finisterre*, the end of the world." He smiled. "Patrick's place."

"Patrick?"

"Patricius the Briton, have you heard of him?"

The secretary suspected he was being patronized. "My grandmother's brother knew Patricius very well," he claimed through tight lips. "They were the greatest of friends."

"In Rome?"

"Of course in Rome." The reply was too hasty.

Liar, thought the older priest. He mopped his brow again. "Your grandmother's brother was fortunate in his friendships," he said dryly. "Patricius has become something of a legend. After he went to Ireland he ordained over three hundred bishops. Some of them are still living, I believe, such as . . ." He ran his eyes down the list. "This one. Erc, bishop of Altraighe-Caille. Make a note: he should receive a copy of the new Missal when they become available."

The secretary gave a derisive snort. "What extraordinary names those people have. 'Erc' sounds like a bone caught in the throat. Why is he on the list?"

"It is puzzling," his superior agreed. "He must be quite old by now. Such decisions are made higher up, of course, and we have no way of knowing the reasons behind them." *Just as I will never know why I have been burdened with a clod like you,* he added silently. "All we need do is sign and stamp the document and pass it on."

"Our good deed for the day," the younger man grumbled.

His colleague gave him a sharp look. "Do you have any objection?"

"I never heard of this man before. How can we know he is

worthy? I should not like to have my good name connected with a mistake in judgement."

It already is, the older priest thought to himself. He gazed out the nearby window at the dusty, torpid street, where a lean brown dog cowered before a group of boys who were taunting it. The leaves of the trees drooped in the heat.

The dog abruptly bared his teeth and snarled at his tormentors. They backed away.

The priest laced his fingers across his chest. "Why not take the day off," he suggested, "and visit your relatives? Surely they can tell you everything you want to know."

The young priest gave a disdainful shrug. "When I have served my time here I might like to travel like Patricius, and make the whole world my classroom. Surely I could arrange such an appointment for myself."

"I'm certain you could," the other man replied. Under his breath he added, "and the sooner the better."

In his journal Brendán wrote, 'During the years I spent at Tearmónn Eirc Ireland prospered. Life remained hard on the rim of the Western Sea, but elsewhere, to use the words of the poets, "the rivers were fish-full, the kine milk-full, the trees heavy-headed."

'In the Year of Our Lord 496, Pope Gelasius, the bishop of Rome, introduced the Gelasian Missal, a book of prayers, chants, and instructions for the celebration of the Mass. By the time copies of the Missal reached Ireland, Gelasius would be dead, but another decision of his was having powerful repercussions.

'In late autumn of 496 Erc learned he had been appointed bishop of Slane. The appointment came as a surprise to us.

Surprise is an understatement. We were thrown in a heap.

"Why are they doing this?" Eithne wailed when her husband gave her the news.

Years had passed since the last time Rome responded to any of his reports on conditions at Tearmónn Eirc. Erc was as baffled as his wife by the new appointment. "Rome never explains, Eithne," he reminded her, trying to conceal his own dismay.

But she knew. "How dare they transfer you to another diocese after all this time and all the work you've put in here!"

"I assume they need me," Erc said quietly.

"There are plenty of other men."

"Few with my experience, and certainly none who have such an intimate connection with Slane."

"What about your intimate connection to me!"

"Ah, Eithne," said the bishop. That was all. "Ah, Eithne."

Brendán happened to witness this exchange. He made no comment, but he remembered.

That night Eithne greeted her husband at the door by saying, "You're not being asked, you're being ordered. Even a fish can decide where to swim, but not you. Rome decrees, so we must leave our home and these people and the church you helped to build with your own hands. *Your* church, husband!"

A muscle twitched in the bishop's jaw. "It is Christ's church," he said.

When he awoke the following morning the first words he heard were, "I'm too old to be dragged across Ireland and start over again from nothing."

Erc tried to placate her. "I have been thinking about that, and decided not to ask it of you. You can stay in this house, where you feel at home, and Brige will remain behind to look after you. When a new bishop is appointed for the diocese you will be given the house at Fenit to live in. It's a fine house, Eithne."

Under her tongue his wife kept a list of the many small injustices her husband committed against her over the years. Unremarked, his crimes had multiplied to fester in the darkness of her mouth like a miser's fortune. Treasures hoarded against the time of greatest need.

The time was now.

"How dare you suggest such a thing?" she shrieked at him.

"Would you abandon me as if I have no value? My father was a cattle lord, or have you forgotten? You're very good at forgetting what's inconvenient to remember. When we married my father provided me with a dowry of gold because the Druids predicted you would be chief brehon someday. What happened to that dowry, Erc? *What happened to it?* You can't tell me you've forgotten about that!"

He looked away.

"For our wedding I had a silk gown dyed with sloes and embroidered with gold thread. Do you remember my shoes laced with silver? And how your fingers trembled as you unlaced them?"

Erc braced himself like a man facing into the teeth of a storm, but said nothing. A man cannot lose an argument if he does not take part.

The storm gained force. Eithne began pacing back and forth, wringing her hands as she spoke. "When the high king summoned you I thought we would join the court at Tara, which shows how wrong a person can be. I expected our daughters would marry princes of the *Uí Néill* someday. But oh no. Instead you met some lunatic on the Hill of Slane and came running home to tell me you'd found a new god. The high king was furious and so was I—not that you asked my opinion.

"Before the year was out I'd been half drowned in cold water to make me a Christian and you were calling yourself a bishop. We left the mildest climate and richest soil in Ireland to come to this bare, bitter place. For a while we were in actual danger—did you think I was unaware of it? People gathered outside the lios, muttering and burning fires.

"I've worked myself grey-headed turning this house into a home for you. Did you ever notice? Did you ever say 'Thank you, Eithne'? You thank God for every little thing but you never thank me.

"And that's not the worst. Instead of joining the clan of the high king, our girls married into the Ciarrí Luachra and we never see them anymore. We are an embarrassment to them, Erc! Crazy Christians ranting at the end of the world!"

Eithne stopped walking; turned to face her husband. Her voice sank to a moan. "Once I ate apples and soft bread every morning, and fat meat and honey wine at night. I used to be plump and pretty; when I arranged my hair young men begged for strands from my comb. Do you remember?"

Erc dare not show pity. She would cry if he did, and he had no defence against a woman's tears. "Come with me and you will have apples and soft bread again, Eithne," he coaxed—though for all he knew it was a lie. The documents from Rome in their precise Church Latin had carried no practical details. Nothing concerning living arrangements.

His wife's body, so vulnerable a moment before, went rigid. "I won't go with you, ever, and that's that. I simply will not go."

In the end, she did. It was Eithne who packed their clothes and necessary household goods—pitifully few of either, she thought to herself as she worked. With Brige's help she loaded them into an oxcart; the same cart that had brought the priest who would take over the parish of Tearmónn Eirc. Both men assumed a new bishop would soon be appointed for the diocese of Altraighe-Caille. In the meantime Ruan was to continue his studies along with the other novices, under the guidance of Erc's replacement.

"An ordinary priest," Eithne muttered under her breath to Brige. "As if just anybody could do what my husband does. And an oxcart! Everyone who is anyone rides a horse or has a chariot at his command, but not a bishop, oh no. If my husband were still a brehon . . ." She set her lips in a thin line.

Brendán was almost as unhappy as Eithne. What could replace the beloved smell of the sea, or the belling of the silver-horned stags?

With heavy heart he sailed one last time to the narrow harbour at the foot of Diadche. As usual, the summit was concealed by a swathe of mist. During the years Brendán lived at Tearmónn

Eirc he had planned to explore the peak, yet somehow never did. He always promised himself, "Tomorrow."

Now his tomorrows were claimed.

We think we have forever. But we don't.

Brendán made his way around the bay to say goodbye to his friends the fishermen. Sundown found him on the little promontory, standing with bowed head beside the cairn of white stones.

Goodbye. God be with you. Goodbye.

The following morning Brendán assured Ruan, "I won't forget you."

"I won't forget you," his friend echoed. Ruan stood in the road and watched the oxcart dwindle into the distance. A long time passed before it disappeared. Oxen walk slowly.

The bishop's family began their journey in silence, cocooned in their private thoughts. Erc rode in the front of the cart with a bundle wrapped in sacking carefully placed between his feet. Eithne sat behind him, facing backwards by her own choice, while Brige and Brendán walked with the yoked bullocks. From time to time Brendán tried to provoke them into a trot by slapping their haunches with a willow rod.

The cart lurched and jolted on its wooden wheels.

Eithne clenched her teeth.

As they left the sea behind, the sky lost its nacreous glow. For the sake of hearing a human voice in the midst of wilderness, Erc said, "We have a lot to think about. A Christian community should provide a perfect home for religion, education, and industry, and is best established in a location with no outside distractions. That may be difficult in the Boyne Valley, which is good ploughland and well populated. Yet we must aspire to what our brothers in the east call a 'desert'; a *diseart*, a deserted place where one can hear the voice of God. Monasticism was born in the desert for good reason."

Eithne sighed.

Brendán thought about the headland of the High Grave, and the harbour below Diadche.

Furze yielded to forest. When the trees closed around them the bishop stopped lecturing. The bullocks swung their tails at tiny, sharp-biting flies.

"Is this the right direction?" Brendán asked. "Are we going outwards?"

Erc's temper frayed. "Must you question everything? A Christian submits. We are going in the direction the Church sends us."

Night caught them in the mountains.

The only hostel they found was a damp timber hut with sleeping pallets laid on the bare earth. The only luxury provided was the mandatory basin of water for washing.

The bishop lay awake much of the night. The more he thought about his situation the worse it seemed. The hopes he could nourish by daylight evaporated in the dark.

They resumed their journey at daybreak. Plodding along, half listening to the creaking of the cart's wooden wheels. From somewhere in the depths of the forest came a deer's plaintive cry.

"Do deer have souls?" Brendán wondered aloud.

"Of course not," the bishop said testily. "They are animals."

"But . . ."

"You have too much imagination, lad. Pay attention to the trail. We have to climb that slope on a slant."

That evening they were guided by the smell of roast venison to a hostel with raised sleeping shelves and thick blankets. The bishop reproved Brige for being greedy and ate almost nothing himself. Afterwards he went outside and stared gloomily into the darkness. Eithne went out to him and touched his arm, but he did not notice.

At their third stop Brendán overheard a conversation between the bishop's wife and their host. "You are giving hospitality to a most prestigious man," Eithne told the hosteller.

"Ah?"

"Oh yes. My husband, Bishop Erc, is the founder of a renowned Christian centre at the edge of the Western Sea. I'm sure you've heard of Tearmónn Eirc?"

"Ah." The hosteller scratched his head. "Don't think so."

"You must have; men came from far and near to study with him," Eithne went on, sounding a little desperate. "Surely some of those pilgrims stopped with you?"

"A lot of people stop with me," the man said. Not to be outdone he added, "They also come from far and near." Noticing the arrival of a new party of travellers, he hurried rather too quickly to greet them.

The bishop's family fell asleep to the sound of rain on thatch.

On our journey I was not troubled by my dreams. Motion seemed to keep them at bay—or perhaps I was too tired to dream.

The rough track the oxen were following gave way to a well-trodden road. Traffic increased. Some travellers were on foot but men and women of the noble class rode horses; stallions for the men and mares for the women. Large hounds trotted behind their masters. Meanwhile traders with their carts shouted greetings or imprecations, and stopped in the middle of the road to make deals.

Erc was exhausted. Riding in an oxcart was tiring enough; depression added a dreadful burden. He dozed fitfully.

When they encountered a family walking along with a number of children, the bullocks stopped of their own accord and lowered their heads to be scratched. Brendán struck up a conversation with a boy about his age who claimed they had never met a Christian before.

The bishop made a mighty effort to shrug off his weariness. He stood up in the cart and spoke to them of Christ.

And God.

The mother of the brood asked, "Which god are you talking about? Where is his dwelling-place? Is he young or old? What makes him different from other gods?"

Erc's eyes, bloodshot from the dust of the road, grew bright again. "Our God is the God of all mankind, God of heaven and earth, of the seas and rivers and lakes, God of the sun and moon and stars, God of high mountains and low valleys, God beyond heaven and within heaven and below heaven." As he quoted Patrick, Erc's voice slowed, deepened. Became music. "God has his dwelling in sky and earth and sea and in everything they contain. He breathes in all creatures and makes all creatures live. He surpasses all things and supports all things, he illumines the sun and the stars, makes wells in dry earth and islands in the sea. He is the God of all creation and all creation lives in him. Youth begins and old age ends with God, who always has been and ever shall be."

The conviction ringing through the bishop's words was irresistible. Even Brendán, who had heard this many times before, was entranced anew.

Erc was only a breath away from Patrick. It was Patrick's God speaking through the bishop in the oxcart. I can still see the upturned faces staring at Erc while incomprehension gave way to excitement. . . .

. . . and then to rapture as they accepted the all-embracing love of God.

Watching the bishop, I realised I could never do what he did.

Their trek continued. One step at a time, dictated by the pace of a pair of bullocks. Cold and rain but sunshine too; brief flashes of warmth. Even in winter the land was green and the birds sang. Brige could mimic their songs perfectly. An escort of flashing wings accompanied the oxcart.

As word spread, Erc frequently was stopped by crowds wanting to hear him preach the Gospel.

The Word.

I loved the sense of forward motion, however slow, and the constantly changing scenery. No forest was like any other forest, every tree was different. Every river, every meadow. The earth was as various from moment to moment as the sea.

I was happy because I was no longer having the dreams.

The landscape through which they travelled was shaped by territorial claims as much as by nature. Promontory forts of stone and earthwork stood atop rounded hills—often manmade—that emerged like islands from the forest. Sacred burial mounds contained chieftains committed to protect their tribeland even in death.

On open grassland, roughly shaped standing stones defined territorial boundaries.

Brendán began noticing standing stones carved with Christian symbols. Once the bishop got out of the oxcart and went to touch the stone, resting his hand against his surface as if he could read God's word through his palm.

Close to the *Slighe Mór*, one of the five royal highways leading to Tara, they came upon an extraordinary sight. Stalks of mullein dipped in tallow blazed in tall iron holders, guiding travellers to the door of a palatial inn. The oaken exterior was painted in vivid colours. The interior was lighted by beeswax candles as thick as a child's arm. Beams and crossbeams were carved with abstract Celtic designs. Portable screens set with bands of silver and copper were arranged around the walls to partition off private spaces.

Outside the hostel, icy rain penetrated the skin and chilled the marrow of the bones. Inside was a fragrant fire of applewood logs. The rain was reduced to a muted song played upon thatch, accompanied by a harper with closed eyes who caressed his harp like a lover. Two huge wolfhounds sprawled at his feet. Scattered about the room were benches set with platters of polished yew wood and beakers of green glass, holding more food and drink than Brige and Brendán had ever seen in one place. Wild boar sausages and blood puddings and carved wildfowl; freshly baked bread and thick oat stirabout sweetened with honey; apples and nuts and ale and buttermilk; stone bottles containing a clear liquid that was not water.

At the invitation of the hosteller the children ate until their stomachs hurt. They teased each other with bits of food whose nature was unfamiliar to them, but tasted wonderful. They laughed a lot. And yawned. And ate some more.

Eithne drank an impressive amount of ale and all of the liquid in one of the stone bottles, then stumbled across the hall to sit at the harper's feet. Without opening his eyes, he smiled down at her. One of the great hounds licked her face. The other put its head in her lap and heaved a contented sigh. She began to hum tunelessly, waving her hand with the chords of the harp.

The bishop lowered his aching bones onto a mattress stuffed with goosedown and instantly fell asleep.

"Are we going to live like this from now on?" Brige whispered to her brother.

Brendán shook his head. "I doubt it. I don't think this qualifies as a desert."

On a barren, rocky island we had searched for food for three days without success. We fell asleep exhausted. The following morning we found a smaller island separated from us by a narrow channel. Its cliffs were surmounted by luxuriant vegetation. "My eyes are even hungrier than my stomach," said Brother Moenniu. "They long to look upon growing things."

We sailed around the new island looking for a landing site. The sheer cliffs were daunting, but eventually we came to the mouth of a little river. Taking to the oars, we rowed upstream until we reached a shallow gravel bank. There we moored the boat and went ashore.

To be enveloped by beauty.

A flower-starred meadow stretched before us. The green grass was as thick as wool and hemmed by shrubbery in full blossom. Groves of little trees rang with birdsong from ten thousand throats. Butterflies danced in clear bright air that smelled of grass and flowers and sunshine. But not of the sea. Not of the abyss.

When we went looking for a source of fresh water we found a spring of crystal purity. Above the spring stood a

single immense tree, its outstretched branches weighed down with snowy doves. The emblem of peace and mercy.

Tears filled my eyes. In the silence of my head I began to pray. "God, who knows the unknown and unknowable, you are aware of the burden I carry in my heart. Show me your mercy."

From the multitude on the tree one dove launched herself into the air. She flew straight to me and lit on the grass at my feet.

I bent down to address her. "If you are a messenger of God," I said, "tell me why these birds have congregated here."

In a piping voice she replied, "We are the survivors of a great slaughter wrought upon us by an ancient enemy. The Creator saw the wrong done to us and carried us to this sanctuary in the palm of his hand. In this paradise we recovered and took a sacred vow. Now we wander through the regions of creation in the form of spirits invisible to earthly eyes, like many other spirits who have missions to perform, but on holy days we return here to take on the bodies you see and sing the praises of the Creator. If you and your brothers join us in this endeavour, you will be rewarded with the dream you most cherish in the depths of your hearts."

My companions understood nothing that had transpired. They thought I had been talking to myself—a longstanding habit of mine. When I repeated what the dove told me they were astonished.

"How can you talk with a bird?" Brother Tarlách wondered.

Thinking of Préachán, I said, "By listening."

"And that's all?" Obviously Tarlách did not believe me.

Sometimes the simplest lesson is the hardest to learn.

Brother Anfudán said eagerly, "Will we go to paradise as soon as we praise God?"

"The bird's message was this," I replied. "If we praise God as devotedly as the birds do, we shall realise our most cherished dreams one day."

"What day? When?" This from Brother Fursu.

Before I could answer him Brother Gowrán said, "In God's good time, which is not ours."

When the doves flew down to drink from the crystal spring they tilted their heads back afterward to thank God.

At the hour of Vespers the birds all sang as if with one voice and we sang with them. The same was repeated for Compline. My brothers and I lay down to sleep around the base of the tree and awoke to the singing of the birds at Lauds. And so the canonical hours passed, Prime, Terce, Sext, Nones, Vespers, and Compline again.

We celebrated Easter in that holy place. The island fed us with its natural bounty: berries and roots and herbs, cresses and fish in the stream. We took what we needed but not one bite more, and thanked the fishes for sharing their life with us. It was as if we existed outside of time, in a place that was intended for humankind before we became greedy.

At Pentecost our avian friends abruptly departed in a cloud of white feathers.

"God has dispatched them on a new mission," I told my companions. "This is the signal to be on our way as well."

They were reluctant to leave the paradise of birds, but I reassured them. "We can load our boat with enough food and water to last until God leads us to the next place. He has not failed us yet."

So we turned our backs on comfort and security and set forth on the sea of life once more. As God intended, we sailed on.

CHAPTER 8

The Boyne River was named for Bo-an, the cattle goddess.

Unless it was the other way around. The fruits of creation conversing in the long pagan summer and choosing identities for themselves. Mountain and river and salmon and deer, wind and rain and stars and humans. Nothing really mattered but the names God gave them. And everything was God.

'On the final leg of our journey,' Brendán wrote, 'we followed the river. If we not already known we were in Royal Meath we knew it then; promontory forts stood watch atop every bluff.'

The oxen were tired, though we had acquired a fresh pair halfway along. When we stopped for the night I always saw they were fed before feeding myself. Standing with the beasts in the dark as they lowered their heads to the corn. Smelling the clean scent of their skins and the sharp tang of their manure. Rubbing their shoulders where the yoke had pressed.

Wondering what the morrow would bring.

'Three days before Christmas we came up valley of the Boyne and saw the Hill of Slane rise before us.'

Erc gave a sharp intake of breath. He recognised the shape of the hill but little else. The grassy slope was scored with footpaths. Where Patrick had lit his fire on that fateful morning there stood a rectangular timber church. The building comprised a single but spacious chamber with the door at one end and a single window at the other. The steep-pitched roof was covered with oak shingles. The interior walls were bedecked with linen hangings embroidered by local women. Close to the pebble-bordered path leading to the door was a large stone cross, deeply carved with Celtic knotwork and scenes from the Gospels.

Word of the bishop's arrival had preceded him. A crowd had been gathering since before dawn, huddling together for warmth. When the oxcart finally appeared they ran forward, jostling one another in their eagerness to greet Erc and his family. The wise oxen, realising their job was done, halted mid-step. Erc was lifted bodily from the cart and carried in triumph up the hill. His wife and the two youngsters followed on foot.

The local Christians had been busy for weeks preparing for their new bishop. No sooner had Erc inspected the church than he was hustled along to admire his freshly-constructed residence.

Secular dwellings were still round, following the ancient pattern. The bishop's house was unusually large. The construction was wicker and daub, with fleeces affixed to the interior walls to keep out draughts. The roof was thickly thatched with reeds from the river, prized for their insulating qualities. Household accoutrements included mattresses stuffed with down and blankets woven of the softest wool. A full range of newly-crafted utensils hung from thongs around the walls. The central hearth boasted elaborate iron fire-dogs.

A dozen strides to the north was a bread oven made of clay; a dozen strides in the other direction was a sizeable guesting house. As a final touch, the bishop's dwelling had its own well.

Eithne could not take it in. She had expected the worst, had armored herself against resentment and hardship. Standing in the doorway of her new home—a house fit for nobility—she began to weep.

Erc was too busy to notice, but Brige did. She put her arms around the woman and whispered, "It's all right now, don't you see? The bishop and God have organized it between them and everything's all right."

In his journal Brendán wrote, "The newly designated diocese of Slane was delighted to have as its first bishop a man ordained by Patrick himself. There were even a few who remembered him from the days of King Laoghaire, and greeted him as "Erc, the sweet-voiced judge." *To his visible embarrassment and secret pleasure.*

We who had been sharing the hardships of a subsistence life were overwhelmed with plenty. Apart from the western coast, most of Ireland was cloaked with primeval forest. There was never a shortage of firewood. Nor of red meat. Vast herds of cattle and deer grazed the grasslands; wild boar fattened on acorns beneath the oak trees. Countless varieties of birds made the trees and meadows their home. In addition the land provided all the raw materials needed by craftsmen of the highest standard, whose products were then traded for imported luxuries of every description.

I could only imagine the splendour of the high king's court at Tara.

He did not deign to pay an immediate visit to Erc, which disappointed the bishop, but every other chieftain and person of importance within a day's walk of our hill soon arrived. Bearing gifts. We received more fur cloaks and baskets of fruit than we could ever use, so many that Erc sent me out to find "needy people" to give them to. Except there were no needy people. This was Ireland in her prime: a bounteous island that could support its inhabitants a thousandfold.

That year at Slane the Feast of Christmas was a feast in truth.

I began to wonder how Erc could reconcile this with his avowed austerity. I knew better than to ask him.

Ireland always had been pastoral; cities and towns were nonexistent. Now the Christians were establishing new, vibrant communities around their religious centres. Tearmónn Eirc had been an early example of what was becoming a mighty movement.

Slane was meant to be Erc's reward.

His new congregation filled the church to overflowing and knelt outside on the cold earth. Their prayers swelled to a joyous chorus that echoed along the valley.

On the Feast of Epiphany, King Lughaidh finally paid a call on the new bishop of Slane. Lughaidh was the last living son of Laeghaire, and had reigned at Tara for twenty-five years after killing his father's successor in battle. A tall, broad, big-bellied man with a body as hard as hewn oak, he retained the habits of war: balancing on the balls of his feet; constantly shifting his gaze.

Lughaidh listened with grave courtesy to Erc's attempts to bring him into the Christian fold. Then, with grave courtesy, he declined. "Your concern for the fate of my spirit does you credit," he said, "but my strong right arm is all I need to gain admittance to the Isles of the Blest, the paradise of warriors. I doubt if your Christian heaven could compare."

Erc hid his disappointment behind a smile. "Should you someday feel otherwise . . ."

Lughaidh smiled too; a smile he carefully measured to correspond to the exact degree of cordiality expressed by the bishop. "In that unlikely event, I shall know where to find you," he said.

As the days passed Erc discovered a physical energy he had thought long lost. He spent the dark months travelling around his new diocese and making plans for its future. When summer came he intended to create a major ecclesiastical community around the Hill of Slane. New priests would be trained for the new parishes he would carve out of the surrounding forest and grassland. Erc also planned to found a monastery which he would endow with a pure gold chalice and paten for the chapel altar.

There was a certain coolness between the bishop and his wife in the matter of that chalice and paten. The bishop had brought them from Tearmónn Eirc wrapped in sacking, and let no one else touch them.

The organisational abilities of the new bishop of Slane were soon recognised. Erc's geographical proximity to Tara made him the most central senior cleric in Ireland. Other bishops conferred with him about the hierarchal arrangements of the Church; abbots visited him to discuss canon law.

The former brehon was in his element.

Meanwhile life at Slane was easy for Eithne, as her husband had promised. Too easy. She had spent long years learning how to pare a rind of cheese to release the tiniest scrap of nourishment; how to boil fish bones and skin and seaweed together into a glutinous soup that would fill the belly, even if it disgusted the palate. All that was soft in Eithne had long since been discarded. Now when she had enough to eat, she had no appetite. Now that she slept in a cushioned bed, she could not sleep. Nor did she have work to do. The women of the parish fought among themselves for the honour of cleaning and maintaining both the church and the bishop's house, and were constantly bringing gifts of food.

Even Brige complained—good-humouredly—that her hands were idle. At the bishop's suggestion she devoted herself to the study of Holy Scripture and long, earnest prayers from which she derived a placid satisfaction.

As soon as winter's mud began to dry, work began on the new monastery. The site Erc had selected was some distance from his church—and visible from Tara. The bishop laid out every detail with great care. The monks' huts and refectory would be built of timber, but Erc insisted on a stone chapel. "Christianity must build for the ages," he said.

Unlike Finnian of Clon Ard, Erc rejected the dual role of

abbot and bishop. An abbot's control was limited to his monastic parish, while a bishop's control was territorial.

Brendán went to watch the construction of the monastery chapel. He knew nothing of the stonemason's art but fishing had made him strong, so he offered to help. At first he only lifted and carried. After a day or two a mason gave him a chisel and explained the rudiments of shaping stone. As the walls rose he felt a growing sense of pride.

In my imagination those walls already resonated with music.

On the first day of spring a deputation of nuns led by Brigid, the abbess of *Cill Dara*, paid a courtesy call on the bishop of Slane. The group included women from several nunneries who jointly contributed a set of embroidered linen altar cloths, the work of their own hands.

I recognised her immediately, even in the distance. That quick, eager step, the roundness of her bosom, the waterfall of hair revealed when her hood fell back . . .

The abbess of Cill Dara was famous. Some called her "the Mary of the Gael." Her father, Dubthach, was a king in Leinster, and she had been fostered by a highly respected Druid; a man converted to Christianity by Patrick himself. As soon as Brigid was old enough to return to her family Dubthach had sought a husband for his daughter. His requirements were rigid: a man of property who had the grazing of at least five hundred cattle and was also a poet. Poets were the equal of princes.

Defying her father's will, Brigid had sought out Mel and Macaille, two of the many bishops ordained by Patrick. She convinced them that she wished to commit her life to Christ. Brigid and seven other noble women then knelt at the bishops' feet and took solemn vows of poverty, chastity, and obedience.

The nunnery the women subsequently established at Cill Dara, the Church of the Oak, was the first of its kind in Ireland.

Brigid had become a familiar figure on the high plain where the warrior aristocracy raced their horses. Unimpressed by titles,

Brigid repeatedly confronted chieftains and kings, blocked their view of the track, and preached the Gospel to them. She was an indefatigable traveller who founded one religious community after another, sought freedom for slaves and captives, and was renowned for her many acts of charity. Her wise counsel was sought by the leading chieftains of her time.

The bishop often spoken of Brigid in reverential tones. He admired her as he did no other woman. They were of the same class and had made the same leap of faith. Giving hospitality to the Mary of the Gael would bestow vast prestige upon Erc. As he went out to meet her he positively glowed.

The historic nature of the occasion was lost on me. I had eyes for only one woman that day. Brigid and her nuns dressed all in white, but Íta was wearing the grey wool she always wore.

Íta.

She must have been old enough to be my mother, yet she possessed the ageless beauty Christ often bestows on his brides. When I saw her at Slane after so many years I could only stand and stare. Trying—desperately—not to remember my dreams, the torment and ecstasy of my dreams.

My dreams of Íta.

Lost in conversation, Brigid and Erc walked up the hill towards the church. The other nuns followed at a respectful distance while Brendán's sister trotted at their heels, enthralled.

Brendán approached one of the nuns. "Do you not know me?" he asked.

There had been a time when Íta had to crouch down to meet my eyes. Now she had to look up to me. There was a network of fine lines around her eyes. Tracks left by laughter. They made her even more beautiful to me because I loved her laughter.

"Braon-finn?" she said hesitantly.

"They call me Brendán now."

"I know. Bishop Erc has kept me informed of your progress. I hoped you would be here with him today."

Hoped. She said she hoped! My imagination ran away with me.

Íta recognized the blue eyes and black curls, but all else was changed. The little boy she remembered had grown into a strapping youth taller than his years. Strong, masculine features were emerging from the childish softness of his face. He was almost old enough to take up weapons.

Her skin tingled the way it did when there was thunder in the air.

She continued following the bishop towards the church. Brendán fell into step beside her. Neither of them spoke.

At the doorway of the church Erc fell to his knees to pray. Brigid and the other nuns knelt behind him. They look like a flock of white doves, thought Íta. She turned to share the thought with Brendán. When she met his eyes her skin tingled again, almost painfully this time.

"I never forgot you," he said.

With an effort she looked away. Lowered her eyes and folded her hands in prayer.

Inside the church, Íta managed to interpose other nuns between herself and Brendán. Yet she could feel his eyes on her. Like sunbeams. Like daggers.

Following Mass, the bishop conducted a tour of the still-incomplete monastery. Afterward, the party converged on the bishop's house for a feast. Eithne had heard Brigid's name often enough over the years, and was gratified to discover that the celebrated woman was older than herself.

Brigid had a gift for making others comfortable. Upon entering the bishop's house she made a point of admiring the flowers in the pitchers and the burnished copper bowls piled with apples. She credited every charming detail to Eithne. Before the day was over the abbess of Cill Dara was asking the bishop's wife for advice on the domestic arrangements in her own abbey.

She also gave Eithne a cross woven of rushes; an elegantly simple design of her own.

Throughout the day, Brendán was acutely uncomfortable. He

felt certain that Íta was avoiding him. He had to talk to her. But whenever he came close she engaged someone else in animated conversation, or slipped away with other nuns to look at this or that or something else. The woman who had always taken time for him now had no time for him at all.

No one paid any attention to the morose youngster who loitered around the edges of the group. No one but his sister, who brought him a cup of wine and asked if he was hungry. "Not now and not ever again," Brendán growled. She raised her eyebrows and left him alone.

After Compline the nuns retired to the guesting house. Brendán followed them, sauntering along as if he had no particular destination in mind. Once or twice he tilted his head back to admire the panorama of the evening sky. Arriving at the guesting house as if by accident, he peered around the door.

Íta was crossing the room with a pile of blankets in her arms. She felt, rather than saw, his presence, and turned towards him. The acute distress on his face prompted her to hand the blankets to another nun to distribute. "I'll be back as soon as I can," she promised.

Spring was in the sunlight but winter lingered in the darkness. She paused long enough to put on a woollen cape before emerging from the guesting house. She had only gone a step or two when Brendán caught hold of her arm.

Gently but firmly Íta disengaged his fingers. "Explain yourself, Braon-finn," she said in a low voice. "Tell me what's the matter with you. Perhaps I can help."

Her face was a pale oval in the darkness. Memory filled in the features. "You're beautiful," he blurted.

He had intended to speak as one adult speaks to another, impressing her with his maturity. When the moment came, the words tumbled out beyond his control. He sounded like Erc talking at top speed. "I'm going to be a priest and the bishop will ordain me and I want to take a wife and be part of the community so will you marry me?" He stopped, alarmed by sound of his own words. It had all gone wrong somehow. "Will you marry me *then*?" he amended.

Íta laughed.

He was so young, so funny and earnest that she could not help herself. The laughter rippled out of her.

Brendán was horrified. He took one step backwards. Then another.

Turned and ran.

Chapter 9

Her woman's heart realised the situation too late. Íta ran after Brendán, calling to him, but his long legs swiftly carried him beyond the range of her voice. She returned to the guesting house distraught. When she knelt beside her pallet she appeared to be praying, so no one disturbed her. No one noticed the tears running down her face.

Brendán hid in the woods west of the hill until the nuns left Slane, then returned to the bishop's house. "I went out to see a friend," he told Eithne. "We had a . . . misunderstanding, and I needed some time to think it over." It was as much truth as he could manage.

Eithne made no comment. She understood that the male has things on his mind which do not concern women.

After several days—and nights—of silent suffering, I set out to repair the damage in the only way I knew: through the word.

How I agonised over that letter! I spent an entire morning on the riverbank, selecting gorgeous, poetic words, and stringing them together like beads to make irresistible phrases.

When I was satisfied I spoke my message aloud, the way I thought Íta would hear it in her head. Disaster. The effusive composition was totally wrong; not like me at all. Not like anyone Íta would want to know. I began again, still reciting aloud, changing words here and sentences there, then throwing everything out and starting again until I was weary of the sound of my own voice.

The final text of the letter was simple in the extreme. "Forgive my childish outburst," I wrote. "I was so glad to see you that I failed to express myself properly. Be assured I seek only your friendship, and offer only the true and unfailing love of a friend."

Brendán entrusted his epistle to a trader who regularly travelled as far as the Meadow of Deep Soil. He did not fear the man would read it. Traders were good at numeracy but otherwise illiterate.

No reply was made to the letter. Nor did he expect one.

It was high summer in Meath—a lusher, leafier summer than ever experienced at Tearmónn Eirc—before Erc learned a new bishop still had not been appointed for Altraighe-Caille. "My people must think I have deserted them," he moaned.

"These are your people now," his wife reminded him, but he was in no mood to listen. He prepared to return to the Altraighe at once.

The members of his new diocese were outraged to think their bishop might travel in an oxcart. They insisted upon equipping him with a pair of fast horses and a high-sided, four-wheeled chariot, plus his own charioteer.

Erc was embarrassed. "Christ lived as did the poor, for he served among the poor. I can hardly do otherwise."

A local chieftain with more sense than tact pointed out that Erc was not a young man. "If you hope to spend any more years as bishop of Slane, you need to take care of yourself now," he told the bishop.

Before Erc was a priest he had been a brehon; he could never argue against logic. He accepted the chariot.

Eithne warned, "You will wreck your health entirely."

"What better sacrifice could I offer to Christ?"

"Then take me with you."

"Do not be ridiculous, woman; I would not dream of taking you away from your comforts here. Besides, chariots are not appropriate for women."

For travelling companions Erc had only Brendán and a charioteer with large, square teeth, like those of his horses. The man was a skilful driver but never stopped talking. He even answered his own questions, eliminating conversation. Afterward Brendán retained only two clear impressions of the journey: the speed of a galloping team, and the nonstop monologue of a man with nothing to say.

To the bishop's dismay, Erc's sanctuary was growing shabby. The timber-framed gateway was sagging on its hinges; the structures within the lios were giving way to the constant assault of the weather.

The priest Erc had left in charge of the parish was well liked and the Altraighe thronged to the little church, filling it to overflowing, yet they never seemed to notice that the buildings were in need of repair. Their boats were in more need of repair, as were their nets. And the dwellings where their families lived.

Bishop Erc set to work on the same day he arrived. He drew up a long list of tasks and organised a work party that included every able-bodied person in the parish.

Ruan was glad to see Brendán again. "I can read and write!" the dark boy exulted as the two worked side by side clearing a drainage ditch. "Not a lot yet, but enough."

"You still want to enter a monastery?"

"It's all arranged. Next month I'm going to Clon Ard."

"I don't want to discourage you," said Brendán, "but . . ."

Ruan rushed forward on the wave of his excitement. "At Clon Ard they'll teach me to illumine manuscripts!"

"Ah. Of course." Brendán decided not to mention Ninnidh. Instead he smiled approvingly and clapped his friend on the shoulder. "I'm really happy for you," he said.

The highlight of the bishop's visit was the ordination of seven new priests; two of them members of the Ciarrí Luachra. Afterwards Erc announced to the congregation, "I plan to divide my time between Tearmónn Eirc and Slane until Rome assigns a new bishop for this diocese. It is an oversight they will soon rectify."

I think Erc was secretly delighted to have two dioceses. The work was too much for a man of his age, yet after he made the announcement the years seemed to fall away from him.

Is the concept of time something that man invented? Like truth, or justice? Are we as old as we think we are? If the soul is immortal, then the essential Me inside my body is timeless.

As soon as he could slip away unnoticed, Brendán visited the cairn on the headland. He felt no urge to pray; the site had no connection with Christianity. Yet the Gael in him recognised a sacral place.

Sister Íta, will God ever speak to me?"

"Perhaps, Braon-Finn. If you open your heart to him."

"When will he speak to me?"

"When you least expect it."

"But how will I know his voice?"

Íta had taken the little boy's hand and held it to her ear. With his small forefinger she traced the intricate whorls. Next she moved the finger to the child's ear and followed the pattern there. "Every person is unique, Braon-Finn. Every one is made to hear God in a different way."

Brendán wrote, 'During that visit to Tearmónn Eirc I made a momentous decision.' *It did not come easily. I tiptoed around in my mind for a long time, afraid of disturbing the new idea being born there. When it was fully fleshed I took it into the light and studied it. Saw the roundness and rightness of it.*

Brendán waited for several days before confronting the bishop. He was hoping for a right time but there was never a right time, so he finally plunged in anyway. "You want me to be a priest," he said to Erc as the bishop was donning his vestments for Mass, "but I'm convinced that God has fashioned me for the contemplative life."

Erc drew himself to his full height—an effort, because his damaged shoulder restricted his posture—before replying. "You are still only a boy. How can you presume to know what God intends?"

"How can you?" Brendán shot back.

Erc said evenly, "This is a childish rebellion, you will forget it tomorrow."

"It's not rebellion, I'm simply acknowledging something I've known for a long time. I'm strongly attracted to solitude. That's the way God made me, so it must be for a reason."

The bishop's expression had hardened like drying mud. "Years of work have gone into preparing you to follow in my footsteps; you have been more thoroughly educated than any member of the Altraighe. Listen to me, Brendán. You are going to enter the priesthood. Make no mistake about it." The mud softened a little; hinted at a smile. "But I promise you this: when the time comes I shall ordain you myself here in Tearmónn Eirc, and invite your entire tribe to share in a great celebration."

Over the years Brendán had become familiar with the bishop's style of coercion.

The covert threat of force sweetened with honey, but force all the same.

He folded his arms across his chest. "I'm freeborn. I have the right to make my own choices."

The bishop's voice rose. "I am responsible for your spiritual well-being. You must obey me in this matter."

Brendán slitted his eyes. "All right. If I can't be a monk I'll become a Druid; I might even study to be a brehon, like you. Following in your footsteps, as you said."

Erc's suddenly livid face would have alarmed his wife. "You blaspheme! May God forgive you!"

"Where's the blasphemy in being a Druid?" Brendán asked, as casually as if he were inquiring about the weather. "Aren't Druids ordinary men and women with special gifts—gifts which our God gave them, even if they don't recognise him?"

Veins throbbed visibly in the bishop's temples. "Be careful what you say, young man! Hell yawns beneath your feet!"

Brendán looked at the ground as if searching for something. Looked up again. "I don't see it."

Erc's forced smile was like the rictus of a corpse. "If you refuse to be serious, we can talk about this at a later time. I have work to do now. Other people need me." He walked away.

Brendán made a rude gesture at his back.

Each had said things he regretted. Neither would undo his words even if he could.

When the bishop made his rounds of the parish he asked Brendán to accompany him. It was a formal request, formally accepted. No other conversation passed between them. Erc watched the boy out of the corner of his eye. Brendán was his to shape and mould, and he would not—could not—accept rebellion. He had allowed his godson considerable leeway in the past but it was time to reaffirm his authority. The lamb must not stray from the flock.

He was determined.

As they approached the dwelling of Gaeth's family, the fisherman's youngest daughter recognised Brendán and ran out to greet him. They had played together in the past, frolicking like healthy young animals.

He was older now.

So was she.

After a moment's hesitation, the girl flung her arms around Brendán and pressed her parted lips against his. Her mouth was wet and warm. Her breath mingled with his breath.

Brendán thrust the girl away from him with such force that she sat down hard on the sand. "Don't do that!" he said in a hoarse voice. "Don't ever do that again."

As they walked back to Tearmónn, Eirc the bishop said, "Your chastity does you credit, Brendán."

The boy shot a glum look in his direction.

I didn't want to be harsh with the girl, but the ardour of my nature was now apparent to me. My rejection of Gaeth's daughter wasn't about chastity. It was about Íta.

In his journal Brendán related, 'After informing Bishop Erc of my desire for a monastic life I returned to Slane with him.'

Being Irish, they found it impossible to make the journey without speaking to one another. After the first few miles they were talking again. Politely. About safe subjects. By the time they reached Slane no one would have been able to tell they had quarrelled.

The breach between them was not healed but patched over. Neither mentioned it, and after a time the relationship continued—almost—as before, with the exception that Brendán's future was never discussed. He continued his studies with the bishop. When Erc paid his quarterly visits to Altraighe-Caille, Brendán accompanied him and never complained about being pressed into hard labour.

Whenever possible he took a boat out on the bay. Letting the sea carry him. Watching the horizon.

Or standing on the headland of the High Grave. Watching the horizon.

In the Year of Our Lord 500, the use of incense was introduced into Christian church service. Across the Irish Sea, the native Britons celebrated a major victory over the invading Saxons at Mount Badon. And at Slane, the bishop's wife coughed her life away in a bloody froth. Eithne died as she had lived: unobtrusively.

Brige commented, "She never really settled here, Brendán. In her heart she yearned to go back to Altraighe-Caille, where life was hard and the bishop needed her."

Eithne was laid to rest in the burial ground behind the church, with Brigid's cross on her bosom, beneath her clasped hands. After the funeral I walked back to the house with Bishop Erc. The years he had thrown off had returned to him in full measure. His face was ashen; he dragged his feet and stopped several times to catch his breath. Brige had a fire on the hearth to warm him and a pitcher of honey wine to comfort him, but they did him no good. As we sat by the fire, Erc said in an almost inaudible voice, "Eithne was with me at the beginning. She was with me through everything. Now everything is over." I was shocked to realise he was crying. Huge, silent tears poured down his otherwise impassive face.

Within a week Erc's flesh began sagging from his bones. The ruined shoulder stood up higher than ever, a hook from the sky upon which his body hung. His parishioners predicted, "The bishop will die before spring."

He did not. He merely stopped being alive.

While Brendán's real life was about to begin.

CHAPTER 10

Following Eithne's death, the bishop carried out his duties as scrupulously as ever, though with an abstracted air. When every bud was pregnant with spring, Erc summoned his godson. "Eithne used to say I was being unfair to you," he admitted to Brendán. "She thought you had a right to live your own life."

Brendán could not help smiling. "I've never disagreed with Eithne about anything."

No smiles were left in the bishop, who said sombrely, "There comes a time when a man must reflect on what he has done well and where he has failed. If I have made a mistake with you . . . let me put it this way. You have learned all I have to teach you, yet still you ask questions. Perhaps you can only find your answers in the wider world. Towards that end I have decided you should undertake a peregrination. . . ."

"From the Latin *peregrinator*, meaning a pilgrim," Brendán interrupted excitedly. "You're saying I can go on a pilgrimage?"

"If your foster mother approves."

Unaccountably—from the bishop's viewpoint—Brendán's windburned cheeks flushed red at the mention of Íta. "I'm a man now. Do we have to ask her permission?"

"Of course we do; Sister Íta's place in your life is indisputable. I have sent her a letter about the matter and await her reply before proceeding. It is always possible she will not agree, you know. There are dangers to consider. Not only wild animals in the forests, but also outlaws who will kill you for the sake of your few belongings. You could fall in a boghole and drown. Or you might sicken and die in a place where no one will ever find you.

"There are other less obvious hazards, Brendán. You may meet others who are undertaking spiritual journeys similar to yours, but you should travel alone. I cannot stress this too much. You need to be able to observe and contemplate without distraction. The way of a pilgrim is an education in itself, and the search for truth and enlightenment can lead down many different roads. The value is in making the journey."

I had stopped listening. Imagination is a wild horse and mine was running away with me again. I watched Íta reading Erc's letter, staring into space in deep thought, then putting quill to paper and . . . no, coming in person to ask . . . to say . . .

What could she ask? Or say? The walls between us had been in place from the beginning. Only a child would think it possible to breach them. And I was no longer a child. I could dream a man's dreams in the privacy of my head; in my vault of bone.

Erc was saying, "The experience will be of inestimable value to you in your priesthood, Brendán."

Suddenly recalled to the moment, the young man looked blank. "Priesthood?"

"Why would I send you on a pilgrimage if not to prepare you for the priesthood?"

As part of the maturing process, Brendán had learned to think before speaking. "You know my desire for a contemplative life," he said after a pause, "and you have remarked on my chastity. Surely you must agree that God has fashioned me for the monastery. What do you suppose Eithne would say about it?"

Erc knew Brendán was attempting to manipulate him; behind those innocent eyes lurked a guileful mind. But the fight had gone out of the bishop. It was enough of a battle to get up every morning, put clothes over his aching body and force food down his unwilling throat; fulfil the endless ecclesiastical obligations he had so willingly undertaken; crawl back into a cold and empty bed at night and struggle in vain to fall asleep. Eithne would say. . . .

What would Eithne say? He tried to hear her voice but it was very faint. Fading away.

Gone to God. Fortunate woman. She always had the easier path, Erc told himself.

"The purpose of a pilgrimage is to seek truth and spiritual enlightenment," he said aloud, passing an age-spotted hand over his eyes, "which you obviously need. If Sister Íta grants her permission, you may go."

"Go where? In what direction?"

"Wherever God sends you," the bishop snapped. Would the lad never outgrow his constant questioning? "When you accept that you are meant for the priesthood, come back to me for ordination."

In a low voice Brendán said, "Not when. If."

Erc pretended not to hear.

After several weeks the bishop received a reply from Íta. Erc did not show her letter to me. "You have her permission," was all he said.

'My lessons with Bishop Erc concluded,' Brendán wrote in

his journal, 'I became a *peregrinator*. A pilgrim needs a stout heart, a strong walking stick, and sturdy sandals. I equipped myself with these, plus a cape of oiled leather and a belt to which I attached my necessaries: a hand axe, a razor, my pouch of flints, a few strips of soft leather for making small repairs, and a packet of iron fishhooks. Slung over my shoulder was a bag containing bread and smoked fish.

"Securely strapped to my back was my manuscript satchel, or *cumhdach*, containing a precious Psalter which I had copied out myself in neat but not particularly artistic Latin script. My cape would protect it in inclement weather."

I had also—and without asking the bishop's permission—copied the list of ecclesiastical communities he had compiled to aid in soliciting recommendations for an abbot for the new monastery at Slane. Monastic foundations adopted the constitution devised by their founder, so the chosen man would be expected to conform to Erc's tenets.

Except for Clon Ard—I had no desire to see Ninnidh again—I planned to visit a number of the monasteries on the bishop's list.

'Religious communities were springing up everywhere. At the edge of the Western Sea a hardy order of monks inhabited offshore islands barely big enough for seabirds. Abbeys in the boggy midlands were being built on narrow strips of solid land surrounded by vast marshes, corresponding to Erc's dream of a "desert." Wherever they could, monks and nuns opened schools to offer the gift of literacy to the local population.'

A person taught to read through the Scriptures became Christian by absorption.

On the bright morning when Brendán left Slane, only his sister was on hand to bid him goodbye. "The bishop slipped out during the night to visit one of his parishioners," Brige explained. "He said not to wake you."

I interpreted Erc's absence as a rebuke for my refusal to submit to his will. But as I walked away the bishop already was receding into the past. The unknown future lay ahead. I could hear the sun singing.

It was good to be travelling again.

Eschewing roads, Brendán set off across country. Roads were primarily for trade; he was looking for something which could be neither bought nor sold.

The first monastery Brendán visited was a couple of days' walk from Slane. Mochta, a Briton and disciple of Patrick, had been in Meath until opposition from a local chieftain forced him to move northwards. There he had been allowed to establish a monastery at a settlement called Louth, in honour of Lugh, the god of the sun.

Christian peacefully supplanting pagan. Patrick would approve.

Mochta's monastery was known as *Teach Naomh Mochta*—Mochta's House. Almost as old as Erc, the abbot was a short round loaf of a man, warm from the oven and given to expansive gestures. When he flung wide his arms to greet Brendán the nearest monks hastily stepped out of the way.

As was required of an abbot, Mochta had shaved the top of his head in an ear-to-ear tonsure and wore a hooded robe and sandals. "Dear brother!" he cried as if he had known Brendán all his life. "Dear, dear brother, how happy we are to welcome you! What news of Slane? And dear Bishop Erc, how is he? I keep promising myself I shall visit him but you see how things are, we are terribly busy, it seems as if a new man arrives almost every day to take his vows here, not that I expect that of you, of course. But come along, we must give you some bread and salt and then there are a few of the brethren I want you to meet . . ." Without giving Brendán a chance to reply to any of this, Mochta hustled him into the heart of Teach Naomh Mochta.

The large monastery was thriving. More than three hundred monks lived and prayed and worked among numerous structures of timber, or wattle-and-daub, scattered across a rolling meadowland. Mochta personally conducted Brendán on a guided tour. "You have to see everything," he kept insisting, "in case you change your mind about Slane."

"But I haven't decided . . ."

"Well that's all to the good then, isn't it? Here's our chapel, I know you'll appreciate the wonderful light inside, everyone does, and . . ."

Mochta did not walk; in spite of his age and the dignity of his office, he bounced. He hummed like a hive of bees. I found his joviality, so different from Bishop Erc's restraint, delightful, and searched my hard-won Latin vocabulary for words to describe the abbot. Ebullient. Effulgent. Effusive. Then, as the day wore on and he was still in full spate: excessive.

In the dusk we came to the edge of monastery land. A grove of apple trees marked the boundary. Wild and gnarled, each tree growing in its own chosen shape.

The heady smell of fruit ripening sweetly in the dark.

I wanted to sit in silence on the grass, just being there. Mochta would not hear of it; we returned to the church to add our voices to all the others singing the praises of God.

A week later I finally succeeded in extricating myself from Teach Naomh Mochta. I had never been more warmly welcomed. But it was not my place.

Every day at sundown the pilgrim read from his Psalter. No matter how weary Brendán was, the beauty of the Psalms refreshed him. On clear nights he also read the map of the sky to orient himself. If darkness overtook him in the vicinity of a hostel he accepted hospitality, though he ate sparingly. More often than not, nightfall caught him in the open. Partially covered by his cape, he fell asleep under a bush or in a cave or—once—in the crotch of an immense tree.

He always set out again before the last star vanished.

Dawn was a sacred time. The earth held its breath as if waiting to be born. Then sunrise lifted the lid of the day, releasing a flood of light to push back the darkness. In gratitude, a single sweet, piping note of birdsong was followed by an explosion of jubilation as thousands of small choristers defined their territories for the new day.

Every day required a new definition.

Freed of supervision, Brendán's true nature began to assert itself.

When the sun shone and the earth smelled sweet, I so rejoiced in the goodness of God that I thought my soul would burst from my body.

If rain brought melancholy—an emotion as common among the Gael as exuberance—he slouched along with his head down, letting the water stream off his leather cape.

Far too often the wind carried the sound of battle. It might come from any direction but there was a deadly sameness about it. Men roaring and taunting one another; the clash of iron; the screams of pain.

War defined the Gael. A tribal people on a small island, they fought for territory and status. When too many young men had been killed and the women were grieving, the warriors might, for a time, practise a highly stylised warfare that resembled sport, but sooner or later they reverted to a more deadly form of combat.

They gloried in it.

As a small child I had believed the life the nuns led was typical of life everywhere. Íta's warrior kinsmen were, I thought, a gaudy exception.

I had it backwards.

The first time Brendán heard the cacophony of battle he considered following it to the battlefield and preaching Christ's message of peace to the combatants. Erc might have. Patrick would have.

Brendán went in the opposite direction.

I wasn't physically afraid. Irish warfare followed explicit rules: during a battle, warriors only attacked warriors. Any other behaviour was dishonourable. But I didn't have Erc's gift, much less Patrick's, and I was very afraid of making a fool of myself.

Brendán might walk for days without seeing another human

being. The major event of his day could be an encounter with a red squirrel who sat on a tree branch and scolded him. At first he tried to interpret every incident as a message from God, but soon realised he was trying to force a meaning where none existed.

There were mornings when I awoke turgid and brimming with the force that had set the stars alight. Mornings when I was grateful to God for giving people bodies with which to experience, even in a tiny way, the rapture of creation.

When his food supplies were exhausted, Brendán fished. Tearmónn Eirc had accustomed him to a meagre diet, but walking required considerable energy. By spreading a net at the mouth of a stream during the dark of the moon—eels only travelled in the dark—he caught a bagful of the silvery creatures. He subsisted on these and watercress until the merest thought of eel turned his stomach.

Fortunately he found a farm where the woman of the house filled his bag with cheese and blood pudding and freshly baked bread. "We've had pilgrims here before," she said cheerfully. She was squint eyed and flat chested, but her voice was as sweet as a meadowlark's.

"Are you a Christian?" asked Brendán.

"I believe in everything," she said.

He began to meet other wanderers. The first of these was an exceedingly thin man with a round red face, like a ripe apple on a spindly branch. The man was sitting crosslegged on the ground, dolefully examining the sole of his foot.

Brendán sat down beside him. "I am Brendán, son of Finnlugh. If you are in difficulties can I be of some assistance?"

"I am Gowrán, son of Echrí," the other replied. "God has put a splinter in my foot."

Brendán was intrigued. "How do you know God put it there?"

"Who else could have?"

"I would assume you stepped on the splinter yourself."

"I did, Brendán. But God ordained that my foot should touch the ground on that exact spot."

"Is the splinter causing you pain?"

"Only when I put weight on my foot. Perhaps that means God doesn't want me to go any further. What do you think?" Gowrán looked earnestly into his face.

"I think you can't sit here forever. Let me have a look." Brendán took the grimy foot into his hands. "Have you no sandals?"

"I had soft leather boots until I met an old woman who was barefoot."

At first impression Gowrán appeared to be slow-witted or holy or both, as sometimes happens.

After Brendán removed the splinter from his foot Gowrán said, "God sent you to rescue me. That means he wants me to go on walking."

"Are you a pilgrim, then?" Brendán asked.

"I don't know yet. I'm just . . . going."

Disobeying Erc's injunction—when did I not?—I invited Gowrán to accompany me for a way. Not out of charity, but of curiosity. Good acts don't necessarily arise from good impulses.

Gowrán was not a talker. He preferred to listen, and replied only if a reply was expected. Brendán knew how to communicate with a quiet man, so he carried the bulk of the conversation yet listened attentively when Gowrán spoke, and was content to share long, undemanding silences.

Gowrán, Brendán learned, was six years older than himself and the youngest son of devout Christian parents. He possessed a rudimentary knowledge of Church Latin. His thinness was deceptive. In hilly country they found a narrow defile which would save them a steep climb, but a boulder blocked the way. Gowrán lifted the massive stone as if it were a pebble and set it aside. When Brendán remarked on his strength he was embarrassed.

Gowrán had nothing of the warrior's arrogance; modesty ran all the way through him. Brendán hazarded a guess: "Do you come from a clan of farmers?"

"I do," Gowrán affirmed. "They don't travel."

"Then why do you?"

"To see more," he replied.

Gowrán could find food and drink whenever he wanted. He was adept at extracting soft fruits from a thicket of brambles without getting scratched, and could scamper up a tree and shake down enough nuts for a meal by the time Brendán had spread his cape on the ground to catch them. His keen nose could usually lead them to the nearest stream, but if none was available, he could detect an underground spring by a change of temperature in the bare earth.

Brendán knew how to fish but Gowrán was an expert at snaring small game. He adjusted each trap to its intended prey, utilising angles and leverages without any training in mathematics.

My first impression of the man had been wrong. Gowrán was intelligent, not merely educated. His body was attuned to the world around him; his spirit saw far beyond. On an afternoon when rain played the drums of forest leaves, Gowrán stated with absolute certainty, "Heaven smells like summer rain."

I believed him.

After a few days in Gowrán's company Brendán concluded that he himself talked too much; to his own ears he sounded as pompous as Bishop Erc. "Have you ever noticed," he remarked to Gowrán, "that we tend to talk like the people we know?"

"Adults do," Gowrán replied. "Children talk like themselves."

When they came to the shores of a large lake, Brendán turned south. Gowrán turned north. "I'm going this way," said Brendán.

"I'm not," responded the other man.

Brendán did not question his decision. The friendship they had developed was based on respecting each other's boundaries.

"I'll be sorry to lose such amiable company," said Brendán as they parted.

"We live on an island," Gowrán pointed out. "If you keep travelling and I keep travelling we'll meet again sometime—provided we don't jump off."

Yet many years later, that is exactly what we did.

After many days at sea we came to a rock-ribbed island that contained the ruins of a village and a stone fortress. We searched the island and found no living being, yet inside the fortress were beds stuffed with clean straw and covered with woollen blankets. The larders were filled with cheese and butter. The stone ovens, still warm to the touch, contained loaves of freshly baked bread. Silver bowls of summer fruits and golden goblets brimming with wine were on the table.

In the best tradition of Gaelic hospitality, a cauldron of heated water waited just inside the door, so we could bathe our hands and feet.

"This feast is a reward for our faith," I told my companions.

They ate and drank their fill, making up for many days on short rations. Afterwards they went to bed, covered themselves with the soft blankets, and soon fell into a deep sleep. Just as I, the last of them, was about to close my eyes, I saw one of the uninvited monks get up. I said nothing but lay in the shadows, watching. Moving stealthily, he approached the table and took one of the gold goblets. He hid it in his clothing and then lay down again.

I did not sleep well that night.

Three days later, as we were about to leave the island, I asked my companions to return anything they might have taken from the place. "Nothing here is ours," I reminded them. "Everything we have used must be returned to its rightful owner."

"But who is the rightful owner?" Fursu asked. "We have seen no one since we arrived."

"The owner's name does not matter, nor do we need to see his face," I said. "These things do not belong to us."

They assured me they had taken nothing. "One of you has been tempted to steal," I said with a heavy heart, "and must return what he has taken. Then the devil will leave you. We cannot allow a man who is possessed by Satan in our boat."

The brothers exchanged glances. The man who had stolen the goblet contrived to look more innocent than anyone else. "I for one am an honest man," he announced. He looked around as if daring anyone to contradict him.

I waited, unmoving, prepared to wait until day turned to night and back again if necessary. At last the thief fumbled with his clothing and withdrew the golden goblet. "Forgive me, Little Father," he said in a broken voice. A moment later he gave a great cry. Dropping the goblet, he clutched at his chest and fell forward onto his face. He never moved again.

I knelt beside him and felt his throat; turned him over and listened to his chest. My eyes filled with tears. "Our friend is dead," I told the others. "The devil has left him and he is at peace."

We buried the first of the three uninvited monks on the island and raised a cross to mark the spot.

Then we sailed on.

Chapter 11

Brendán rambled on, accepting hospitality where he found it, tilting his face up to the sun, baring his head to the rain. Listening to the calls of inland birds, the melodious lark and thrush and warbler, and missing the screech of the gull. The belling of the silver-horned stags.

Perversely, once I had attained the solitude I craved I began to long for the sound of a human voice. Once or twice I doubled back to revisit some clan I had met earlier, to warm myself by a family hearth and share the trivia of family life.

When he came to a river too deep or too rapid to ford he went looking for someone with a boat. Talking with men who fished the river was like coming home.

He could spend the better part of a day examining the construction of a boat; learning its strengths and weaknesses and how it differed from the vessels he knew. He might help to mend a damaged boat or tie a torn net. Or go home with a fisherman and spend the night with him and his family, still talking boats. And water. And weather.

The great constant: weather. A man walking across Ireland learned to know weather as intimately as the lines on his own palms.

Mindful of his calling, Brendán always sought a way to introduce Christianity into the conversation. He might not have Erc's gift for preaching to a crowd but he was comfortable talking on a more intimate level, where he could get direct responses.

When he came upon a man tending a flock of sheep he noticed a clumsily fashioned wooden cross on a thong around the shepherd's neck. Pleased by this sign of the spreading faith, Brendán said, "I see you believe in Christ."

Without taking his eyes off his flock the shepherd replied, "No. But I believe in men who believe in him."

How does one acquire faith? Is it taught or does it come from personal experience? Does the source make a difference in the quality?

How had I come by my faith?

Responding to an intuition, one morning he threw down his staff and stretched his body full length on the ground. He was not tired. He was wide awake and full of energy, as a man should be when he seeks to absorb knowledge.

The way of a pilgrim is an education in itself.

Lying on the grassy hillside, he listened to the frantic scrabbling of insects scurrying away from the sudden giant in their midst, the faint sigh of the grasses he was crushing, even the tiny shifts of grains of earth adjusting to his weight. Brendán focussed his entire attention on the unfolding events around him. . . .

. . . until he became aware of another sound, at the furthest reaches of audibility. He strained to hear.

The earth was humming.

The earth was humming!

The sound was faint yet distinct, similar to but not the same as water running through an underground river. Or blood through veins. From time to time the sound climaxed in a discernible pulse.

Why did I never notice before? All of Creation sings. Countless different voices but one song.

He lay enraptured. The sun above sang, the earth below hummed, and Brendán was a pinpoint of consciousness transfixed between them, not merely himself but part of an immense Whole.

The emotion he felt was too enormous for joy.

At last the awareness of time passing dragged him to his feet. Dark clouds were gathering over the distant line of mountains and a cold wind had sprung up. He began walking again.

Time.

Do we progress through time? Or . . . and did I not wonder about this before . . . do we circle around it?

Consider the act of walking. One step after another. During just one step an entire life can be lived in the imagination; indeed, entire but miniscule lives are being lived under our feet. In God's time are our lives no longer than theirs?

God's time . . .

Brendán was so preoccupied he failed to notice the standing stone half-hidden by a growth of holly. Unaware, he passed from one tribeland to another. Grassland gave way to woodland. When the moan of the wind became a howl, Brendán hurried towards a stand of ancient oaks. He could shelter among them until the storm blew over. Propping his staff against a tree, he searched in his food bag for a bit of cheese.

Why is it you can find everything else, but not the one thing you are looking for?

As silent as fog, they came up behind him.

The point of an iron spear touched the back of Brendán's neck. With a violent start, he whirled around.

The spear was levelled at him by a man so tall his feet almost touched the ground on either side of his small brown stallion. He was arrayed in the multicoloured regalia of a Gaelic warlord. The solid gold torc around his neck was as thick as an infant's wrist. Accompanying him were a dozen warriors on foot, armed with spears and short swords.

"Your name and tribe," their chief demanded. Brendán did not recognise his accent.

"Brendán of the Altraighe."

"Judging by your speech, you're a long way from home," the man observed. "What sort of name is Brinn-donn?"

"Latin. I mean, it's the Latin version of . . ."

"You're a foreigner," said one of the warriors. He drew his sword from its sheath with a rasping sound.

"He's not a trader, though," another observed. "No cart and no merchandise. And no weapons." He spat on the ground in contempt.

Their chieftain shifted weight on his horse. "What are we to do with you?" he asked Brendán in a conversational tone. "You're trespassing on our territory. We could kill you, but is there any benefit to be gained by it? I can see from here you have nothing worth owning."

"I'm only a pilgrim."

"A pilgrim." The man on the horse sneered beneath his extravagant moustache. "And what's that when it's at home?"

"A person who travels in search of . . ." Brendán hesitated, aware how ridiculous this was going to sound to a dozen heavily armed men. ". . . in search of truth and enlightenment."

The chieftain turned to his followers. "Now where would a man find truth around here?" he asked with exaggerated seriousness. "We're all honest, aren't we? Perhaps Brinn-donn would like to meet our friend Innatmar. There's a man who knows a thing or two about enlightenment. Bring him!" He slammed his legs against the horse's sides and trotted away.

Two burly warriors seized Brendán. He was strong but they were stronger. They bent his arms up behind his back with seasoned expertise and hustled him along after the man on the horse. His protests were ignored. He might as well have been a bullock going to slaughter. To avoid being dragged he straightened up as best he could and broke into a shambling run.

One warrior followed close behind Brendán, reaching out every few steps to poke his neck with the tip of a sword. The skin in that area became acutely sensitive. "Stop that!" Brendán shouted.

Up ahead, the chieftain gave a harsh bark of laughter.

He led them deeper into the forest.

There were no bushes in the deep shade; only ferns and brilliantly green moss amidst timeworn stones. The air was damp and peaty. Brendán noticed an unpleasant residue of acrid smoke. Something had burned here recently.

No birds were singing.

In a small glade lit by a slanting sunbeam, the chieftain halted his horse. "I strongly advise you to show respect, Brinn-donn. You wouldn't want to insult Innatmar. He has unpleasant ways of retaliating."

The men who were holding Brendán released him and stood back. He straightened his disarranged clothing and ran his fingers through his hair. His staff was lost; left far behind. Perhaps when this was over he could find it again.

He waited.

His captors looked expectant.

Nothing happened.

Brendán felt sweat trickling down his back. At last he said, "Where is Innatmar?"

"Here," replied one of the trees.

It took a moment to realise that the speaker was not a tree, but a man wearing a hooded robe the colour of tree bark. He emerged from among the oaks with a peculiar, gliding gait. The chieftain saluted him with a nod of the head. His warriors did the same, though they nodded twice instead of once.

The robed figure did not salute anyone. "What have you brought me?" he asked the chieftain. His voice was the rustle of leaves.

"This person is called Brinn-donn, and claims to be looking for enlightenment. I thought he might require the services of a Druid."

The warriors sniggered.

Innatmar thrust his face into Brendán's. His breath was like damp earth. "You are not of our tribe," he stated flatly.

"I come from. . . ."

"Therefore I am not obligated to give you the benefit of my gifts."

"I'm not asking for. . . ."

"Hospitality must be observed, however," the Druid continued inexorably. "Tell me what you need."

"Actually I have everything that. . . ."

The Druid looked towards the chieftain. "Enlightenment?" he queried.

"That's what he said."

"Ah. Light for the head. Wisdom." Innatmar turned back to Brendán. "No one can have enough wisdom, nor could you begin to contain a fragment of the knowledge I possess. What do you most want to know?"

After all the years and the unanswered questions, a real Druid stood before me, offering explanations. I could not help staring at him. He was clean shaven; even the hair of his head had been shaved away in front to make his forehead a high, bare dome. The hood prevented me from seeing if he was entirely bald. His face was unremarkable, with deeply lined skin and a gently curving mouth . . .

. . . that smiled at me.

Suddenly I was chilled me to the bone.

Until that moment I did not realise that Erc's prejudices had become mine. The questions I should have asked dried on my tongue.

Brendán forced himself to speak. "Your knowledge means nothing to me, pagan." He meant to sound defiant but his voice faltered.

The Druid raised his hand. Brendán shrank back. The warriors seized him again and held him immobile.

Innatmar touched the young man's right temple with one bony forefinger. Pain lanced through Brendán's head; he felt nauseous. Tiny swirls of blue and green light danced around the perimeter of his vision.

Innatmar took a step backwards. "Release him," he instructed. The warriors obeyed. The Druid slowly turned around three times, like a dog preparing to lie down. He examined the palms of his hands. Spat copiously into the left one. Studied the result. Lifted his head and gazed up at the surrounding trees.

"Mm-hm," said Innatmar.

"Mm-hm," murmured the warriors in unison.

"Ash-lin," said Innatmar.

"Ash-lin," his chorus responded.

The Druid returned to Brendán. He deliberately came a step too close, invading the space between them. Brendán wanted to draw back but held his ground.

Innatmar looked amused. "I have a riddle for you," he said. "Imagine a quiet pool, shining like a disc of polished silver. Slap the disc with the flat of your hand and it shatters into ripples. Although they all sparkle, no two ripples are the same; each reflects the light in its own, individual way. But in time they form a single surface again."

Fixing Brendán with a penetrating gaze, Innatmar whispered, "Now tell me: what became of all those separate sparkles?"

The Druid's stare was unbearable. Brendán looked away, searched desperately for some avenue of escape.

The trees surrounding the glade formed an impenetrable wall.

"I don't need anything from you!" he cried. "Let me go!"

"We don't need anything from you," Innatmar said softly. "You have always been free to go."

Where the trees had blocked his way a moment before, Brendán saw a gap wide enough for a human body. He bolted.

Armed with a new staff cut from a sturdy blackthorn, a shaken Brendán eventually continued his pilgrimage. Sometimes he wandered aimlessly for days, only to discover he had gone in a large circle. Yet sooner or later he would hear bells announce the canonical hours, and follow them.

The monasteries Brendán visited treated him as an honoured guest. They urged him to stay and join their order. His answer was always the same, "I'm not yet ready to make a decision."

That was true as far as it went, but I never explained the real reason. None of them gripped my spirit with both hands, like the promontory of the High Grave.

A monastic community was a reflection of its founder, who set down official rules for his order in accordance with his own interpretation of Holy Scripture. In early sixth century Ireland, these communities were hardly regulated at all. The influence of Rome was just beginning to make itself felt.

Having inculcated a sense of sin in its followers, the Church had recognised the need for relieving the unbearable burden of guilt. According to the Gospel of Matthew, Christ had forgiven sins. Rome claimed the same power had descended by apostolic succession to its anointed. Penance, preceded by confession, was about to become a sacrament.

Some abbots dedicated their lives to saving souls from hell. In their monasteries the penitential rituals included reciting the Lord's Prayer three hundred and sixty-five times a day, every day of the year, and twice on feast days. Sleeping on a bed of nettles could be the penance for a single lustful thought. To overcome gluttony a sinner undertook self-induced starvation. Seeking forgiveness for sloth required one to climb a mountain on his knees.

Other monasteries took a more benign view, concentrating on Christ's message of loving kindness. They balanced discipline with humour and asceticism with an occasional measure of honey wine. Piety and poetry received almost equal attention. Their rituals might include marching around a large stone a specific number of times on holy days while praying continually. In this way the monks sought to imbue formerly pagan objects of devotion with Christian values.

Brendán explored monasteries at both ends of the scale. After each encounter he took time to reflect. Lying on his back on the grass, looking at the sky. Huddling in a cave, listening to the rain.

I concluded that the Celtic Church was making up its own version of Christianity as it went along.

Our Gaelic forebears interacted on a daily basis with the unseen world. They were well aware of the important activities that take place in invisible spaces. Dreams and visions were not illusion to them but an aspect of reality, so it was easy to accept the miracle of Christ's resurrection.

The rigid theology of Rome did not allow for any miracles other than its own, and was growing in influence.

If we tried to impose a more concrete form upon our inherited spirituality we might lose its essence. Erc was an able administrator but he did not appreciate the miraculous articulation of a bird's wing or the soulful plaintiveness of a deer's cry. That was his blindness; his inability to recognise the hand of God.

Perhaps what he felt for the Druids was not hatred, but jealousy.

Whatever their ethos, Irish monasteries set high standards for idealism and self-sacrifice. Not everyone could live up to them. If he obtained his abbot's permission a monk might leave a strict order for one less strict—or, on rare occasions, the other way around. A few even moved for the sake of movement, responding to a force older than Christianity: the apparently random disorder of life that blew seeds across the earth and stars through the heavens.

In the same random fashion Brendán continued his pilgrimage. Seeking without knowing exactly what he sought.

At the abbey of Clon Tuaiscirt he met his only surviving brother, Faitleac. He looked like an older version of Brendán, though he was less muscular and not as tall. At first the two men were so excited that their words got tangled. Neither could understand what the other was saying.

The abbot, a round little man with a round red face, smoothly interceded. "Any student of Bishop Erc is welcome here, Brendán. We are great admirers of his. Faitleac will see that you are comfortable. Please stay with us as long as you like. Perhaps you would consider joining our order?"

The guesting house was built of timber and smelled of the cedar shingles used for roofing. Faitleac spread a blanket on the bed and hung Brendán's cape and bag on wooden pegs. Then the two men looked at each other. The words that had tumbled out in the beginning were lost now.

"So," Faitleac ventured. "You're here."

"I am here."

"And you're well?"

"I am well. You?"

"I'm well too."

"This abbey is impressive," said Brendán. "A model ecclesiastical centre, in fact. Very . . . impressive."

"It is."

"And you're happy here?"

"I am content."

The silence dragged. Both were relieved when the bell summoned them for prayer.

Their next conversation took place after the single meal of the day; Clon Tuaiscirt might be impressive in size, but the order it housed subscribed to a strict asceticism. As Faitleac accompanied his brother back to the guesting house he asked, "Our mother, how is she?"

"I haven't seen her in a long time. She went back to her own people, you know."

Faitleac nodded. "I'm not surprised. She had suffered all the grief she could bear. When our brothers were killed she tried to be the proud mother of warriors, but it nearly broke her. So Finnlugh gave her his promise."

"What promise?"

"To stop fighting the Ciarrí Luachra and devote himself to fishing. That's when he built the new house at Fenit where you and Brige were born. I remember the first time he took us to see it, and how happy my mother was."

Brendán was thunderstruck. "I didn't know," he said faintly.

Why did no one tell me this before? Did they think I wouldn't be interested? Children only look one way—ahead—until they start to grow up and wonder what's behind them. Then the past matters. My brother had lived a different childhood from mine, with parents I would never know.

An entire world was in existence before I was born. On the other side of the darkness from which I emerged.

The two men sat on the ground outside the guesting house with their backs pressed against its walls and the bottomless well of the sky above them. Night sounds. A brief patter of rain on leaves. The smell of the earth.

Faitleac declared he would remain at Clon Tuaiscirt until he died. "I came here straight from Altraighe-Caille and will be buried in the shadow of our High Cross when I die," he said contentedly. "The good brothers will remember me at every divine service, for as long as the abbey stands."

"But didn't you want to do anything else with your life? Even for a few years?"

"I never thought about it. By the time I was born our parents had converted to Christianity, and from early childhood I knew I was destined to be a monk. Just as Brige will be a nun and you will be a priest."

Brendán stiffened. "How can you be so sure?"

"Because we are Finnlugh's children."

"What do you mean, Faitleac?"

"Don't you understand? We are Bishop Erc's offering to God."

We had been at sea for a timeless time, cradled by winds, blanketed by stars. Our supplies had dwindled; we were eating only a few bites every third day. On the morning, we drank the last of our water, sharp-eyed Aedgal reported an inhabited island ahead. As we drew near its shore the wind turned against us and pushed us away. I ordered my crew to lower the sail and make a second approach using the oars. This effort was successful, but we could find no landing place. Massive boulders formed a bulwark that held the land tantalisingly out of reach.

We had circled the island several times before the brothers cried out in frustration, "God give us help!"

A great wave broke against the boulders and crashed down over us. Instinctively, we flinched. When we opened our eyes again we saw a narrow landing place just ahead, with barely enough room for our vessel. The brothers quickly clambered over the side and moored the boat.

A narrow path led up from the landing place to a stretch of level grassy ground. A short walk would bring us to several low buildings. Upon starting towards them we discovered two wells: one held clear water, in the other the water was dark and muddy.

My men clamoured for a drink of the clear water but I told them, "We must ask permission of the inhabitants of this island before we can use their well." Some of the brothers grumbled; Tarlách the loudest of all. "If God brought us here to obtain water then we should drink water!"

A man with snowy hair and shining face, and wearing the garb of an abbot, approached us and prostrated himself on the earth at my feet. We promptly raised him from the ground. He then embraced me warmly, but said nothing. Instead he beckoned us to follow him to the nearest building, whose doorway was surmounted by a wooden cross. With gestures of the utmost meekness and humility, he urged us to enter.

My companions showered him with questions. "What place is this?" Aedgal wanted to know. Moenniu said, "Can you replenish our supplies?" "Is there any water? I'm parched with thirst," Liber complained. The abbot only smiled and shook his head. Then I realised that silence must be one of the rules of his order. "Be quiet," I admonished my monks, "lest you profane a holy place."

No sooner had I spoken than eleven men in the robes of monks approached us, carrying basins of warm water. The abbot himself gravely washed our feet. When this expression of hospitality had been bestowed the eleven monks embraced each of my companions in turn.

Their abbot then led us to a small refectory which was furnished with an oaken table and benches. He silently invited us to seat ourselves around the table. One of his monks served us with a dozen loaves of bread, whiter and softer than any we had ever seen. A second brother passed a large bowl heaped with pounded roots sweeter than honey. A third brought goblets of sparkling water. The abbot and his monks then sat down with us, but did not touch the food.

While we ate and drank the abbot spoke at last. "I am called Ailbe, and I found this monastery eighty years ago, just as you see it now. One of our wells is muddy because it contains warm water which we only use for washing. The other provides the water you are drinking; it is always pure.

"There are twenty-four monks in the monastery. Every morning we find twelve loaves of bread in the larder. On Sundays and feast days there is an entire loaf for each of us. We eat nothing that is burned by a fire. We suffer neither heat nor cold. We do not age here nor do we sicken."

I was embarrassed to realise my brothers and I had just consumed their whole day's ration. My face must have revealed my dismay, because Ailbe said, "Do not concern yourself for our sakes. Whatever we give in charity is always returned to us.

"Now let us go to the church for Vespers. The only time a human voice is heard on this island is when we sing the holy offices, or when God sends one of his saints to visit us and I can speak as I do now."

I shrank from his kindly-meant imputation of sainthood. Ailbe did not know me.

My monks arose, and together with the other eleven, silently preceded Ailbe and myself to the church. From the doorway we saw twelve more monks inside. They genuflected and went outside to make room for us.

Their church was exactly the right size to accommodate twenty-four men, kneeling on cushions arranged around the central altar. The building was perfectly square and lit by seven lamps, three in front of the altar and two in front of each of the two small side altars. "We brought seven beeswax candles with us from our homeland," said Ailbe. "On this island they acquired special properties. We have never needed to replace them."

The patens, cruets, and chalices on the altar were all cut from crystal, but I was more moved by the beauty of the voices raised in prayer. When the abbot intoned, "God, come to our aid," the congregation chanted in response, "We have acted wrongly, we have sullied our souls with iniquity. We ask our faithful Father to spare us. Let us sleep in peace this night, knowing that you, Our Lord, have given us hope."

We did indeed sleep peacefully that night. The burdens on my soul did not trouble me, and when I awoke at dawn I felt fresh and new.

As we broke our fast I asked Ailbe, "Does the rule of silence ever become too much of a strain?"

"In this place we are in harmony; we do not need to debate or quarrel or question," he replied, "so we maintain a friendly silence. Quietude bestows peace, and rest."

Ailbe's community seemed almost perfect to me, if perfection could be obtained in this world. I inquired, "May I stay here and spend my days with you?"

The abbot paused, as if listening to a distant voice. Then he said, "You are meant to return to your own monastery in Ireland and be buried there. But first you will see amazing things. When your journey is over you may come to us again and spend Christmas and Epiphany here."

I promised that we would accept his invitation.

Then we sailed on.

Chapter 12

Brendán remained at Clon Tuaiscirt long enough to satisfy the requirements of hospitality and familial obligation, then went on his way again.

Days passed. Weeks. Seasons. Sun and sleet were all the same to him. His sandals wore out and he repaired them, then repaired them again. His tunic frayed around the bottom. He tore his sleeves on briars.

If he came to a crossroads where a market was being held, he lingered for a time. Men bargained, wives gossiped, craftsmen extolled their wares and children scampered about like mice on a meadow. Swirl of colour and smell of life. Cattle bawling, pigs squealing. And always talk, rolling tides of talk. Standing on the fringes, Brendán listened with thirsty ears.

When the silent call came he went on his way.

The silent call was very low and whispered, and as loud as rolling thunder. It was a voice and a cry and a command that rose up out of the land around me and was irresistible.

Outwards. Always outwards.

In the scriptorium at Clon Fert, Brendán wrote, 'While on pilgrimage I encountered Tarlách, from the kingdom of Ulster, who claimed to be a pilgrim like myself. We shared our food and exchanged views.'

At first Brendán warmed to Tarlách. The man's huge hands and feet were out of proportion to the rest of his body; he resembled a young hound that was failing to fulfil the early promise of giant paws. Mournful, downturned eyes and habitual sniffling added to the illusion of a lonesome puppy looking for someone to scratch his ears.

Tarlách's first words dispelled the illusion. Even in normal conversation his voice had a truculent tone. "My father has a hostelry near Ard Macha, Patrick's holy city," he told Brendán, "but I never liked the place. Too many hills; no matter where you want to go it's always uphill. I didn't like the hostelry business either, it's full of idiots who make unreasonable demands. After one quarrel too many I decided to become a pilgrim."

"Did your father encourage you?"

Tarlách gave a sour smile. "Let's just say he didn't discourage me. He thought I'd come running back as soon as I got hungry, but he was wrong. People feed pilgrims," he added smugly.

"Surely you've learned more than that during your travels," Brendán said.

"I've learned everything I wish to know. For example, I spent enough time in Leinster to become an expert on the eastern tribes. Ask me anything about them. I can tell you this much: they're as slippery as eels. Every Leinsterman is worse than the next."

It was Brendán's turn to smile. "That's a slippery remark itself."

"Not at all, it's absolutely accurate. I'm an excellent judge of character."

When Brendán offered to walk with him for a way, Tarlách agreed. "But only until we fall out," he stipulated.

"Are you so sure we will?"

"I fall out with everyone," said the Ulsterman.

I soon discovered why. Tarlách's only idea of conversation was debate. He contradicted every statement I made. With him it was possible to avoid an argument only by exerting infinite patience—and my patience wasn't always infinite.

Every person we meet is an opportunity to learn. Tarlách taught me that there are some people who know everything. Unfortunately they don't know anything else.

Tarlách had been baptised and called himself a Christian, yet disagreed with almost every aspect of Holy Scripture.

Exasperated, Brendán finally asked, "Do you even believe in God?"

"On good days I do. Most of the time I don't."

"How can you say you're a Christian when you have no faith?"

"On the contrary, I have infinite faith. I believe that everything is shadow and smoke."

"Including you and me?"

"A collection of dust motes," Tarlách said dismissively.

In Brendán's mind there appeared a quiet pool like polished silver. And then a hand, slapping. "Still water cannot move by itself, that is not the nature of water," he said to Tarlách. "It must be acted upon by another force. Would you agree?"

"I suppose so," the Ulsterman reluctantly admitted.

"And dust motes cannot gather of their own volition to form a human being; that is not the nature of dust. So some other power is at work."

"If I grant that—and I'm not sure I do—are you saying that power is God?"

"What else could it be?" asked Brendán.

"Accident." Tarlách extended his huge hands palm up, as if the gesture explained everything. "It's nothing but an accident."

"Look at your hands, Tarlách. No, I'm not criticising their size, I'm admiring their strength. Consider all the things they can do. What 'accident' could shape such complex and useful tools?"

Tarlách wanted to accept the compliment without agreeing to the premise. "That doesn't prove the existence of God."

"I myself am the proof. My imagination . . ."

"You imagine God exists because you want to believe in him!" Tarlách interrupted triumphantly.

"That's not what I mean," said Brendán. "My imagination comes from God, who created me in his image. Before there was me, God *imagined* me. I was kindled by God. And so were you."

I did not consciously choose those words. They rose unbidden from a deep well of belief I had never explored. Yet it was there. A strength and a sanctuary given to me in my earliest childhood.

By Íta.

Brendán wrote, 'Tarlách and I traveled together for ten or twelve days, during which time we talked so much we grew hoarse.'

Some might find it hard to like the Ulsterman, but I did. Tarlách was the dash of vinegar which cuts the sweetness of honey. Only after we had parted company did I realise what he really wanted. He wanted to be convinced.

Am I convinced?

Looking down at myself after all these years I see a belly like a small cooking pot, a pair of knobbly knees, and feet as twisted and gnarled as oak roots. Surely Brendán, with all his imperfections, is not a replica of God.

What has happened to my faith along the way?

CHAPTER 13

Wherever Brendán's peregrinations took him, he heard music, soaring above the valleys and floating like mist around the mountains. Birds sang the day awake and sang it asleep again at night. Hunters sang around their campfires; farmers sang as they ploughed their fields; women at their looms sang weaving songs; youngsters at their play sang game songs. Traders even taught their children counting songs.

One cold, starry night a single human voice, unaided and pure, was carried on the wind to Brendán as he slept. Singing of love with a passion that permeated his dreams. Singing a lament that broke his sleeping heart.

The Gael fought. But they also sang.

Although Brendán tried to avoid warfare during his pilgrimage, in time it came to him—in the form of a red-haired, freckled man with a hawkish face, a young warrior who had been knocked unconscious during combat.

Colmán awoke to find that the tide of battle had rolled on without him. He lay flat on his back on trampled grass. Leaning over him was a clean-shaven man of his own age, holding a wooden staff.

"Hit me with that stick and I'll kill you," Colmán growled.

"Not from your present position," observed Brendán. "But don't worry, I'm not a warrior."

"I'm not worried. You're the most harmless creature I've seen today."

"Is that meant to be an insult?"

"Do you take it as an insult?"

"I take it as a compliment. I am Brendán, son of Finnlugh."

"Well then, Brendán, give me your hand, will you? My head's still ringing. I am Colmán, son of Lennán," he said as an afterthought while Brendán helped him to his feet. "Have you seen my sword around here? Or my shield?"

"What does your sword look like?"

"A bit longer than your forearm, with a leaf-shaped blade. Who are you that you know nothing of swords?"

"I'm a pilgrim," said Brendán. "I don't fight."

"That's hard to believe," Colmán retorted. "The shoulders of you belong on an ox. You have to be a warrior."

"I don't have to be anything other than what I am. If a man's future was determined by his origins, no bird that comes from an egg could fly."

"I think I'd better lie down again," said Colmán.

Brendán put an arm around him and helped ease him to the ground. The warrior sat with his knees raised and his head lowered, breathing raggedly, while dizziness came in waves. Brendán went away. Returned. Pressed a wad of moss soaked in water to his forehead.

Colmán said hoarsely, "I'm in your debt."

"I'm a Christian, I give my help freely. There's some blood on your tunic; I have a small assortment of herbal cures if you need them."

Colmán looked down at the crimson smear across the saffron cloth. "I don't think that's mine." He ran one hand over his body. "No, definitely not mine. Some other poor fool's." He gave a crooked grin, his teeth very white in his freckled face. "I'll be all right, just let me sit here awhile."

He sat. Brendán sat down too, and waited. After a while Colmán spoke again. "Did you say you're a Christian? I've heard of your tribe; they're all over the place these days."

"We're not a tribe. Anyone can be a Christian."

"Even the unfree?"

"Slaves and kings alike."

Colmán responded with a contemptuous snort. "I wouldn't join a band of people who would accept just anybody."

"That's all right," said Brendán. He sat down beside the warrior, reached into his bag, and produced a loaf of bread. Breaking it in two, he offered half to Colmán. "There's a stream in the meadow over there and I've filled my waterskin. Here, have a drink."

The warrior drained the waterskin but ate only a couple of bites of bread. "This tastes odd," he remarked.

"I carry fish in that bag."

"Hunh. A man needs red meat to keep him strong."

"I don't need strength the way you do. What I need is strength of character. Of soul."

"You're as odd as the bread," said Colmán, looking owlishly at his benefactor. He was having a little trouble focussing his eyes.

They sat in silence again, while Brendán covertly watched the other man for signs of improvement. When a faint hint of colour returned to the warrior's cheeks, he said, "Do you live near here, Colmán?"

"Not at all, I come from the far side of the Shannon."

"What brought you to this place?"

"The fighting, of course. The king of Munster demanded a hundred warriors from the king of my tribe, and I was one of them."

"When they miss you they'll come back for you," Brendán assured him.

Colmán looked dubious. "They probably think I'm dead, that's why they went off and left me." His bright grin suddenly flashed. "But we were losing anyway and autumn's in the air, so I think I'll go home for the winter and cut firewood and tell war stories."

Cheered by this prospect, he was soon back on his feet. Brendán helped him look for his weapons. They found his shield half submerged in a tangle of bracken. The small, circular shield was made of boiled oxhide stretched over a wickerwork frame and whitened with a heavy application of lime. When Colmán pounded the shield with his fist a cloud of dust arose, making Brendán sneeze. "There's more than one way to get the enemy off guard," Colmán laughed.

They could not find his sword, though they searched for the rest of the day. "I loved that sword," Colmán said mournfully. "I made the hilt myself and set it with sharks' teeth I got from a trader. I made the scabbard too." He ran his fingers along the embossed leather sheath that hung from his belt. "It's no good to me now, though." He unbuckled his belt and removed the scabbard.

"Save it for your next sword," Brendán advised.

"It doesn't work like that. First you have the blade, then you shape the leather to fit it. Every time I look at this it will remind me what a fine weapon I lost; that some other maggot picked up and ran off with," Colmán added bitterly. He started to throw the scabbard into the bracken.

Brendán caught his wrist. "Give it to me instead."

"If you don't fight, what will you do with it?"

"I don't know. Something."

"You really are odd," said Colmán. "But it's yours if you want it."

They camped that night beside the stream in the meadow. In the morning they set off together, with their backs to the rising sun.

"What's it like to be a warrior, Colmán?"

"Hard work sometimes, occasionally terrifying. Mostly you stand around and wait."

"That's true about many things," Brendán said. "I was wondering how it feels to kill another man."

"I don't kill very often, and I don't feel anything much. It has to be done so I do it. I try not to look at them afterwards."

"Then you do have a conscience."

"I hope not. A conscience is no use to a warrior."

"You could give up fighting if you want," suggested Brendán.

"What would I do then? A man has to fight to prove he's a man."

"I'm a man," Brendán said with certainty.

Colmán was a new experience for me. Two of my brothers—two whom I would never know—must have been very like him.

Colmán proved to be a skilled forager and a merry companion. Brendán had more in common with him than with his own brother Faitleac. The warrior, who had a keen mind, asked almost as many questions as Brendán himself.

"This Christ of yours—is he a god?"

"He's an aspect of the one God, Colmán."

"How can you say there's only one god? What about the gods of fire and water and earth and stone? I've offered sacrifices to all of them. And what about the goddesses of war who hover over the battlefield? I've heard their wings myself."

Brendán said, "They're only superstition."

The warrior turned to face him. Colmán's freckled features might have been hewn from granite. His clear grey eyes were cold. "So if I don't believe what you believe, then what I believe is superstition."

Almost too late, Brendán recalled one of Patrick's axioms: "Never tell the heathens they are wrong. Recognise the validity of their dissent. Their truth is as real to them as yours to you, and you will neither shame nor beat it out of them."

" 'Superstition' is the wrong word," Brendán said hastily, "and I shouldn't have I used it. You could apply it to my beliefs just as I did to yours. Tell me: what do the wings of the war goddesses sound like? Are they loud, or far away?"

The two men discussed many gods and one god, paganism and Christianity, for the rest of the day. Brendán remained mindful of Patrick's injunction; Colmán was increasingly curious about Brendán's viewpoint.

On the following day Brendán did not mention religion at all.

The day after that, Colmán asked him the questions he wanted to answer.

And sometimes the answers came to me without my having to look for them.

Every morning, Colmán awoke well before Brendán. By the time Brendán opened his eyes the warrior was busy stretching his arms and legs; bending and straightening his back; making leaps and lunges.

"Why put yourself through that when you're not fighting?" Brendán wondered.

"Because I will be fighting," said Colmán. "It's what I do."

When they arrived at the upper reaches of the Shannon they forded the shallows together, then parted company. Colmán headed south, and homeward. Brendán continued west, his destination a monastery on the Aran Islands. The warrior remained on his mind. Of the various men who had accompanied him during his pilgrimage, Colmán was the one he missed most.

Autumn was indeed in the air. The pilgrim walked with an easy stride. Thinking, praying, sometimes singing. Happily meeting strangers and happily being alone. Days slipped by. Somewhere ahead was another of the monasteries on his list but he was in no hurry to reach it. The pleasure was in the journey.

The sharp pain that lanced through his head drove the air from his lungs and made his stomach lurch. Tiny swirls of blue and green light danced around the perimeter of his vision. He sat down hard.

This time Brendán *felt* the earth singing: a sustained hum that rang through his bones and made his genitals tingle. He felt incredibly alive yet wonderfully at peace—and then he knew.

The ground on which he sat was an Other Place. A place apart.

He did not—could not move. From experience he knew that sooner or later the world would intrude through his five senses. Until then he concentrated on holding on to the rapture for as long as he could.

When the song finally faded he ached with loss. *Come back, oh come back!*

Shivering, Brendán got to his feet like an old man, joint by joint, and drew his cape around his shoulders. He regretted having left his heavy cloak behind at Slane, to prove how tough he was.

No one noticed anyway.

He looked to the sky to determine how much longer the light would last. A wind from the sea was driving clouds across the face of the sun. As Brendán watched, the clouds assumed the form of an immense chariot decorated with plumes. Nothing appeared to be pulling the chariot yet the huge wheels were turning.

Bright red wheels ornamented with silver bosses.

Brendán rubbed his eyes. When he looked again the chariot was racing across the sky. Then one of the wheels broke into two pieces and plummeted to earth. Clearly visible, the larger piece struck the ground just ahead of him, rebounded once, then settled. He ran towards it.

Instead of a wheel he found two large contiguous mounds of earth. Across them lay a swathe of red flowers with white centres, blooming out of season.

Perplexed, Brendán tilted his head back and looked at the sky. The chariot had vanished; there were not even any clouds. But the wind from the west was growing stronger.

He began to search for firewood.

Many years later at Clon Fert, Brendán pared the point of his quill with the knife he kept in an outsized leather sheath. Dipping the freshly sharpened quill into a pot of sticky black ink, he wrote, 'On the Aran Islands I visited the famed monastery founded by Énda, considered the father of Irish monasticism. The islands had been granted to Énda by Aengus, king of Cashel, shortly after his own conversion.' *When Patrick pinned Aengus to the earth with his crosier.* Smiling to himself, Brendán shook his head. *Patrick certainly did cast a wide net.*

He resumed writing. 'While at *Magh Enna* I formulated a few ideas of my own for a religious order. Founding a monastery in those early days was not difficult. All that was necessary was a bit of land, some willing followers to help with the construction, and a man whose heart brimmed with the love of God.'

My order would not see life as a battle to be won but a gift to be celebrated. We would be a scholarly band of brothers; moderately ascetic, enthusiastically devout. We would adore God, follow the teachings of his Son, and celebrate the Holy Ghost as a motive if invisible force in the world. Under my abbacy ancient wisdoms would not be summarily condemned, but used to illumine the all-embracing nature of the Almighty.

My abbacy . . . I knew I was not worthy. The very scale of my imagining told me I was too proud.

And the dreams that still came in the night told me I was too sinful.

'From the islands I travelled east again, to a monastery in Connacht. There I met a renowned scholar of the Scriptures, a monk called Jarlath. A generation older than I, Brother Jarlath had been educated by Sénán, a disciple of Patrick, and by Énda himself.'

A very wide net indeed.

'I spent the worst of the winter studying under Brother Jarlath's tutelage. In spite of the difference in our ages we became more like friends than student and teacher.'

On a day of bitter wind the two men huddled thankfully inside the stone walls of the scriptorium. Brendán remarked, 'At Tearmónn Eirc the scriptorium was made of sods. The wind used to follow us inside.'

"I was born in a hut of wattle and daub," said Jarlath. "In the booleying time, when my clan drove the cattle to the high pastures, we built temporary shelters of branches. I don't recall any discomfort. Everything seemed . . . softer . . . then. All this stone . . ." He left the thought unfinished.

"Stone is building for the ages," Brendán pointed out.

"It isn't the construction of this place that troubles me. Our abbot is a good Christian but he's not a Patrician. I didn't apprehend the difference when I first came here, but I do now. Blessed Patrick was guided by visions that were as real to him as he was real to God. That's the sort of Christianity which appeals to me."

"And me," said Brendán.

"Like the Roman Emperor Constantine, our abbot places his faith in relics," Jarlath went on. "Because Christianity is an historical religion based on historical fact, he wants tangible artefacts. He has us brothers driven to distraction writing letters to far-flung places in search of a sliver of the True Cross."

Brendán's eyes twinkled. "There's a man called Gowrán you should meet. He might donate a sliver."

"Really?"

"Ah . . . not exactly. I was making a joke," Brendán wryly admitted. "Do pieces of the Cross still exist?"

"I don't know; I'm not even sure it matters. Have you ever had a vision, Brendán?"

The young man hesitated. This was private territory. "Have you?"

"I have not. I long with all my soul for a personal communication from Our Lord, but I'm afraid it will never happen here. We are too preoccupied with the tangible. Personally, I think the saddest story in Holy Scripture is that of Doubting Thomas."

"I agree," said Brendán. "Perhaps . . ."

The words rose up in me again, out of that wellspring.

"Perhaps the act of believing is almost as important as what one believes in. Faith itself has weight and value, Brother Jarlath. The human yearning to believe is very strong. There can be no explanation for it but the existence of God. Because our dreaming souls remember God, our waking minds desperately try to believe in something. The important thing is this: we have to believe *first*. That's what makes miracles possible."

Jarlath was impressed. "How did one so young acquire such wisdom?"

Brendán looked down at his toes: dirty toes with broken nails and thick pads of callus where the sandals had rubbed. "Thoughts come to me during my travels," he said modestly.

"I regret I've never gone on a pilgrimage."

"A pilgrimage takes place in the mind and heart," said Brendán. "Walking stimulates me, but if you really want to, you could close your eyes and go on a pilgrimage without leaving this room."

The older man looked dubious. "The abbot would never countenance such behaviour."

How often has Bishop Erc reproved me when my mind appeared to wander?

"Then why not found a monastery yourself, Brother Jarlath? You have great knowledge and an exemplary reputation. Devout men would flock to you."

"A monastery requires land and I have none."

With a sudden broad smile, Brendán announced, "God has shown me the perfect site for you!"

"Is this another joke, like the splinter?"

"It isn't a joke. You asked if I ever had a vision. I have, but I realise it wasn't intended for me. I'm just the vehicle to take you there."

Jarlath studied his eager face. There was a light in those eyes. Brendán *believed.*

At *Tuam*, the Mound of Two Shoulders, Jarlath prepared to build his monastery. He had permission from his abbot and the support of the bishop of the diocese. The local chieftain, a recent convert, had given him the land. The monastery was to be called *Clon Fuis*, the Exuberant Meadow. A name inspired by the profusion of wildflowers.

Brendán helped set the cornerstone.

"Stay here and take holy vows," Jarlath urged him. "This was your vision also; you said the wheel broke in two pieces. Clon Fuis will be yours as much as mine; we can build it together."

I was tempted. I could imagine staying with that good man in that holy place and welcoming brothers who also sought visions. But Erc had cursed me with a sense of responsibility that I could not throw off, no matter how much I wanted to. It was a greater nuisance than a conscience.

Brendán said, "I have to go back to Bishop Erc first. I couldn't take such a step without this permission."

"We could send him a letter. I'm sure he would give you his blessing."

"Letters aren't always enough," Brendán said sadly.

This time I did not follow a circuitous route. Although I had been travelling for a long time, the distance between Tuam and Slane was relatively short. The most important part of the pilgrimage took place inside the head.

While hurrying towards Meath I composed a number of speeches for the bishop. Seeking for arguments he would have to accept. Except there weren't any. There's no easy way to tell a person what they don't want to hear.

As he climbed the Hill of Slane, Brendán decided the best approach was to be blunt and get it over with.

He was not given the opportunity. The doors which had opened for him were closing.

Chapter 14

The bishop's not here," said Brige. Her hands were twisting together like small animals wrestling. "He left for Tearmónn Eirc ten days ago. I didn't want him to go, but you know how he is," she added plaintively.

Brendán leaned his staff against the doorframe and stooped to unfasten his sandals. His tired feet ached. "I know how he is. Why didn't you want him to go?"

The young woman fought back tears. "He's very ill, Brendán—though he won't admit it—but he insisted on making the journey. He went for you. To be with you."

Brendán straightened abruptly. "I haven't been anywhere near there. A pilgrimage means going somewhere you've never been before. Erc knows that."

"He loves you like a son—though he wouldn't admit that either—and after you left it was like when Eithne died. He slowly shrank down into himself. Finally he even stopped thinking clearly. He was convinced you were on your way home—meaning Tearmónn Eirc—and he insisted he'd promised to meet you there. We could see how ill he was; we all tried to dissuade him but it was like talking to a stump. He summoned his charioteer and off they went." The tears dammed by her eyelids spilled over; flooded down her cheeks. "Oh Brendán, I don't think I'll ever see him alive again!"

I had never ridden a horse in my life, but I borrowed the fastest one in the parish and set off for Tearmónn Eirc. By the time Sliabh Mis rose before me, every bone in my body hated the unfortunate horse. The poor creature's abused mouth must have hated me just as much. But I had learned to ride.

During Brendán's pilgrimage, Rome finally had appointed a new bishop to Altraighe-Caille. Molua was a fussy, middle-aged widower and disinclined to marry again; a conscientious Christian who did everything he was asked to do and never less—but never more; a man of small dreams who considered the bishopric of an obscure diocese to be the achievement of a lifetime.

When Bishop Molua heard that a man on a horse was approaching, he rushed out to meet him. "Are you Brendán?" he shouted before the rider even drew rein.

"I am."

The bishop threw his hands in the air. "Our prayers have been answered!" he exulted. His expression sobered. "The bishop of Slane is dying, Brendán, and he's been calling for you. We feared you might not arrive in time. It's a miracle you did."

"A miracle," echoed Brendán. His lips felt numb.

"I'll take you to him at once. Follow me."

They came to a high earthen bank, passed through an unguarded gateway, entered a space delineated by roof and walls and peopled with shadows. When the shadows spoke to Brendán their words bounced off his ears. He was only aware of the figure on the bed.

Erc had always been lean, but now there was not enough meat on his bones to make hills of the blanket that covered him. His exposed face was ghastly. The skin was thin enough to reveal the skull beneath and had turned an improbable greenish-yellow, while the area around the eyes was the colour of a deep bruise. From across the room Brendán could smell the odour of decay. Some vital part of the man was dying.

Brendán dropped to his knees beside the bed. "I've come home," he said.

Erc opened his eyes. "I knew you would," he said in a barely audible voice. "I have come too . . ." A pause. A wheeze of breath. ". . . to ordain you." He reached out with a hand resembling a bundle of twigs tied together. Brendán took it in his own hand.

Erc closed his eyes.

Brendán looked towards Bishop Molua. "Is he all right?"

"I don't know . . . I can't say . . . we do have a healer here, though." He signalled to an elderly woman with bags of herbs and nostrums tied to her girdle.

She bent over the sickbed, watching the man's breathing, then lowered her head to listen to his chest. When she straightened up again she told Brendán, "He appears to be sleeping. He's been waiting a long time for you; now he can relax. And so can you," she added kindly.

Brendán became aware of the other people in the room.

They reminded me of carrion crows waiting at the edge of a battlefield.

Suddenly the young man narrowed his eyes to slits.

Rome had appropriated the right to appoint bishops, but in the Celtic Church the rules of hierarchical succession followed the secular system established under Brehon Law. When a bishop—or abbot—died, the most suitable member of his family took his place.

As soon as I saw Ninnidh I knew why he had come. The avid expression on his unguarded face gave him away. Clon Ard wasn't that far from Slane. The bishop's cousin would have known about his illness before I did.

Ninnidh assumed Erc would agree with what seemed obvious to him: since the bishop had no living brothers and no sons, his well-educated cousin was the most suitable person to be the next bishop of Slane. Ninnidh was not surprised by Brendán's arrival at Tearmónn Eirc, but neither was he concerned. The bishop's godson was not related to Erc by blood; therefore he was negligible.

When he saw Brendán looking at him, Ninnidh responded with the blank stare of disinterest.

I interpreted his expression as contempt. The iron of resolution took hold of me then.

A dog may chase a man on a galloping horse, but if he catches them he still won't be able to ride the horse.

Brendán leaned over the bed and whispered into Erc's ear, "I'll be here when you feel better. And you will feel better. You promised to ordain me for the priesthood so I can follow in your footsteps." He repeated the last phrase deliberately. "So I can follow in your footsteps."

A faint smile creased the ghastly face.

Brendán spent the night in his old cell, where he did not sleep but sat staring into the enemy Dark. Thinking.

A monk could not serve as a priest but a priest could become a monk, and some did. Accepting ordination would not of itself deny me the right to enter a monastery, and the ordination would give a dying man comfort. It seemed a small sacrifice.

It was not small.

Better than anyone, I knew the strength of Erc's will. He might have been asleep but on some level he had heard—and understood—my whispered words. His smile showed that he had interpreted "so I can follow in your footsteps" exactly as I meant him to. If Brige was right and the bishop loved me like a son, once I was ordained he would never confirm Ninnidh as his successor at Slane.

I was disappointed to discover how petty I was; how mean-spirited. Christian virtue wasn't as well rooted in me as I had thought.

As punishment for my failings, I had tricked myself into the one thing I didn't want.

At sunset the bishop asked for a little warm milk.

On the following day he ate some bread and a bit of fish.

By the end of the week he was sitting up in bed and making plans for Brendán's ordination. Erc still looked dreadful. Because of his thinness the damaged shoulder protruded more than ever, like the peak of a mountain above a rockslide, and his colour was still bad. But his voice was stronger and his mind was clear.

Ninnidh had fully expected to return to Slane with the bishop's body and carrying the bishop's crosier. Erc's recovery was as inexplicable to him as it was to everyone else. Yet he had to appear as happy as everyone else was—with the possible, and puzzling, exception of Brendán.

When he thought no one was watching, the bishop's godson looked as if he had been punched in the stomach.

Ninnidh, who had grown up amid a crowd of rowdy siblings, did not like children; they were too loud, too demanding; they pummelled and pulled and tugged and were relentlessly selfish. Selfishness was all right in its place, Ninnidh felt, but he preferred it to serve him.

In Tearmónn Eirc his distaste for children had been transferred to Brendán and Brige. He had expected the ecclesiastical center to be the sanctuary its name implied, a scholarly retreat peopled by adults. When the youngsters arrived he had ignored them to the best of his ability.

Now Brendán was no longer a youngster. And it was obvious he was in pain.

Ninnidh's curiosity was aroused.

Erc continued to gain in strength, ferociously willing himself to health. The first time he was able to stand up—shaky, trembling, leaning heavily on Brendán's broad shoulder—his eyes were bleary and his skin sagged away from his bones like melting wax.

Three days later he dispatched runners throughout the diocese of Altraighe to announce the upcoming ordination of Brendán, son of Finnlugh.

The ordination took place at sunrise in the sod-walled church. It was crowded to bursting point by the time Bishop Molua entered, followed by the bishop of Slane. Erc was robed in the gold-embroidered vestments he customarily reserved for Easter.

He had brought them from Slane; he was that sure of me.

Erc was able to walk into the church, very slowly, but he immediately sat down on a stool which had been placed for him below the altar.

Brendán was the last to enter. He wore only a plain tunic of bleached linen, belted with a new rope. Without looking left or right he paced solemnly forward and knelt at the feet of Bishop Erc.

The words from the Gospel: "Everyone that hath forsaken father or mother or sister or lands for my Name's sake shall receive a hundredfold in the present, and shall possess everlasting life."

The vows. The anointing oil.

And the bloom of joy that brought a touch of colour to Bishop Erc's cheeks for the first time in months.

Ninnidh, who was watching closely, detected no joy on the face of the newly-ordained priest, either at that moment or during the celebration that followed.

Bishop Erc had been granted a brief respite from his illness—many called it a miracle—but after the ordination he was exhausted. Bishop Molua made him comfortable in his house in Tearmónn Eirc and assured him he could stay as long as he wanted.

Ninnidh waited for several days before confronting him. "I am deeply sorry about your illness, cousin," he said—pointedly calling attention to their relationship—"but under the circumstances, do you not think it would be wise to name your successor at Slane?"

"No."

Ninnidh's carefully arranged smile faltered. "What do you mean?"

"No means no, Ninnidh. I shall rest here until I am stronger, then I intend to take Brendán to Slane and prepare him to succeed me as bishop when the time comes."

Ninnidh's jaw dropped. "But he's only a boy!"

"Coming close to death gives a person clearer vision," Erc said. "I see now that you are not as observant as you should be. Brendán has been a grown man for several years."

"Are you sure it's what he wants?" Ninnidh struggled not to sound desperate. "He seems so unhappy . . ."

"Did he tell you he is unhappy?"

"No, but . . ."

"Then do not make assumptions, Ninnidh. That is another of your failings; you make assumptions. Go now. I need to rest."

"I'll go," Ninnidh said through gritted teeth. "Just don't expect me to come running back when you need me."

That same day he left for Clon Ard.

The bishop of Slane suffered through a cold wet summer while fluid gathered in his lungs and his heart rattled behind his ribs. He delayed discussing the bishopric with Brendán. Not because he feared his godson would refuse—he was confidant Brendán would accept—but because he felt the appointment and its subsequent announcement should be made at Slane.

Day by day Erc insisted he was feeling better. Day by day his strength drained from him. At last he was forced to admit to himself that he would never return to Slane; he could not survive the journey. He could not even summon the energy to give Brendán the intense preparation such a young man would require to succeed him.

Fortunately Erc had trained other priests, older and more experienced men, any one of whom was qualified to become bishop of Slane. But not his godson, not the one upon whom he had set his heart.

When the wild geese flew south in the autumn they took Bishop Erc's soul with them.

On the day he died I felt nothing at first. Numbness in the face of the impossible. Erc simply could not be dead. The man who above all others had shaped my life—how could he be gone?

There had been times when I resented the bishop, a few times when I almost hated him. He had been a boulder in my road, keeping me from reaching destinations of my own choosing. But after his death I began to fill with grief like water in a barrel; a grief so cold and deep it drowned all other emotions.

Once I had thought God was my actual father. Then I learned of Finnlugh but never saw him, had no way of knowing him. Yet Erc had always been there. The father life chose for me.

After he was gone I knew I loved him.

Everything was done as Bishop Erc would have wished. Runners were sent to inform the larger Christian community of his departure for heaven. A funeral Mass was said in the church he had helped build with his own hands. A large number attended the service. Some had travelled a considerable distance—including Ruan, who came all the way from Clon Ard.

Ninnidh was conspicuous by his absence.

The congregation sang "Gloria in excelsis Deo," and "Audite Omnes," a hymn composed in honour of Patrick. The earthen walls absorbed the music. As long as they remained standing they would resonate in memory of Erc, son of Daig.

When the ceremony was over Brendán went down to the bay alone.

I would not grieve for Bishop Erc beside the High Grave; that was not his place. Instead I sought the little harbour at the foot of Diadche and wept for him as I knelt on the damp earth.

It was said of Erc that as a brehon he had always judged rightly. I prayed he would receive the same just judgement now.

My prayers at last concluded, I looked up at the mountain. Why had I never climbed Diadche before? It was always there, waiting for me.

Perhaps that's why: it was always there, waiting for me.

Even with the aid of my staff, the climb was difficult enough. I undertook it as a penance. No matter what others thought, God—unto whom all hearts are open and all desires known—was aware of the true circumstances of my ordination. Was he very angry? I would have been.

As Brendán began his climb the wind became a gale. It pummelled him with furious fists; it drove the breath from his lungs. Every step was a struggle. He hunched down into his shoulders. The gale gathered force; threatened to tear him off Diadche. The roar was deafening.

Near the western base of the mountain Brendán found a slight hollow. Fighting the wind every step of the way, he piled up enough stones to shelter the front of the recess. Within this makeshift cell he knelt to ask God's forgiveness.

Whatever you ask of me I shall do. Without resentment; with an open heart.

Stones and the wind. Dark and the mountain. And prayer.

Little by little, the gale diminished.

When he judged it was safe, he resumed climbing.

Up, and up; boggy soil slipping unexpectedly; be careful! Angle sideways and keep going; up, and up, wading through purple heather, past pink thrift and green samphire and saxifrage. Rough beauty on every hand but he could not stop to admire it. Up, and up . . . abruptly he was enveloped in dense fog. The very air he breathed turned liquid. The mountain below him vanished. The peak above was invisible.

Brendán was totally alone. The only reality was the ground under his feet and the staff in his hand.

And faith. I have faith that the summit is there.

Up, and up. His heart was hammering but he kept climbing. For an eternity, it seemed.

The fog was blown away in a single mighty exhalation.

And Brendán found himself on the summit of Diadche. No clouds, no mist. The air was as clear as on the first day of Creation.

Here. Right here.

He turned around slowly, feasting on the view.

To the east Brendán glimpsed glacier-carved valleys filled with purple shadows. When he raised his eyes to the curving spine of Sliabh Mis he could see half of Ireland beyond, lying in soft folds like a blanket. In the opposite direction was the Western Sea, reaching to the end of the world. And beyond.

On the horizon was the setting sun.

Singing. Like a great bronze bell ringing out over the water.

The sea was singing too, a wild melody advancing and retreating and roaring back again, ever changing, always the same. Great deep rollers falling upon themselves like thunder. White spume flying: the tossing manes of white stallions pulling the chariot of Manannán Mac Lir. Clouds turning rose and gold, birds stitching black patterns across their glowing faces.

As Brendán watched with dazzled eyes, the sun painted a golden road over the sea. Somewhere along that road—he could not tell how far away—tall towers glittered. Clearly visible.

"Hy Brasail," Brendán murmured, awestruck. "The Isles of the Blest."

On the early part of our voyage we had become accustomed to kindness. The beneficence of God was to be found everywhere, it seemed. Our faith grew in equal measure to our sense of well-being. We had nothing to fear. The Western Sea was not an abyss at all, but the road to Paradise.

The shores we approached on that warm, windless day bore no resemblance to Paradise.

The land looked bleak and barren. We could see a solitary mountain wreathed in clouds; clouds which were lit from beneath with sparks of fire. The air rang with the blowing of bellows and the clanging of hammers. "I believe we have found an island of smiths," Colmán announced. "At last I can have a new head made for my axe."

However the rest of my crew observed the forbidding landscape with trepidation.

"There is life here," I told them, "and if not Christian souls, then souls which need Christ. We shall go ashore and find them."

We landed our boat on a beach of glittering black sand. Carrying several full water bags, we headed inland. The ground was littered with lumps of charcoal and heaps of slag frequently blocked our way. Soon our faces and clothing were speckled with soot. The air smelled like rotten eggs. Liber wondered, "What manner of people could possibly live here?"

"Whoever they are," I replied grimly, "they must be in dire need of Christian compassion."

Except for Cerball, to whom caution was unknown, the monks looked apprehensive. I did not want to give in to their fears, but I too felt something was terribly wrong.

Just as I decided to turn back, the mountain gave a deafening roar and burst open.

An immense, blazing demon of crimson and gold sprang from the ruptured heart of the mountain and began hurling boulders into the air. Rivers of liquid fire poured down the flanks of the mountain and ran past us into the sea, sending up great clouds of hissing steam. The ground shuddered as if the island were shaking itself apart.

Then the soil under our feet caught fire.

"Run!" I shouted to my dumbstruck companions. "*Run!!!* We have come to the gates of Hell!" I whirled around and raced for my life. Their vow of obedience saved them; they came pelting after me.

My feet hardly seemed to touch the smoking earth but I could feel its heat through my sandals. Never in my life had I run as fast.

The fire did not extend as far as the beach but the demon was not through with us. As I drew near the boat a shower of burning coals fell from the sky. Some of the coals landed in the bottom of the vessel. I vaulted over the side, tore off my robe, and scooped up the flaming embers with it, then threw them into the sea.

The other monks arrived panting and sweating, thankful to be alive. "We must launch the boat at once!" they cried.

I agreed—but first I had to take a count.

One was missing.

Almost naked, with blistered skin and sandals burned away, I crawled out of the boat and went back for him. The brothers begged me not to go but I ignored their warnings. Just as it is possibly to be so badly hurt you feel no pain, it is also possible to be so badly scared you feel no fear.

It was late afternoon but the sky was as dark as night, save for the lurid flames. The air was almost too thick to breathe. I tried to call the missing monk's name but kept choking.

At last I saw him.

The second of the three uninvited monks who had insisted upon coming with us stood staring at the fiery spectacle. He did not move; he might as well have been a tree. I once saw a fawn stand like that while a wolf approached. There are sights which freeze the mind.

I ran forward, determined to carry him in my arms all

the way to the boat if necessary. Before I could reach him a fresh river of flame came pouring down towards us, encircling him, cutting off any hope of rescue. A great gout of fire belched around the unfortunate man. For an instant I saw his hair standing upright, crisping in the heat.

Then he was gone.

We dragged the boat into the water and rowed away as fast as we could, while the demon smith continued to rage over the island. All through the night we could see his fire. At last, exhausted by terror and pity, we slept.

We awoke in a sulphurous dawn to find ourselves still safe. Our brave little boat was floating in the palm of God.

We sailed on.

CHAPTER 15

Molua was waiting for Brendán when he returned from Diadche. "Bishop Erc should have been the one to tell you," Molua said apologetically, tenting his fingers and hiding behind them. "But he only made the decision shortly before his death, and he made me promise to wait until after his funeral before informing you."

"What are you talking about?"

"You must have known that Bishop Erc wanted you to succeed him at Slane, but he realised you are still too young. I personally thought his cousin Ninnidh would be his choice, but they had a quarrel about something—you remember when Ninnidh stormed out of here—so the bishopric has gone to Ninnidh's eldest brother instead. A good man," Molua added. "Bishop Erc educated him too."

To Molua's surprise, Brendán smiled.

God has a sense of humour; that's another proof that we are made in his image.

A lesser man might be disappointed, thought Molua, but obviously Erc's godson was made of stronger stuff. Brendán grew in his estimation. "If there's anything I can do . . ." Molua began. Knowing there was not.

"Thank you for informing me of Bishop Erc's wise decision," Brendán said with quiet dignity. "And also for your many kindnesses to him during his illness. I shall go to the church now and pray for the new bishop of Slane."

After spending half a day on his knees, Brendán retired to his clochán. Alone in his cell, alone in himself.

Had Erc read my heart and relented at the last moment? Or—and this was far more likely—was he merely being practical?

Did it matter? Sometimes we are too busy looking for reasons to see results.

Was the vision I saw from Diadche a blessing? Or a punishment?

Either way I understood.

I would not have to be the bishop of Slane because that was not what God wanted of me.

Brendán remained at Tearmónn Eirc to assist the bishop as a parish priest. He also sent for Brige to come from Slane. "I didn't want to stay there with the new bishop," she confided to her brother after she arrived. "He's nothing like Erc."

"Have you thought of marrying?"

A shadow passed over her face. "If I had a husband, he might die. Or our children might die. I've seen . . . it's better to stay as I am."

"What happened to our mother wouldn't happen to you."

"You don't know that, Brendán. I could take care of Bishop Erc because we weren't part of each other; do you understand?

I can love Christ without being afraid, but I don't want a husband."

Brendán grinned. "And Bishop Molua doesn't want another wife. But he does need someone to cook his food and sweep his floor; someone familiar with the burdens of his vocation. Would you be interested?"

She hesitated. "I've been thinking about joining a nunnery."

"Don't," said Brendán. "Join me instead."

Stay here so there will be a woman in my life.

Ruan was another who remained at Tearmónn Eirc. "I've worked hard at learning illumination," he told Brendán, "but now the abbot has me studying Greek. It's heavy weather. I need a rest."

Eventually Brendán brought up the subject of Ninnidh. "He's also studying Greek under Finnian, I believe. What do you think of him?"

Ruan shrugged. "He's all right. Why?"

"I thought perhaps he was the reason you didn't want to go back to Clon Ard."

Ruan looked astonished. "Ninnidh?"

When Brige found a butterfly that had outlived its season, she carried it to her brother. Tears glittered in her eyes. "The poor thing is so beautiful and it's dying," she said. "I can't bear it."

Brendán took the exhausted creature onto the palm of his hand. He diluted a single drop of honey with water and touched it to the insect's proboscis. Slowly, the butterfly unrolled its tongue and supped the liquid. It lived for five more days, and attended Mass clinging to Brige's sleeve.

"You saved it only to die again," she mourned when the butterfly finally died. "That was cruel."

Her brother put his arm around her shoulder. "Look up at the sky. God hung those stars there to brighten the cavern of night. They know they're in his hands and they don't protest their fate. Neither do creatures like butterflies, Brige. They don't anticipate grief; they live each hour fully. To them five days is precious. On our own deathbeds we'll plead with God for five more days."

"What will you do with yours, if he gives them to you?"

Brendán laughed. "Find more butterflies for you."

Sometimes his eyes sparkled with mischief, but there was a solid core to Brendán which others instinctively recognised. He had the calmness of power.

A small coterie of admirers began to form around him.

Brendán was puzzled. "What do they want of me?" he asked Ruan.

"Just to be with you."

"Why? There's nothing special about me."

"There is. For one thing, you've seen miracles. Remember telling me about the chariot in the clouds, and the wheel that fell off?"

A miracle? In my memory the incident had the weight of reality.

Brendán's band of followers grew. When the weather deteriorated, they gathered in the refectory and urged him to relate the details of his pilgrimage. They listened attentively to his thoughts and discoveries. Almost before he realised it, Brendán was explaining his ideas for a monastic order.

I let myself be flattered. There is no other explanation.

On the first mild day he set out alone for Diadche.

The wall at the mouth of the hollow was still there, though partially collapsed. He gathered more stones and began creating a grotto, an artificial cave. The inside was as dark as the inside of a clochán. The earthen floor followed the angle of the slope, making it uncomfortable to stand. Kneeling was easier, yet even then there was a sense of clinging to the side of the mountain.

When the work was finished, Brendán stood back to see the structure in its entirety.

I made that, he thought with satisfaction. *Everything that is made has a maker.*

The skin on his arms began to prickle.

Those stones. This mountain. Me.

Everything that is made has a Maker. His Creation is the tangible proof of Him.

'My very first foundation,' wrote the abbot of Clon Fert many years later, 'was a simple stone oratory on the side of a mountain. I went there by myself from time to time, to pray.'

The young bird was awkward, as newly fledged birds are. Its inexperienced parents had built their first nest of sticks upon a precipice and the wind had torn it down. Only one fledgling survived. Flapping helplessly, it tumbled down the western face of Diadche, easy prey for the golden eagles who patrolled the mountains.

Brendán found it first.

As he approached his grotto an erratic motion off to one side caught his attention. The bird panicked even more when it saw him. He called in a soothing voice, "Don't be afraid, little *préachán*; little crow. I won't hurt you."

The bird tried to flatten itself against the earth. Brendán stood still. "It's cold up here, isn't it?" he said in a conversational voice. "And you don't have enough feathers yet. I can take you to a warmer place if you like." He squatted down so he did not loom so large in the creature's eyes. "Préachán," he repeated softly. "Préachán."

The bird blinked.

Snugly nested in Brendán's cloak, the fledgling was carried across the bay in his currach. From time to time it extended its neck and fixed its beady eyes on the man. "I'm still here," he said reassuringly.

When he reached Tearmónn Eirc he found two men wiping mildew off the timber in the gateway. Wood was scarce and valuable; maintaining it was a constant job. "What's that you're carrying?" one asked.

"A young crow."

"Didn't anyone tell you that you can't eat a crow?"

"I don't intend to eat him. I'm going to feed him until he's able to fend for himself."

"Stone the thing," said the other man. "Everyone knows that crows devour the grain in the fields."

"No worries for us, then," Brendán laughed. "Everyone knows that we have no grain nor any fields to grow it in. And before you ask, I'll give little Préachán a share of my food, not yours. A bit of bread soaked in water should do for a start."

"You think it will live?"

"He'll live if he wants to," said Brendán.

He composed a letter for Íta; the first since his unanswered apology many years earlier. He did not mention what had happened between them, nor his ordination, nor even the death of Bishop Erc. He wrote:

> I have an unusual friend, an orphan I rescued on the mountainside. At first I thought he was a crow so I called him Préachán. As he grows it is obvious he is a raven. He has a massive beak, a shaggy throat, a wedge-shaped tail and fingers of feathers at the tips of his wings. Enormous wings, for he is becoming an enormous bird. Whatever his tribe, Préachán is a droll character. He sits with his head cocked, staring into my face, and from time to time he croaks a caustic comment. I do not yet understand his language, but I doubt if his remarks are complimentary. Having a critic at a man's elbow keeps him humble.

Íta did not write a reply to this letter either. But she sent a large sack of corn.

"You've worked a miracle," Brendán told the raven. "I think I may be forgiven."

He debated with himself about taking Préachán to Cill Íde to meet his benefactress, but decided against it.

Behaving like a foolish child had alienated me from her once; I didn't want to risk that again.

Shortly after Erc's death, an increased asceticism, inspired by the *Penetential of Vinnian*, a book written in Rome, swept through the Church in Ireland. Stringent new restrictions were imposed on both clerics and laymen. Married persons were required to refrain from sexual relations not only on Saturday and Sunday, but also for three periods of forty days each in every year, and from the time of a child's conception until its birth. Divorce and concubinage, both common in Ireland, were proscribed. Celibacy became the rule rather than an option, for monks and nuns alike.

And so I really lost her. My waking mind understood but my dreaming mind did not. My dreaming mind remembered God and made love to Íta.

In spite of the restrictions on monastic communities, their populations increased. Many people decided it was easier to take holy orders than to live up to the Church's demands in a secular society.

In time and inevitably, Brendán's admirers discovered where he was going. They followed him by boat and by land. In time and inevitably, his private oratory on Diadche rang with their prayers. A few even built tiny clocháns near the grotto to use during the summer months.

As Préachán matured he still spent every night in Brendán's cell with his head tucked under his wing. When the bell rang to arouse the faithful for the first prayers of the day, the raven hopped onto Brendán and launched a mock assault with beak and talons. He never drew blood.

The raven would let no one touch him but Brendán; not even Brige. If she tried to put her hand on him he shied away. She was hurt by his refusal to accept her. Brendán said comfortingly, "Ravens are a law unto themselves, Brige. The rest of God's creatures love you dearly; allow this one to be faithful to me."

A number of women and children in the parish—and not a few men—began to "set something aside" for the big black bird.

Préachán followed the same route day after day and thanked each of his contributors with a resonant croak.

Préachán would eat anything. Bread, wild fruits such as sloes and brambles, birds' eggs, fish guts—it was all the same to him. If he could get it in his beak he swallowed it. When he was given more than he wanted he carried the excess back to my cell and stuffed it into the recesses where I stored my belongings. Once he replaced my bag of flints with a rotting crab.

The only manmade structure Préachán would enter was Brendán's cell, though he would wait outside the door of the church while his friend was inside. When Brendán went out on the bay Préachán perched on the prow of his boat. His presence infuriated the gulls; they swooped as close as they dared and screamed insults at him, then fled in alarm if he looked at them.

Bishop Molua had misgivings about Préachán. "Crows are vermin," he told Brendán. "You shouldn't keep one."

"He's not a crow and I'm not keeping him," Brendán replied. "Préachán's free to fly away whenever he wants, but he chooses to stay with me. I'm flattered; ravens tend to avoid humans."

The bishop tried a different approach. "Did you know that the pagan goddess of war is a raven?"

"Surely you're not superstitious, Molua."

The bishop bridled. "Of course not. I was only trying to explain the importance of symbols."

"So a bird is a bad symbol? What about a deer? Or a fish? The early Christians used a fish as the symbol for Christ."

"I . . ." Molua hesitated. Dimly he recalled Bishop Erc warning him not to debate with Brendán. "The point is . . ." He hesitated again. Rushed heedlessly forward. "We have to be mindful of tradition!"

"Tradition must be respected," Brendán agreed. "Our forebears attributed magical powers to birds, so we should too. Among the Druids there is a class called diviners, who claim they can foretell the future by reading the entrails of owls. The diviners are invariably right in one respect." His eyes danced. "The owls whose entrails they read have no future."

Bishop Molua changed the subject.

Brendán's name began to be known beyond the borders of Altraighe-Caille. Visitors to the ecclesiastical centre were impressed by the intelligence and piety of the young priest—and intrigued by the raven, his constant companion. When they returned to their homes they told their friends about him.

And their friends told their friends, in the way of the Irish. A good story could not be hoarded.

Autumn and winter and spring again. And change in the air.

Fionn-barr—Fair Top—was a devout Christian who had created a singular retreat in the wilderness to the east of the Ciarrí Luachra. On a tiny, grassy island in the midst of a tranquil lake he had built a stone hut for himself. The shore of the lake was a natural garden of ferns and moss. Beyond was a lush valley studded with massive boulders split from the cliffs that rose on all sides. Shielded from the vagaries of the weather, the location was a veritable paradise.

Such extravagant beauty seemed curiously at odds with the ascetic life that Fionn-barr lived. The local tribes speculated endlessly about him. In the absence of fact, imagination triumphed. People began claiming the hermit could perform miracles.

A local chieftain who visited him late one winter declared, "If with my two eyes I could see some wonder performed by your God, then I might believe in him." The two men were standing on the cold ground beneath a leafless hazel tree. No sooner did the chieftain finish speaking than fully ripe hazel nuts showered down upon him. He was converted the same day.

Or so the story was told.

When Fionn-barr heard of the priest in Altraighe-Caille who built an oratory on the side of a wild and lonely mountain, he recognised a kindred spirit. But it was more than that. According to his informants, Brendán, like himself, could trace his bloodline to Niall of the Nine Hostages. Although he rarely left his island, Fionn-barr set out to meet his kinsman.

His arrival in Tearmónn Eirc was unremarkable. Aside from his unusual silvery-white hair he was just another pilgrim, travel-stained and weary, seeking shelter. When he gave his name and the reason for his visit, however, Bishop Molua could hardly contain his delight. If Brendán was acquiring a small reputation among Christians, Fionn-barr of Gougán Barra was already famous.

"You need not climb Diadche to meet Brendán," the bishop told the visitor. "He's often up there with his band of followers, but he's here today, probably in his clochán. I'll send for him."

"Please don't trouble yourself. I prefer to go to him, just tell me which is his cell."

"Easily identified, Brendán's cell. It's the one with the raven."

Préachán was standing lookout atop the beehive hut. When he saw Fionn-barr approach he gave a loud croak. A moment later Brendán peered out of the low doorway. "A visitor, you say? Why, there he is!

"You're very welcome," he told Fionn-barr, "but do I know you? Never mind, come inside. It will be warmer in here with the two of us."

"You actually do own a raven," Fionn-barr marvelled as he sat down crosslegged on the earthen floor.

"No, I share my life with one," said Brendán. "Préachán belongs to himself."

They began their conversation with Niall of the Nine Hostages, establishing the familial links so important to the Gael. Brendán was touched that a distant kinsman had made such an effort to meet him.

"It was an impulse," said Fionn-barr.

Brendán grinned. "You've come a long way on an impulse, then. That's the sort of thing I do."

"What else do you do?"

"Pray. Fish. Study Holy Scripture."

"You must do more than that. Bishop Molua tells me you've acquired a devoted band of followers. Do you hope to found an order?"

"Oh no," Brendán assured him. "I don't want to be responsible for anyone else, I'm only beginning to find my own way."

Fionn-barr persisted. "Perhaps you should think about it."

"I have thought about it once or twice, but I know my limitations. Tell me, Fionn-barr: what pathway led you to Gougán Barra?"

His visitor tried to rest his back against the wall, which curved as it rose to meet the low ceiling. "My father was a master smith called Amargein, a name which has been passed down through the generations in our family. I inherited his silver hair but not his silver tongue. After his conversion to Christianity he told his family wonderful stories about Jesus Christ."

"I heard the same stories as a small child," said Brendán. *Íta. Íta.*

"Ever since I was a small child I wanted to be a priest," Fionn-barr continued. "As soon as I reached manhood I was ordained, and shortly afterward I married a woman who shared my love of God." He shifted uncomfortably against the wall. "She died giving birth to our son," he added in a low voice.

The two men sat listening to the click of the raven's claws as he walked around on top of the cell.

At last Brendán asked—shyly—"Was it very good? Being married?"

Fionn-barr stared at the rectangle of grey light in the doorway. "Very good," he said.

"Ah."

Fionn-barr turned to look at the other man. Look into and through him, see the hidden pain. "Have you never . . ."

"No."

"Not even . . ."

"No."

The bird above them gave a derisive cry.

Chapter 16

The peninsula northwest of Gaul was called *Armorica,* the Land Facing the Sea. Over countless millennia, sediment from the seabed had been folded and pressed and folded again to form a chain of granite mountains running roughly east to west. During still more millennia, flooding overlaid the granite with ridges of quartzite and shale deposits. By the sixth century after Christ, erosion had abraded the former uplands, creating a countryside of broad, gently rolling plateaux that sloped to the sea. The infinitely varied coastline was deeply indented by river valleys. A variety of soils nourished a wide variety of plant life. Armorica was, if one had the ability to recognise it, beautiful.

The hand of God did this, Malo thought to himself. *Out of old rocks, he made a miracle.*

"How many people know a miracle when they see one?" he wondered aloud.

The only other ears in his immediate vicinity belonged to the mule upon which he rode. The ears were very large but not interested in philosophical speculation. The mule vastly preferred to hear oats being poured into a leather bucket. The animal had long yellow teeth commensurate with its considerable age, and a deadly kick unaffected by the years. As long as he sat on the mule's back Malo was as safe as if surrounded by armed guards.

He was proud of his mule. The creature had come to him years ago and in a rather odd way. Malo's tribe made its living by scooping salt from sand beaches after high tide. They dried the valuable commodity in brick kilns, then packed it into baskets which they carried to market by oxcart. The salt was purchased by seafarers who sold it on in distant ports—making a much larger profit than they would ever admit.

The Armorican phrase for a liar was: "as poor as a ship's captain".

Gathering the salt was backbreaking work, mind-numbingly monotonous. Malo's father had done it before him, and that man's father before him, and so backwards into the fog of unknowable time. It was simply the way things were. Life offered no alternatives.

In spite of this, in his youth Malo had dreamed. A wiry young man whose thick brown hair and bushy eyebrows were permanently grey with salt, he would suddenly stop in the middle of his work, lick the persistent rime of salt from his chapped lips, and wander among his hazy thoughts, searching for something fresh and bright.

Something else. Anything else.

One winter afternoon he had been loading baskets of salt into an oxcart when a brown mule came up the road. A man wearing a heavy cloak and a lugubrious expression sat astride the animal, wedged in place by a mountain of impedimenta. Mules were an uncommon sight in Armorica. Malo was astonished that the beast was able to carry so many burdens with apparent ease. Abandoning his task, he ran to the road to talk to the rider.

After a few false starts they found a common language in the Gaulish tongue. Neither spoke it fluently, but with the addition of extravagant gestures they understood each other.

The stranger identified himself as a priest from Rome. He had undertaken a journey modelled on that of an earlier holy man, but became disillusioned. Now he was anxious to return to his homeland. "The wide world is cold and grey," he complained, "and the people have no culture." With Malo's help he wearily dismounted. As he stood rubbing his backside he asked, "Does this road lead to the sea?"

The Armorican nodded. An affirmative nod was part of the universal language.

"Do you know any captains of ships?"

Malo nodded again. Warily, this time.

The priest gave a relieved sigh. "Good. I have no desire to ride this beast all the way back to Rome. Could you arrange passage for me on an Armorican vessel?"

Rocking back on his heels, Malo assumed a doubtful expression. "This is not the best season for sailing," he said.

"I do not mind a rough voyage," replied the priest. "I have been riding a mule, remember."

"How much can you pay for your passage?"

The priest's face fell. "I have only a little silver left. I am accustomed to the best inns and they are run by robbers."

"If I help you, how much will you pay me?"

The priest turned his hands palm up and appeared embarrassed.

Malo stood where he was and looked at the mule.

The mule looked back.

The priest followed the direction of Malo's gaze. "Would you like to buy this beast?" he asked eagerly.

"I do not deal in animals. I sell salt."

"This mule could carry a lot of salt. Mules are much more useful than oxen."

Maintaining his dubious expression, Malo slowly examined the mule—a creature he knew almost nothing about—while clucking his tongue with disapproval as if he were an experienced mule dealer and had never seen such a bad example.

The animal was well fed and muscular and its hooves were neatly trimmed. Malo did not remark on these virtues aloud, however.

When the mule cocked a hind leg he quickly stepped back.

"Vicious brute," he remarked.

"On the contrary, this mule has been my guardian angel," the priest asserted. "Do you know about angels?"

Malo shook his head.

"Are you a Christian?"

Malo shook his head again.

A broad smile transformed the priest's face. "Then in exchange for your assistance I shall give you a mule . . . and save your soul. The gift of faith is worth more than all the mules in the world. It can fill you with enough joy for a lifetime."

"Joy," echoed Malo, as if he did not know the word.

The priest sensed a possible breakthrough in negotiations. "The animal cannot be used for breeding," he explained, hoping to clench the deal by a demonstration of honesty, "because the child of a mare and an ass is sterile. But this mule is very young and can provide you with sturdy transportation for many years to come."

"And the 'faith' you offer. How long will that last?"

"Until the end of time," the priest assured Malo.

* * *

In his journal Brendán wrote, 'A kinsman of mine, Fionn-barr, son of Amargein, had given his son into fosterage following the death of his wife. He then retired from the world and built a hermitage at Gougán Barra. The first time he visited me I was deeply impressed by the man and we began to correspond. Eventually I invited him to Altraighe-Caille for a longer time, with the intention of asking him to become my spiritual confidante.'

On this occasion Fionn-barr spent a summer in Altraighe-Caille. He barely recalled a time when he had so enjoyed the company of others; had talked, and sung, and laughed. When he laughed out loud at some remark of Brendán's, he felt his long-frozen joy begin to thaw.

The majesty of the sea moved him to tears. "It must be inspiring to live here," he said to Brendán. "I have loved the woods and marshes, but this. . . ." At a loss for adequate words, he made a gesture that encompassed the bay and the ocean beyond. "This," he said simply.

"This," Brendán echoed.

He took his guest to pray in the oratory on Diadche. Afterward they climbed to the summit side by side. With the beauty of God's creation spread out below them, at last Brendán confessed the secret he had whispered only to Préachán in the privacy of his cell.

"What is my penance?" he asked Fionn-Barr. He braced himself to receive a severe scourging at the very least; a permanent bed of nettles; perhaps even anathema.

"How long have you suffered this on your conscience?"

"Fifteen years," was the embarrassed answer.

Fionn-barr said, "Then I give you fifteen years of suffering as your penance, and declare that you have served your term."

If only it were that easy. Confessing eased my conscience; forgiveness soothed my spirit. But nothing granted forgetfulness.

I know now what I only suspected then. The real punishment for sin is memory. Death is the blessing that wipes it away.

A storm roared out of the sea on the night after Fionn-barr departed for Gougán Barra. As the wind gathered strength, proving its malign intentions, Brendán prayed for the safety of his kinsman. It was too late to run after Fionn-barr and bring him back to the shelter of the lios.

When the full force of the storm hit Tearmónn Eirc, debris slammed with incredible force against earthen ramparts. Had the walls been less thick they might have been battered down. Those who had access to clocháns—including Brendán and Préachán—were safe enough; the beehive huts were designed to withstand weather. Elsewhere people huddled together with their eyes shut tight, enduring like dumb beasts.

At first light Brendán joined the work party Bishop Molua was organising. The ramparts of the lios had mitigated the worst of it for the ecclesiastical centre, but the dwellings of the Altraighe along the coast were devastated and most of the boats destroyed.

In the aftermath of the storm a brilliant sun shone. The sky had never been so blue; the earth never washed so clean. The air was crisp and invigorating. People worked frantically to replace what was lost.

Days would pass before Brendán dare take a moment for himself. His boat had been badly damaged but not totally destroyed by the storm surge. It would take time to repair, however. Without a boat, the only way to reach the oratory on Diadche was by taking the landward route along the north shore of the peninsula, followed by a difficult climb up the east side of the mountain.

The promontory of Ard Fert was much nearer.

Brendán managed to slip away without being noticed, though Préachán nearly ruined it by flying after him. He walked to the strand—a totally different strand now, reconstructed by wind and tide—and turned northward.

It wasn't there.

Even from a distance I could tell that the headland had vanished. I began to run.

Préachán flew with me, keeping pace. We went a great distance along the beach until my breath deserted me entirely, then I turned and slowly walked back, scouring the shoreline with my eyes. There was no strip of high ground jutting into the sea. No little cairn of white stones. Nothing but strangeness and emptiness.

The sea had taken the High Grave of the Milesian. And the other memorial as well.

Gone forever.

The Ciarrí Luachra demanded an exorbitant price—three years' supply of salt—for the necessary oxhides, and the fishermen fell to work rebuilding their boats. It might be a long time before they brought in another good catch. Men spoke in gruff voices when they spoke at all. Women, jealous of their food stores, were less welcoming to visitors. Even Brendán was not urged to share a meal.

While his followers went to Diadche to repair any storm damage to the oratory, Brendán set to work on his own currach. Mending the frame, fitting additional oxhides, sealing the joins with holly resin and smearing rancid fat over the hull to make it watertight. The removable mast had survived but he had to make a new sail. Triangular in shape, it consisted of the hides of small animals. Oxhide stiffened when exposed to seawater and lost flexibility, but the skins of wolf and fox were impervious to salty spray.

When the new sail was ready, Brendán wrapped it tightly around the mast and stowed them in the bottom of the boat.

Préachán kept him company, overseeing the labour with a glittering eye. If Brendán was in a mood to talk the raven held up his end of the conversation with a complex repertoire of clicks and croaks and chuckles. If Brendán was quiet the bird was quiet too.

When his currach was seaworthy Brendán rowed to the little harbour below Diadche. "Are you ready to go ashore?" he asked his companion.

Préachán gave himself a vigorous shake and lifted his wings as if to fly. Instead, he settled back onto the prow and fixed unblinking eyes on Brendán.

The man stared back at him. Turned to gaze up at the mountain. "Perhaps you're right," he said. "This isn't our place. Not really."

Brendán beached his boat and climbed towards the oratory. Préachán followed, though reluctantly. Ruan saw them first and hurried to meet them. "There's been no damage, Brendán," he reported happily. "We built well—I mean, you built well. The oratory is just as it was. It looks like one of the clocháns leaked a little, but we've fitted new stones. We've even dug a cess pit."

"Stay here as long as you like, all of you," said Brendán. "You have my blessing."

"Aren't you going to stay with us?"

"Not now, Ruan, I've decided to make another pilgrimage."

"I'll come with you!"

Brendán shook his head. "I'm going by water this time and you hate the sea; I wouldn't ask that of you. Besides, a pilgrimage is best undertaken alone."

The remainder of the little band was now crowding around them. Molais and Sechnall, and Aedgal the sharp-eyed, Liber and Anfudán and Dianách the runner, Eber the tall, and Cerball the clever.

They implored me not to go; not to leave them.

Why are the most important things the most difficult to explain?

If you do explain, they don't believe you.

Chapter 17

Brendán put a new edge on the knife he kept in his scabbard and mended a long-neglected tear in his heavy woollen cloak. He scraped the hair from six deer-skins and stitched them into bags to hold fresh water. The manuscript satchel containing his Psalter was treated to an extra coating of wax to keep it waterproof and then fitted into a carved wooden box. He would carry no maps.

I had no particular destination in mind. I would simply go, entrusting myself to the will of God.

Bishop Molua was unhappy about his impending departure. Brendán was a great asset; his presence attracted new people to Tearmónn Eirc, a gift which the bishop lacked. "I don't understand why you're going," he complained to Brendán. "You've already been on one long pilgrimage."

"I have been on a long pilgrimage. I've eaten food too, but that doesn't keep me from needing more."

"We need you here," Molua stressed.

"I'll be back."

"How can you be sure? The sea is unforgiving."

"I know that as well as anyone does."

"Have I said something . . . done something . . . is there any way I could persuade you . . ."

"You've been the soul of kindness, Molua, but please believe me: the journey is necessary. If I stay in one place I can teach, but when I travel I can learn. How can I do one without first doing the other?"

"The only lesson you may learn is how to die," warned the bishop.

On the afternoon of Brendán's departure a crowd of old friends and recent followers gathered to wish him well. As he was about to launch his currach a little boy gripped the side of the boat and clung with all his might. "Take me with you, Brendán! I won't be any trouble, I don't eat very much."

The child was not yet ten years old. His audacity reminded Brendán of himself at that age. Smiling, he asked, "Why do you want to go with me, Fursu?"

"Just to be going!" cried the boy.

Fursu's mother was running down the beach to reclaim him. "Don't worry," Brendán called to her, "Your son will stay here."

As he gently removed the child's clutching fingers from the boat, Brendán whispered, "Finish growing and study the patterns of the stars, Fursu. I'll be back."

He shoved off as the bells were chiming Terce.

We went out with the tide, Préachán and I. When the big waves near the mouth of the bay hit us I half expected the raven to fly away but he stayed with me. Like myself, he was not easily frightened.

"Now we wait," I told him.

Since childhood I had been able to recognise different currents not only by their colour, but also by a subtle change of water texture against the boat. Dubán had laughed the first time I made that claim. Gaeth had believed me.

We did not have long to wait. Through the leather hull of the boat I felt the water change. A powerful current took hold of us and swept us around the coast of Corca Dhuibhne, between the last outstretched finger of land and the flock of tiny islands that lay in the Western Sea.

We were away!

A series of deeply indented peninsulas extend from the southwest corner of Ireland. The Irish have fished these waters for millennia, but no human has mastered them. They are obedient to only one power.

In his journal Brendán wrote, 'After leaving Altraighe-Caille we journeyed along the southern coast of Ireland, relying on a combination of sail and current. At night I beached the boat wherever I could and Préachán and I slept ashore. Sometimes I was offered hospitality.'

And sometimes I had to make a run for my boat with my robe flapping around my legs and the raven flapping above my head. Ireland was becoming Christianised—not pacified. Among the Gael one did not necessarily imply the other. The majority of baptised warriors continued to seek battle, and saw no contradiction in their behaviour.

We clerics were fond of referring to ourselves as "Warriors for Christ." Perhaps that was a mistake.

By assiduous employment of the currents, Brendán rarely needed to raise his sail. There was time for contemplation.

Viewed from a boat, Ireland took on a different aspect. Her eroding ramparts predicted the future. Land was intractable, but sea was relentless; constantly moving and endlessly adaptable, it combined a bold frontal assault with subtle undermining. The sea was destined to win the battle.

Ireland, Brendán realised, would disappear.

"I mourned the destruction of the promontory of the High Grave," Brendán said to the raven, "but nothing will survive forever—except our souls. And the Church, of course."

Préachán cocked a questioning eye at him.

Is the Church the creation of Our Lord? Is it not, at least partially, the creation of the men who write its laws?

But . . .

God is implicit in the fact of having created Man. He also gave us the imagination to develop a religion which satisfies our emotional needs. Therefore he made the Church.

But . . .

What about the religion of the pagans? Was it not developed in the same way?

Do trees and rocks have a religion?

What about animals?

I wondered if deer have souls, but that was before I found Préachán. He taught me that he is a person in his own right. So is every living creature. We are all God-kindled.

The animals were not thrown out of Paradise—only humans were. Unconfused by trying to make their creator resemble themselves, birds still sing their morning song to the true God.

One evening they camped in a sandy cove encircled by low cliffs. The wind tingled with the possibility of sleet. Brendán tipped his boat onto its side and propped up one end with driftwood to provide shelter for the night. At dawn the raven began searching for edibles along the fresh tide line. The man left the cove and walked inland with two empty water bags.

Instead of fresh water Brendán found a solitary ash tree. Straight as a spear and leafless. Silhouetted against an amethyst sky were twelve large blackbirds perched on the outermost twigs: tiny twigs which could not possibly bear their weight.

Evenly spaced, they formed a perfect halo around the top of the tree.

Below them on the grass was a broken circle of standing stones.

Brendán felt a dizzying convergence of pagan and Christian time.

Or was it all the same?

He ran back to the cove to tell Préachán, "I have seen the twelve apostles!" His face was lit with wonder.

"Churrk," commented the raven.

They resumed their voyage.

As the boat reached the last outcrop of land the waves gathered strength. The colour of slate and crested with foam, they rolled on towards an empty horizon. Yet the sea between the island of the Gael and the much larger island of the Britons was said to contain a number of lesser islands, many of them ignorant of Christianity.

Brendán shaded his eyes with his hand and gazed towards the east. Nothing; nothing but water.

The traders said otherwise and the traders knew their business. They were as trustworthy as the stars when it came to geography.

"If God desires it, we might reach an island before sundown," Brendán said to Préachán. "We could be out of sight of land for a long time, though. You can turn back now if you want to."

The raven's staccato croak sounded remarkably like a laugh.

Brendán studied the waves, mentally pitting his strength and that of his boat against the power of the open sea. He was about to make the outward leap . . . when intuition bade him re-set his sail and head north along the Irish coast instead. Past hill and forest, past fishing harbours and the trading settlements of the Leinstermen.

For once he regretted listening to an intuition. When he beached the boat for the night he found no hospitality, only unrelieved darkness and the cry of some helpless animal caught in the grip of a predator. Man and bird huddled close to their tiny fire at water's edge. The raven did not tuck his head under his wing. He stayed awake. Watching.

The next day was much the same. The night was worse. When the sun rose it gave no warmth. Brendán's exhalations formed a silver cloud in the air.

The voyage continued. Past river mouth and tidal bay, past the war camps of the Ulaid and deserted promontory forts from an earlier era. The waves grew higher, piling upon one another. The leather boat rode the crests but dropped sickeningly into the troughs. Préachán muttered to himself .

"I'm sorry I brought you here," Brendán told him. "You were safe in Altraighe-Caille."

Releasing his grip on the prow, the raven flapped onto Brendán's shoulder. His size and weight made handling the boat awkward. When he gently stroked the side of Brendán's face with his beak, all was forgiven.

When the waves eased, Brendán briefly closed his eyes to rest them. They opened on a changed scene. Dense fog lay like a shroud over the sea. The water was flat. Instead of wind there was silence. The transformation was shocking.

Usually I am impervious to the weather. It is part of God's creation; even the most miserable day is beautiful to me. But fog fills me with foreboding. Fog distorts reality. What is near appears to be far away; what is small appears immense. Thought is suspended in favour of instinct.

Like a sail without wind, my piece of iolite was useless. I turned it every which way, hoping for some tiny ray of reflected sunlight to reveal our position, but the stone was dull. Dead. I began to row with absolutely no idea in which direction I was going.

I wondered if we were still in the world at all. Préachán was a shapeless shadow at the front of the boat. In my imagination he suddenly vanished. Leaving me alone in Nowhere.

The terror I had never expected to feel again clenched my bowels. "Préachán!" I cried.

He answered immediately. I knew his vocabulary by this time; his resonate croak was unafraid. My own nerves steadied. I rowed on.

There are only two directions: forward and back. I was not going back.

'My first landfall outside of Ireland,' Brendán wrote in his journal, 'took place on one of forty islands, many of them uninhabited, off the coast of Alba—the land the Romans had called Britannia Minor. Cúchulainn of Ulster was trained in the arts of war on an island in this group, and was now called Skye.

'Like the Gael, these islanders belong to the Celtic race. Those in the west make their living from the sea; those who live on islands further east hunt red deer and wild goats and weave a sturdy cloth from the wool of small sheep. Their climate is too cold for many crops, so root vegetables are a staple. The islanders do not think of their lives as hard, but of themselves as hardy.'

Fortuitously, Christianity was already established on the first island I visited. As I beached my boat I noticed several beehive huts on a hillside. I went ashore with a wooden cross prominently displayed on the leather cord around my neck—and the raven on my shoulder.

I was met with broad smiles and outstretched hands. Préachán's welcome was even warmer than mine. Missionaries were no novelty to the islanders; tame ravens were. When they spoke to him he talked back, in his fashion. The children loved him. They trooped along behind us, laughing. Like an eddying current we drew in their mothers too, and then their fathers as well.

It was like a homecoming. Tangible proof that we World Enders belonged to a much larger tribe. Not only Gaelic, or even Celtic, we were part of the expanding network of Christians—enthusiastic participants in a radical revolution.

I was eager to see how far it extended.

And help to carry it further.

Brendán spent many weeks sailing among the islands, searching out and evangelising those who were still ignorant of the word of Christ. He founded a monastery which he called *Ailech* and helped a grieving widow to establish a nunnery so she could begin a new life.

Brendán's sandaled foot left a lasting imprint on many shores.

Inevitably the day came when the wind from the west smelled of Ireland. He provisioned his boat, including a supply of strips of dried meat for Préachán, and the islanders assured him that the northern coast of Ireland would be visible on the next clear day.

So he set sail.

But there were no clear days, only mist and rain. At night Brendán beached the currach on a spit of land and built a fire. By its wavering light he made some necessary repairs and adjustments to the currach before setting out again. While he worked, Préachán preened himself, making repairs and adjustments to his own travel equipment. From time to time the raven rolled an eye towards the man to see if he was watching.

Brendán sat back on his heels and laughed.

The following day a fisherman told him, "Look sharp. Do you see where I'm pointing? That dark line is a peninsula and the last stepping stone before Ireland. It's no great distance; you can camp there tonight and cross the channel fresh in the morning."

In the morning. Ireland, in the morning.

Brendán was dragging his boat ashore on the peninsula when disaster struck.

Chapter 18

From the corner of his eye Brendán saw a sudden blur of dark wings close to his head. A moment later he heard a deadly thud.

He made a dive for Préachán, catching him just before he hit the ground. "No! No no no God no!"

The arrow had passed through the raven's wing and pinned it to his body. Brendán found the arrowhead embedded beside the jutting breastbone. Préachán was limp in his hands. Grief stricken, he spread his woollen cloak on the ground and placed the bird on it, then gently folded the fabric over him.

He straightened up and screamed at the empty land,

"Where are you, you maggot! Come out and face me!" His hand sought the knife in its scabbard.

Préachán gave a muffled cry.

Brendán dropped to his knees and turned back the cloak. "I'm here, I'm here! Keep breathing." He fumbled among the feathers until he felt the stuttering beat of the raven's heart. "I'm here. Keep breathing. You can live if you want to."

If he removed the arrow he had to be ready to staunch the flow of blood. He cut a section of fabric from the cloak and folded it into a thick pad. Then, with infinite gentleness, he began trying to work the arrowhead free a little at a time.

Préachán's beak opened in a silent scream.

"All right," said Brendán. "All right."

Praying is the easiest thing in the world. Simply talk to God. Aloud or in your head; either way he will hear you. After that it's up to him.

Brendán braced the bird's body against his thigh. Took hold of the arrow shaft with both hands. Closed his eyes. And pulled.

Help us.

From the height of Diadche, Aedgal saw the currach approaching. Sechnall and Anfudán heard his shout and scrambled down towards the harbour.

A year after Brendán's voyage began there were streaks of grey in his hair and his clothing was ragged, but he managed a smile for his friends. "Where are the rest of you?" he asked in a hoarse voice.

"At Tearmónn Eirc with Ruan," Sechnall said. "He's begun illuminating a Gospel and they wanted to watch."

"He never returned to Clon Ard?"

"He's been waiting for you," said Anfudán. "We all have. Now that you're back to stay . . . you are back to stay, aren't you?"

Before Brendán could answer, a wild cry came from the bottom of the boat.

Sechnall hastily signed the Cross in the air. "What manner of demon makes such a sound?"

Brendán reached into the currach and tenderly retrieved a large bundle wrapped in damp wool. "This demon is the friend who took an arrow meant for me," he said. He turned back a corner of the cloak to reveal the injured raven.

After staunching the initial bleeding he had packed the wound in Préachán's breast with moss. He tried to stitch it closed as he would mend a hole in the boat, but the skin was too thin. The stitches tore loose immediately. His only option was to cut wide strips from his tunic and snugly bind the entire torso.

Next he turned his attention to the bird's wing. The arrow had splintered a bone as it passed through. When Brendán removed the splinters of bone protruding through the feathers, Préachán roused enough to try to bite him. He carefully washed the wing with seawater and folded it into a normal shape, then bound both wings to the body. Only the head and feet were left free. Brendán wrapped the immobilized raven in his cloak and immediately set sail for home.

As the fisherman had predicted, his next landfall was on the north Irish coast. But the voyage around the island became a nightmare. He could not find a friendly current; the wind was always against him. Every moment he could spare was spent in caring for the raven. Brendán did not remember eating or sleeping, urinating or moving his bowels. He must have gone ashore for fresh water but he never recalled that either.

For most of the journey Préachán lay in the bottom of the currach with his eyes closed. His long toes clenched and unclenched in pain. Brendán talked to him almost constantly, using his voice to anchor the bird to life. He recited Holy Scripture and the pagan tales of the seanachie. He even tried counting, first in Irish and then in Latin.

Occasionally the raven struggled to get his head free of the cloak and called out to him. As they neared the Corca Dhuibhne peninsula, the calls grew stronger. Brendán began to hope.

"It's a miracle you got him here alive," said Aedgal.

"A miracle is a decision God makes," Brendán replied. "We are all miracles."

"Is he still in pain?"

"Probably. It was a terrible wound and we've had a rough voyage. The wound seems to be healing, but he'll never fly again."

Anfudán offered helpfully, "I could wring his neck for you. It's very quick."

Brendán rounded on him. "Can you fly?"

"Of course not."

"Then shall I wring your neck for you?" Brendán growled.

Préachán would remain with me for twenty-two years, sharing every voyage I made during that time. I built a secure perch for him in the prow so he could enjoy the wind on his wings and imagine he was flying. Sadly, he missed the greatest adventure of them all. One morning I awoke to find his body cold and still beside my bed.

I buried him in consecrated soil. At Ard Fert.

The number of Brendán's followers had increased in his absence; more clocháns had been built on Diadche. A fish oil lamp was kept burning night and day in front of the oratory. "That was my idea," Aedgal said. "Had you had sailed into the bay at night, you would have seen it."

"No matter how far away you were, we could feel you with us all the time," Liber assured Brendán.

I was embarrassed to realise how rarely I had thought of them. My faithful companions—erased by distance and circumstance. I did not deserve such good friends.

The people of the parish gathered in Tearmónn Eirc to celebrate Brendán's return, while Dianách the runner carried the news to more distant members of his tribe. Catching Brendán—briefly—alone, Ruan said, "There's something I'd like to show you."

In one corner of the scriptorium a table and stool had been

placed behind a screen of rushes. On the table lay an open manuscript. Ruan's dark face lit with the simple joy of competence as he indicated the uppermost page. "This is what I'm working on now, Brendán. It's for the Gospel of Matthew."

The sheet of vellum was not just a page; it was a work of art.

The black ink was composed of soot bound with fish oil. Vibrant colours had been produced by pulverising minerals such as red lead, malachite, and folium. "In Clon Ard they use lapis lazuli for the Virgin's robe," Ruan said apologetically, "but it's expensive. We have nothing like that here."

Brendán recalled other gospels he had seen on his pilgrimage, their pages ornamented with gold leaf as if the light of God shone out of the vellum. *Ruan would have had access to unlimited materials if he had stayed at Clon Ard. But he chose to be with me.*

I have to love him. I have to love them all.

My unexpected family.

An unexpected message for Brendán arrived a few weeks later. Íta wrote, "We were unaware of your voyage until after your return, but give thanks that Our Lord kept you safe on your travels."

Brendán read the few lines again and again. Then he folded the letter into a tiny square and tucked it between pages in his Psalter.

While he was away the number of people attending the ecclesiastical centre had dropped substantially, but with his return people flocked into Tearmónn Eirc to hear about his journey. Afterwards they hurried back to their clans to repeat the story.

Because they were Irish, word borrowed word. The details of the voyage changed. In time, saving the raven was transmogrified into raising the dead.

This was never repeated in my hearing, but I knew about the rumour. And in my terrible pride I made no effort to stop it.

The first time someone suggested that I found a monastery I laughed. Given my many sins, it seemed impossible. But the third or fifth or tenth time, I listened.

There is something rather sad about a man who lets other people persuade him to do what he really wanted to do all along.

When Brendán approached Molua about the possibility of founding a monastery, the bishop pounced on the idea. "Not just a monastery; a complete abbey! You will build it in Altraighe-Caille, of course?"

"I haven't thought about the location yet, Molua. I'm still considering the idea."

"The abbey must be here, where you were born," the bishop insisted. Even as he spoke, the buildings were rising in his mind. "There's plenty of land available within a cock's crow. You will be the first abbot and Tearmónn Eirc will be your mother church." Molua's thoughts raced on. "I shall write to Rome and request funding for essentials—we are always woefully short, but perhaps with the promise of an abbey where none has been before—and then too, the monks who join your order will bring their own property, those who have any, and of course they will make their own robes and raise their own food and. . . ."

As he chattered I imagined the tide going out, and me with it. Away, away . . . then the tide returning with inexorable force, carrying me on its silver crest, thundering onto the defenceless beach.

The sea always wins.

I shaved the forefront of my head in a monk's tonsure and put on one of the hooded robes I would wear for the rest of my life.

Brendán spent several days selecting a site close to Tearmónn Eirc. He finally decided on a low ridge that overlooked the bay and Altraighe-Caille, but also offered a view of Ciarrí Luachra to the north.

He had seen enough abbeys; he knew what he wanted to build. The rectangular chapel would consist of a nave and chancel, and form one side of a rectangle. The other three sides would contain dormitories, offices, refectory, and scriptorium. The centre would be a courtyard open to the sky.

There was much discussion about a burying ground for the

monks. Some thought it should be adjacent to the chapel. Others wanted it at the foot of the ridge. When Brendán told the bishop he planned to have a crypt dug under the chancel, Molua was upset. "There's plenty of space available outside. The chapel should be reserved for the living, as God intends."

Brendán narrowed his eyes. "He hasn't told me that."

"Are you implying God speaks to you on any subject at all?" Molua demanded. His feelings towards Brendán oscillated between admiration and irritation. He had expected Erc's godson to be more respectful; malleable, even. But there was a stubborn streak in the man.

"What passes between me and God is private," said Brendán. He folded his arms across his chest and looked the bishop in the eye. His own eyes were twinkling; a clue the bishop overlooked.

"I can tell you why I've decided on a crypt, Molua. In a separate burying ground a person is in exile; cut off from all he held dear. The pagan Gael have never acknowledged a barrier between death and life. They celebrate the dead along with the living; they even bury loved ones beneath their doorways. The dead continue to be included in the lives of their families and I think that's how it should be."

Liber and Cerball paced out the dimensions of the proposed abbey; Sechnall wrote them down. Anfudán dug a hole at one corner; Eber and Moenniu sank a long stone into the earth. Ruan carved the top of the stone with the ogham symbol for friendship. Aedgal said, "What shall we call the monastery, Brendán?"

I thought of Diadche. And the bay of Tra Lí. And the promontory which was no longer visible to human eyes but always visible in my memory. I thought of the past and the future, and the brothers who would be buried here someday. On the high ground.

"This monastery shall be known as Ard Fert," said Brendán.

Many years later Brendán wrote, 'Founding a monastery was not difficult; establishing it was much more demanding. The ongoing survival of the community would depend upon the quality and character of the brothers.'

Although my followers were good men, there were three more I hoped would join us. I sent Dianách the runner to look for them. He was given their names and description and instructed to seek them among the tribes of Munster. After so long a time they might be anywhere, however.

Or even dead.

Fleeing the Island of Smiths, we sailed southwards. I was too shaken to consider a course; I only wanted to get as far away as possible. Our hearts and prayers were full of the man who had died. Some of the brothers wept. The rest of us gazed wordlessly at the sea.

My grief was doubled; I mourned for the lost monk and for my sense of invulnerability. The terror I thought was almost fifty years behind me had returned in full measure. When the fire demon bore down on me I had recognised my mortality.

Burning to death would have been much worse than drowning in the sea.

But the sea went on and on.

For three days we sailed under clouds so dense the iolite stone could not capture a single ray of sunlight. At night the stars were hidden. I had no idea where we were. The supplies we had with us would soon be gone, though I rationed them strictly. When I tried to sleep I had ghastly dreams. When I awoke my body ached with every one of my years.

Dawn on the fourth day brought a clear but windless sky. The sea was perfectly still. I instructed Eber to climb onto the side of the boat and reach down into the water. When he held up his hand we saw gobs of slimy weed clinging to his fingers. "It is as thick as curds down there," he informed us.

Without wind the sail was useless. My crew took to the oars but their best efforts failed against the masses of weed. We were becalmed. Cerball remarked, "I wouldn't give two balls of roasted snow for our chances of getting out of this."

"Remember we are in God's hands," said Gowrán. "In his good time he will act on our behalf."

So we waited. Nothing happened.

The grumbling, led as usual by Tarlách, grew louder. I began to fear my crew was losing faith in me. What is leadership but the ability to inspire confidence? If I had no confidence in myself how could I captain my men?

The sky was full of blood that night—a pulsing angry crimson like the sky over Armageddon.

"We're all going to die," moaned Solám, "and I am too young to die. But the world is ending just as the prophets predicted and we are stranded in the middle of nowhere, far from our own people. Who will bury us? Who will mourn us? What have we done to deserve this?"

"We are going to die sometime, but not yet," I told him. "We are alive now; we will be alive tomorrow when the wind begins to blow."

"The wind will never blow," Tarlách asserted. "There is no more wind. No more hope, no anything. Leave us in our misery, Navigator."

"Each of us carries within himself the seed of happiness."

Tarlách gave me a sullen look. "I don't."

I could not allow his attitude to poison the others. Taking hold of Tarlách's face, I forced his lips into a smile. "Now," I said, "I command you to hold that expression. Gowrán, you smile too. And you, Eber, Cerball—all of you. Crosán, you are always the readiest to laugh. Do so now."

"At a time like this?"

"This is the best possible time. I command you: laugh."

Crosán responded with an hysterical giggle that set the rest to laughing in earnest.

The mood in the boat improved.

Waiting for God is all very well for a lazy man, but throughout my life I had been a man of action. In the morning a seagull came close to the boat. I hit it with an oar. I parcelled out its few drops of blood and its stringy, oily flesh. We used its feathers to make lures and drew more birds from the sky. I prayed that Préachán would forgive me. He never liked gulls anyway.

When their hunger and thirst were satisfied, the monks were less despondent. "Tell us what to do now," they demanded of me.

They did not want to hear about my problems, the pains I suffered, the nights I spent trembling and afraid. No. Definitely not. My brothers expected me—no, they *needed* me—to be invincible. Anything less threatened them. Their abbot was their sword and their shield in the temporal world.

The insecurity I felt—and now I realised that I had walked through life on a tenuous cobweb, suspended above disaster—I must keep to myself. I could not bare my soul to my companions though they regularly bared theirs to mine.

During his lifetime, had Christ's apostles demanded invulnerability of him? And did he find it as much a burden as I do? I, who am so much less than Christ. I who am no saint, not even a good man. I have no expectation of Heaven. I lose my way more often than I find it.

I stood tall in the boat and squared my shoulders. "Past a certain point," I told my crew, "grief is an indulgence. We have allowed it to incapacitate us for long enough. Raise the sail again; unship the oars. We are going on."

And we did.

CHAPTER 19

Tarlách was in a sour mood when he arrived. "That runner of yours, Brendán—what's his name, Dianách?—caught up with me on a good day or I would have knocked him flat. Instead he made me accompany him to this dreary place for no good reason."

"There is a very good reason," said Brendán. "We're building a new monastery here and the brothers need a contrary, irascible man to help them learn patience."

Tarlách snorted. "Enough of your flattery. Why did you really send for me?"

"On my pilgrimage I met several exceptional men whom I hoped would join me in God's service. You're one of them."

"More flattery. Why do you think I'd have the slightest interest in being a monk?"

"What do you have the slightest interest in?"

Tarlách scowled. Wiped his nose on his sleeve. Scratched his jowls. "Not much," he admitted.

"If you're not happy with your life as it is," said Brendán, "I'm offering you a chance to change it."

Brendán wrote to Íta, "God has led me to found a monastery. Ard Fert is being erected near Tearmónn Eirc. When it is ready, Bishop Molua will perform the consecration. The brothers and I hope you will attend."

To his amazement, she responded immediately. "Your letter filled me with joy, Braon-Finn. I cannot attend the consecration, but you will be in my thoughts and prayers, on that day and always."

And always. And always.

"Your friend Gowrán is impossible to find," Dianách reported to Brendán. "I never caught up with him, though any number of people told me, 'You just missed him.' Apparently he's been wandering around Ireland for years and no one knows why. Perhaps he's mad."

"He isn't mad," said Brendán, "and don't worry about it. We live on an island. If Gowrán keeps travelling and I keep travelling we'll meet again someday."

"But you're not travelling," Dianách pointed out.

'In the construction of Ard Fert,' Brendán wrote many years later, 'we combined earth and stone. The base of the rectangular earthwork walls was buttressed with upright stones set in trenches. Within the walls we constructed a drystone oratory similar to the one on Diadche. Our clocháns were stone, but our refectory was made of tightly packed sods sealed with mud.

'The ethos for the our order—the mission which would underlie the rules—was to search for God in ordinary things.

This was the most valuable lesson I had learned on my pilgrimage.

'As with all monastic communities, solemn vows of obedience and humility were essential.

I needed them as much as anyone else; perhaps more.

'All labours were communal. The day was divided into three parts: five hours for prayer, five hours for work, and five hours for studying Scripture or other spiritual writings.

Erc had instilled the need for balance in me.

'The brothers were allowed clothing appropriate to the climate. Our food was plain but sufficient in quantity.

No one at Ard Fert would suffer from hunger.

'We were celibate but not sexless; our manhood found its full and joyful expression in our passion for God.'

We remain good friends, my little apostle and I. His only purpose is to relieve me of urine, but in spite of being covered by clothing he is a keen observer of our surroundings. Many times he has responded with a throb of pleasure to delights I failed to notice: a bird's song, the fragrance of a flower, hot sunlight falling across my groin. My little apostle may not participate, but he appreciates.

After explaining the rules of the new order to the nascent monks, Brendán said with a smile, "You've never been monks and I've never been an abbot, so we'll be learning together."

All of life is a school.

I was so startled to hear the voice that it took me several moments to recover. I did not understand what it was trying to tell me; not then. But I would remember the words. And often repeat them.

"One more thing," Brendán told his followers. "There must be music. I want us to sing until the sound soaks into the walls."

"I can't sing," protested Anfudán.

"Crows sing and so do nightingales," Brendán said. "You may think you sound like a crow, but it's all music to God."

Ruan smiled. His dark eyes often followed Préachán in flight. In the perfect design of the bird he saw something of God's own art. He caught frogs and crayfish to offer to the raven, and felt privileged when Préachán finally accepted them from his fingers.

On the morning of the consecration, while Bishop Molua was sprinkling the four corners of Ard Fert with holy water, Gowrán came running up the slope. He was breathless and red in the face. "Am I too late?" he called when he saw Brendán.

Tarlách shouted, "Be quiet, you fool! You're disrupting a consecration!"

Brendán ran to the newcomer and seized his hands in welcome.

Later Gowrán told him, "After we parted I wandered. Years passed; I fell ill. I remember collapsing beside a low stone wall. God sent some nuns to find me and carry me to their abbey."

Brendán sat up very straight. "Nuns?"

"The sisters of Cill Íde. Their abbess is . . ."

"You met Íta?"

"She was very kind to me. I would have died but for her ministrations."

Brendán could not help himself. "Is she still beautiful?"

Gowrán was baffled by the question. "Beautiful? She's a *nun*."

"I . . . she . . . of course she is, I know that. We're old friends, I was just asking about her health."

"Her health is excellent as far as I know," Gowrán replied, watching the other man closely.

Brendán felt that a further explanation was necessary. "Sister Íta fostered me."

"Ah. She didn't mention it."

"You talked about me with her?" Brendán did his best to sound casual.

But he had already given too much away and Gowrán was far from simple-minded.

In the years to come, it was not Gowrán's physical strength I relied on, but his sensitivity. He said little, observed much, understood everything.

The nuns had rescued ailing travellers before, nursing them

back to health—or burying them in consecrated ground when they were beyond help. Íta saw nothing unusual in Gowrán's arrival until she sat beside his bed and heard his feverish ramblings; the disjointed recounting of his conversations with Brendán, son of Finnlugh.

When he began to recover she urged him to talk more about Brendán. "He's a friend of mine," Íta explained, without going into detail, "and I am glad to have news of him."

"Brendán was good to me," Gowrán told her. "People are not always good to me. I've been called a fool but I am not a fool."

"I'm sure you're not."

"Brendán made me aware that I am a pilgrim too. I need more guidance, Sister Íta. I've been wandering and wandering and I know God talks to me, but I don't understand what he says."

Íta looked sympathetic. "I'm afraid that happens to us all, Gowrán. The important thing is to want to understand. Being with others who are on the same journey helps. Brigid of Cill Dara has recently opened her abbey to monks as well as nuns, and I am inspired to follow her example. Perhaps your friend Brendán will join us. Would you consider the monastic life, Gowrán?"

"I might."

"Think about it," she suggested.

But before Gowrán could make a decision, Íta received Brendán's letter.

The abbess of Cill Íde went to the chapel alone. As she knelt in the house of God, her lips framed the word: "abbot."

Past a certain point, there is no going back.

"If you do decide to join a monastery," Íta had told Gowrán, "I can tell you where to find your friend Brendán."

From the beginning, Ard Fert blossomed.

'There were not enough hours in the day to contain our

happiness,' Brendán wrote many years later. 'We prayed together and studied together and worked together, and no task was difficult because it was shared. God was our silent but supportive companion in all our endeavours. Lacking fields to farm, the brothers farmed the sea. Most of them were local men to whom boats were almost another limb, but a few of those first monks came from further inland and had to be taught the skills of seamanship. They rejoiced in their learning as I had once rejoiced in mine.

'They did indeed sing as they worked, and their joy spread outward in concentric circles. When I began receiving applications from would-be novices, the guesting house in Tearmónn Eirc was appropriated as a novitiate for the monastery. Next came the scriptorium, to which we added a separate workshop—Brother Ruan needed space for his illuminations.'

Two of the three I sought had joined us. It was too much to hope we might add Colmán to our brotherhood. The warrior might well be dead.

The dissolution of boundaries between Erc's Sanctuary and Ard Fert resulted, in a practical sense, in the expansion of the diocesan seat. Bishop Molua appointed an energetic young parish priest for Tra Lí and spent more of his time on organisational matters, though he lacked Erc's ability in that regard. Brige's duties also were enlarged; soon she was asking other young women to help her.

When Brendán caught a glimpse of his sister in full sail, performing the never-ending tasks appropriate to her station, he felt comforted. They had almost no time together and yet they *were* together; there was a female presence in his life.

It would have been a desert otherwise.

In the refectory Brendán did not sit at the head of the table but halfway down the side, between Brother Gowrán and Brother Ruan. The abbot enjoyed good conversation but preferred to eat in a companionable silence. He was taken aback when he heard one of the brothers tell a prospective novice, "The abbot is so humble he eats amongst us rather than ruling from above."

Brendán confided to Brige, "I'm not comfortable with my reputation; it's based on the tales other people tell about me and the Irish tendency to embroider a story."

"Both of your pilgrimages," she reminded him, "were real."

He patted her hand. "Thank you for reminding me."

The arrival of a letter was always an event, whether it came in the hand of a runner or the pack of a trader. Fionn-barr wrote, "You have brought me out into the world again, Brendán. Inspired by your achievements at Ard Fert, I have founded an ecclesiastical community in the *Corcaigh*, the marshy place, on the River Lee. There is a growing demand among the Irish for centers of worship."

We yearn to believe, but do we also yearn to worship? It seems so, which prompts the next question: why? Would an omniscient, omnipotent God require us to worship him merely to satisfy his vanity? I think not.

Perhaps we were given the need to worship to impel us to do something for ourselves. To seek that which we worship; to grow.

Chapter 20

As one year gave way to the next, Brendán feared he was no longer growing. He was always busy but it was external busyness, not the inward burnishing of a soul. With Préachán clinging to his shoulder, he began visiting the strand again, and the boats. And the sea.

One evening Ruan saw Brendán returning from the bay with a far-off look in his eyes. "You're going on another pilgrimage, Brother Abbot," he remarked.

"How did you know?"

Ruan shrugged.

Bishop Molua was less sanguine. "An abbot cannot keep going on pilgrimages because he's restless—you have responsibilities."

I was beginning to hate that word.

Molua was disappointed and I could not blame him. I wasn't conforming to the model my predecessors had created for abbots. But a conformist is not creative. A conformist only does what others have done before him. Bishop Erc believed creativity identified a person as being spiritually alive. I agreed.

God made me restless for a reason. It was up to me to find out why.

For his second voyage Brendán had a definite destination in mind. He wanted to visit the land the Romans called Brittania. Patrick's birthplace was an appropriate subject for a pilgrimage. He constructed a larger, sturdier boat and invited four monks—Eber, Aedgal, Cerball, and Gowrán—to be his crew.

After Brendán made the announcement, an angry Ruan burst into the abbot's cell. "You can't leave me behind again! I was your friend before any of the others, Brendán. I insist on going with you this time."

Brendán raised his eyebrows. "You insist? Obedience is the first rule of the order, Brother Ruan. I had a good reason for not choosing you; we've been over this before."

Ruan was not mollified. "You think you're being kind to me because I hate the sea, but I don't hate it half as much as I hate seeing you and Préachán sail away without me." It was the longest speech Ruan had ever made. Brendán's eyebrows went a notch higher.

"What about your work?" he inquired. "You can't illuminate manuscripts in a boat."

"Serving God is my work," Ruan said with dignity. "I can do that anywhere."

Still Brendán hesitated. "We are made as we are for a reason," he told his friend. "I was made restless. You were made to hate the sea. God has his reasons; I don't think we should go against them."

"Let it be on my head, then," said Ruan.

Certain bright spots gleam in the memory when all else fades. Some are important, some just . . . are. The day we first put the new boat in the water, a wide high sky and a sharp wind blowing, and the brothers as excited as the boys of Cill Íde. Four men at the oars and one at the rudder. A raven in the prow. And myself at the sail.

Glancing over my shoulder and seeing Ruan smile.

The direction the voyage took was not left up to wind and wave. Brendán studied the night sky intently, reading the map of the stars.

I overheard one of the brothers call me 'the Navigator' behind my back. He could have said it to my face; I considered the title a compliment. The name stuck.

They made landfall on the western coast of Brittania close to the border of Alba. After securing the boat they wandered some distance inland, seeking Patrick's birthplace. Préachán was more interested in the huge fat moths he kept seeing. He awkwardly abandoned Brendán's shoulder for a hunting expedition, hopping along as if pedestrianism were natural to him. Brendán started to intervene, then decided against it.

He has to live his life.

In time Préachán caught up with them again, looking very pleased with himself. Part of a moth's wing still protruded from the side of his beak.

The monks had no success in finding Patrick's birthplace. None of the natives they encountered had even heard of the man. The Irish had to be satisfied with a limited tour of the land that had endured the invasion—and departure—of Caesar's legions.

The latter had been more destructive than the former.

In Britannia the foreign conquerors had found a complex, and in some ways highly sophisticated, tribal culture and torn it apart, replacing the ancient ways with strict order. Roman order was anathema to the free-spirited British Celts, but over almost four centuries they had learned to adapt. They had accepted Roman social structure, Roman bureaucracy—and, when it came, Roman Christianity. Then the Romans pulled out.

Anything remotely resembling civilisation went with them.

We picked our way across fallow fields and stumbled along a broken Roman road. It was an education to see what could become of iron and ambition: the trappings of empire. Rusting bits of metal half buried in the dirt. Weeds pushing up through cracks in the pavement, and the forest crowding in. I told Préachán, "The end of the world will look like this."

Christianity had survived in this place, but with a unique texture. The strands were woven by passionate Gaelic highlanders descended from the Irish *Dal Riada*; by clever, lowland Picts who used ogham; and by the remnants of British tribes who no longer knew how to form a cohesive society. The monks encountered a few Christians, but they were not made welcome. The natives were understandably suspicious of outsiders.

When Ruan heard a rumour of abandoned books in a deserted Roman villa, Sechnall and Cerball went with him to look for them. They returned to the boat with armloads of plunder.

Brendán seized upon Athanasius's *Life of Antony.* Bound in mildewed leather, the manuscript itself was still intact.

"Athanasius was the bishop of Alexandria during the fourth century," Brendán told his companions. "I studied about him with Bishop Erc. Athanasius gained fame through his opposition to the 'Arian Heresy,' which denied the divinity of Christ and made him subordinate to God the Father. The heresy had seized the imagination of powerful intellectuals such as Emperor Constantine. Constantine forced Athanasius into exile not once but twice, yet he never recanted and ultimately triumphed. Here in my hands I hold that triumph. Words, brothers. Written words!"

The discovery set the tone for the voyage. Brendán and his monks slowly made friends among some of the half wild natives; visited Roman forts disintegrating from weather and neglect; chanted the divine office in churches where only two or three old women comprised the congregation—and searched for books. Searched for the spoils the conquerors had left behind.

The Isle of the Britons had been claimed for Christ, but the

Christians were too busy trying to survive in a changed world to learn how to read. They let the Irish help themselves to manuscripts that they would only burn for fuel.

"Does every addition require a subtraction?" Brendán wondered aloud to the raven.

Préachán busied himself preening his feathers. He might never fly again, but he remained prepared.

When they returned to Ard Fert, the abbot assigned a new task to Brother Ruan and Brother Sechnall. "I shall send Dianách to find a bard and bring him here; not a Christian, but one of the . . ."

"Pagans?" Sechnall interrupted.

"I wasn't going to say that. I just want a bard who hasn't been influenced yet by Christianity—someone who can recite the ancient tales as they have always been told, warm with living breath. And I want you to write them down."

Occasionally Brendán slipped away from his duties to stand in the doorway and watch. Listening to the bard. Hearing the deep sure voice of a man whose soul still lived in another time.

The words, the words, the precious words! The memories of individuals and the history of our race, caught like a flower in ice and preserved for the time to come.

When Brendán announced he was planning yet another voyage, Bishop Molua realised, even before he spoke the words, that they had been inevitable for a long time. "Continuity is important in a monastic community, Brendán. If your travels mean more to you than administrating a monastery, I think the time has come to consider another abbot for Ard Fert. It is customary to appoint new abbots from within their own order. Is there one above others who . . . ?" He left the question open, offering Brendán the tribute of naming his successor.

Brendán studied the backs of his hands. They were broad and strong, with flexible fingers and powerful sinews; hands capable of much more than the gentle duties of an abbot. "The brothers here are all good men," he said thoughtfully. "Yet none of them has the exact combination of qualities needed for an abbot."

Molua's eyes tightened at the corners. "And you do? I'm not so sure anymore. There is too much rebel in you, Brother Abbot."

Brendán looked up. Met Molua's eyes. "There is one man who would be ideal in my opinion," he said. "He's not in Ard Fert, but he could continue what I've begun and probably do it better."

The bishop was clearly angry now; Brendán had pushed him too far. "If you expect me to flatter you into staying, you're making a mistake. I suggest you write a letter to the person you mention—preferably tomorrow."

I contrived to look contrite.

The very next day I wrote a letter to Fionn-barr. He knew of the burdens on my soul, and I knew he had completed the establishment of his Christian community by the Lee and was looking for a new way to serve God.

I understood very well.

God shapes each of us to suit his plans.

We were pursued by a storm so ferocious that we had to run downwind to avoid capsizing. Ropes were dragged behind the boat to keep us from going too fast. We rigged a canopy of oxhides to provide a little protection, but the icy water hardened the leather to the strength of stone. Our weary heads ached from the noise of the storm drumming above us.

When the waves grew mountainous and threatened to swamp the boat, some of my crew beseeched, "We are terrified, Brother Abbot! Give us your faith!"

"I cannot give my faith to anyone," I said. "I can only tell you that I have it. The choice to believe or not is yours."

At last Aedgal sighted an island in the distance; the monks raised a weary cheer. "God is good!" cried Brother Gowrán.

My crew lifted their oars and made in all haste for the island. Unfortunately we grounded in the shallows before we could reach the shore. I ordered the monks out of the boat and instructed them to tie our trailing ropes to the sides of the vessel so we could drag it onto solid land. We all put our shoulders to the ropes. A few mighty heaves, and we were safe.

The dark, storm-wet earth was devoid of sand but studded with molluscs and bits of driftwood. It was a blessing to know we would not fall asleep in the boat, at the mercy of wind and wave. We could close our eyes secure in our stability. Only a man who has spent a long time at sea can appreciate how good it is to stop moving.

I stood in the prow to say Mass while the brothers knelt on the ground around the boat. Curtains of black rain marched forward, rank upon rank, and swept over us. The wind whipped the waves around the island into mountains, but I did not need to raise my voice. God could hear me.

At the conclusion of the Mass the storm abated.

In the ringing silence: God.

I knelt in the prow of the boat and bowed my head.

The giant is Iasconius. He pleases Me. Whatsoever harm is visited upon him will be visited upon those who harm him.

The cold and weary brothers took their sodden belongings ashore and began gathering wood for a fire so they could dry their clothes. The driftwood was too wet to burn. They had a little tinder and a lot of determination.

Crouching around the few sparks they managed to strike, they blew them into life.

The first flame leaped upwards.

Brother Crosán, as was his wont, made a joke. The others laughed.

The earth heaved upwards.

The monks abandoned their things and ran to the boat, begging my protection. I stretched out my arms and helped them aboard. Brother Cerball was the last. After everyone else was safe, he climbed over the gunwale just as the island moved out from under us.

We were afloat again.

The monks moaned aloud.

"There is nothing to fear," I assured them. "While you were busy kindling the fire I heard the voice of God."

Liber, who was deathly pale from his quivering chin to the dome of his bald head, said, "I didn't hear anything."

"You have to listen to the silence."

"There is nothing to hear in silence," Eber protested.

"On the contrary," I told the tallest of the monks, "in silence everything can be heard. It is noise which deafens.

"We were not on an island, my brothers, but a living creature. He is called Iasconius. These waters are his kingdom. He tolerated our invasion until we lit a fire on his back, but who among us would allow such behaviour from a visitor?"

"A living creature?" Moenniu was incredulous. "No fish was ever that large."

"I did not say he was a fish. All I know is that his name is Iasconius and he will not harm us. Nor," I added sternly, looking from face to face, "should we ever harm him."

We sailed on.

Chapter 21

When Brendán and his crew returned to Ard Fert following his third voyage, they were welcomed by the new abbot, Fionn-barr of Gougán Barra. "I'm grateful for this opportunity," he told Brendán. "I've sent for my son Mernoc to join me and act as steward for the poor. He and I have been estranged for years, but perhaps in a new place we can make a fresh start."

"There's no need to thank me," said Brendán. "You've given me something of equal value, I assure you." *The freedom of the sea.*

On land, however, Brendán's freedom evaporated.

People were eager to hear the details of his voyage.

Brendán tried to oblige, but the more he talked about his journeys the less real they became to him. Telling and re-telling seemed to squeeze the juice out of them, while his imagination kept trying to interject images he did not want to share. After a few days he directed his would-be audience to Sechnall. Sechnall had a gift for straightforward narration.

Brendán did send a letter to Íta, telling her where he had gone and assuring her of his safe return. When words were written down he had more control over them; thoughts could not tumble out of his mouth before they were fully formed.

Íta's reply was gratifyingly prompt. "I read out parts of your letter in the refectory," she wrote, "and it was much enjoyed."

Which parts did she read aloud? And which did she leave out?

Brendán had difficulties slipping back into monastic life. Some of the brothers seemed vaguely uncomfortable with him. They sat a little distance from him in chapel and did not walk with him in the courtyard. They replied with genuine warmth when he spoke to them but did not initiate conversations. After a few weeks of this, Gowrán articulated the problem. "You were the abbot here, Brother Brendán. Now you're not. The new abbot is well liked, but so are you."

Put so simply, the problem was obvious. It was a matter of loyalty, which is subtly different from allegiance. The monks were confused about their personal loyalties and I could not blame them. Fortunately the solution was equally simple.

I was not ready to be planted like a tree. I wanted to visit Gaul, part of which was now under the rule of a Christian king, Clovis of the Franks. I wanted to meet the creative, questing Greeks and the pragmatic Romans; wanted to ask more questions and listen to more answers and discover truths for myself. I had seen just enough of the world to want more.

I had yet to learn that more is never enough.

When Brendán returned to the sea, he felt he was being born again; immersed in a watery element out of which he would emerge to a new dawn. But no matter where he sailed, he never went far inland. The boat was both his freedom and his umbilical cord. He changed his crew from journey to journey, giving different brothers an opportunity to travel with him. There were only two constants: Ruan and Préachán took part in every voyage.

Three constants. When we returned to Ireland I always sent a letter to Íta. At first they were little more than assurances of my safety. Any inadvertent emotion was carefully expunged. When I was satisfied, I committed the final draft of the letter to parchment and entrusted it to a runner—usually Dianách.

When he returned, I never asked any questions about Sister Íta. Unlike Brother Gowrán, Brother Dianách liked to talk. And his mouth ran as fast as his feet.

Brendán visited Cymru—known as Wales by the Romans—a mountainous kingdom west of Roman Britain. In Britain the native tribes had won a temporary victory over the Anglo-Saxons, but other Germanic invaders were crowding in—barbaric pagans who worshipped barbaric gods. The Christian missionaries now flocking into Britain had their work cut out for them.

The land of the Cymry was different. There had been a time when Irish raiders looted settlements all along the British coast and frequently took slaves, but the establishment of Christianity in Ireland had changed that. Brendán and his party were warmly welcomed.

The Irish monks could almost but not quite understand the language, which had similarities to their own. The Cymry were an intensely Celtic people and poetic to their souls, and Brendán longed to converse with them. Fortunately he met a British Christian who was able to translate for him.

Gildas had been to Ireland himself. Well-travelled and weleducated, he had lived through momentous times. He had witnessed the heroic—and disgraceful—events surrounding the final war between Briton and Saxon, and described the battle of

Badon Hill as 'almost the last slaughter wrought upon us by that scum of the earth, the Saxons.'

"We have not heard the last of the Saxons," he warned Brendán darkly. "They are like weeds. Cut off one head and two pop up."

Gildas was compiling a history of recent events. "Men in ages to come will learn much from observing the way this island has fallen into a hundred petty kingdoms with a hundred petty kings squabbling over bones," he predicted.

Brendán told him, "When your manuscript is completed I would be grateful if you have a scribe make a copy for me."

"You must do something for me in return," the Briton replied. "Keep a journal of your travels and send me a copy."

I promised I would. But it was one of those things you put on the long finger, always meaning to get around to it when you have time.

In Cymru, Brendán heard of the great winged dragons that slumbered in caves in the mountains, waiting to fight titanic battles of good and evil beyond the realm of mortal men. "Are they distant relatives of yours?" he asked Préachán teasingly.

The bird gave him a disdainful look and defecated on his sandal.

The more I travelled the more I wanted to travel; to see and hear and experience for myself. Sometimes I identified himself as a missionary, sometimes as a pilgrim. But always as a Christian.

And there was always a letter to Íta when he returned. More and more of himself went into those letters.

More and more of herself went into the replies.

'Does God have a face like mine?' Brendán wondered. 'Is his skin as lined and weathered, are his muscles stiff in the mornings? I'm being fanciful, Íta, but sometimes I wonder.'

Íta was amused. The child she knew as Braon-finn was still inside the man called Brendán, and she was thankful. She replied, 'God experiences everything you do—in his own way. I believe we are the sensory organs of the Divine. Love means being part of. Those who love you are always part of you.'

Those who love you.

Brendán made a journey to Armorica, west of Gaul, which had been recommended to him by Gildas. The newest member of his crew was Brother Fionán, who was barely sixteen, but strong for his age. Brendán gave the other monks specific orders to look out for him. "I've known his parents since I was a young lad," he told them. "Keep him safe or I can never return to Altraighe-Caille."

Armorica was another Celtic country that had been conquered by Caesar. Here Brendán had the same problem as with the Cymry—the natives spoke a language that was disturbingly familiar, but not quite comprehensible to an Irishman. They were hospitable people and great fishermen. Once Brendán found someone who could translate for him, he spent happy hours talking about boats and fishing. As he had done among the Cymry, he also built an oratory and encouraged the growth of several Christian communities.

"The best thing that happened to us in Armorica,' Brendán wrote afterwards to Íta, 'was meeting a pilgrim called Malo. He rode up and down the countryside on a long-eared horse, singing Psalms at the top of his voice. I have never seen a more joyful man, nor one happier in the service of the Lord. Malo reaffirmed my belief in my vocation.'

My letters changed as I was changing. I had begun revealing my emotions to Íta.

Some of my emotions.

After leaving Armorica, Brendán and his crew sailed along the coast for a time. When they came upon a huge rock like the top of a mountain rising from the sea, young Fionán caught Brendán. "See that, Brother Brendán? It reminds me of the drowned mountain off the coast of Altraighe-Caille. Wouldn't that be a wonderful place for a monastery?"

Brendán shaded his eyes with his hand and squinted at the great rock that towered like God's own fortress. "Perhaps it would be," he agreed. "But I'm not sure my legs are young enough to make the climb."

Despite his disclaimer, Brendán appeared indefatigable. After every voyage he returned to Ireland long enough to speak with Fionn-barr, to send a letter to Íta, and to gather enough men to build a church or an oratory or develop Christians where none had been before.

He explained to his followers, "Some hold that Christianity is immiscible, by its purity rendered incapable of mixing with any other religion. Patrick refuted this. He discovered that the most satisfactory—and lasting—way to convert pagans was by demonstrating the similarities between their beliefs and Christ's teaching. He encouraged the two religions to flow together as two streams run into one river, and we shall do the same."

In his journal Brendán wrote, 'I always found Christ's work to do. Foreign coastlines abounded in small islands waiting to hear the Word. Missionaries such as Patrick devoted their lives to one place, but our mission was dictated by the sea.'

My life was dictated by the sea.

'At sea there are only two hours, light and dark, and only two seasons, summer and winter. It is easy to lose count of the years. It is also difficult to recall all the places we visited. I remember some of them by the names we gave them: the Island of Mice, the Coast of Blowing Sand, the Island of Fleas.

'Wherever God sent our boat we went ashore. We never set sail again until we felt we had done some good.'

For a number of days we had been sailing through an ocean of fog and gloom. Our spirits were as heavy as the clouds louring over us. Then from afar we spied a crystal pillar

rising straight up out of the sea. With great excitement my crewmen pointed it out to one another. Brother Cerball said, "It is a city made of glass."

"Or perhaps it is the palace of a mighty king," suggested Brother Aedgal.

"Truly, we are looking at the house of God," Brother Gowrán proclaimed. He fell to his knees in the bottom of the boat and began to pray in a loud voice.

I prayed silently within myself. This was not what we had been searching for . . . or was it? There was only one way to find out.

Propelled by awe as much as wind, we set sail for the pillar.

The glittering edifice proved to be larger and further away than it first appeared. The winds were capricious. Eventually we lowered the sails and relied on our oars, but after rowing throughout the remaining daylight we still had not reached our destination. We shipped the oars and rested ourselves for the night. Frost glittered in the dark as if the light of day were trapped inside.

No one slept much. We took turns peering into the gloom to see if the pillar was still there. Some object was still there—an object that glimmered palely through the darkness. Every man had a different idea of what it might be.

I said nothing. By keeping my mouth closed I could avoid being mistaken.

The rising sun illumined a towering structure beyond human imagination. Brother Tarlách declared, "No human hand could have constructed this," and for once I agreed with him. Only God could have conceived it.

Ten thousand jewels flamed with the solar fire. Our eyes were dazzled by polychrome light. The grandeur of creation left me speechless. Such an object could not exist in the middle of the cold ocean. Yet there it was. Such an object could not exist anywhere. Yet there it was.

At my command we raised our sails again and bent to the oars as well, until we fairly flew over the water. At last we were within hailing distance—if there had been anyone to answer our cry. Our shouts rang unanswered over the water, returning to us with a hollow echo.

A sense of emptiness swept over me. Vast sea, vast sky, one tiny boat, a few tiny men . . . and nothing else. Nothing else in God's cosmos except what stood before us. Implacable. Impossible. Incredibly beautiful.

There was not a single pillar but a whole forest of them, rising in an immense crystalline cluster, shrouded by what appeared to be a delicately-patterned silver net that obscured the finer details of the structure. For a time we simply rested on our oars and stared at it, filling ourselves with wonder.

Silence rang in our ears like chimes.

At last I gave the order to go forward. By shipping our oars and lowering the sails and their masts we were able to pass through one of the gaps in the net. We entered a shimmering space so cold we could hardly breathe.

Our exhalations made patterns upon the air. Almost like a swirl of stars.

Upon finally reaching the great pillars we tried to find a landing site, but there was none. The crystal dropped in a vertical wall to the sea. There were a few openings like archways which might have led to the interior, but we dare not enter in case we could not get the boat out again.

Instead we decided to sail around the object to determine its size. This circumnavigation took an entire day. Wherever the crystal came between us and the sun a dark twilight fell over us. Some of my crew were frightened. Others claimed to see marvels among the pillars, such as a jewel-studded chalice. They pleaded to go closer but I refused.

"If God wanted us to explore his sparkling city he would have provided a landing site," I told them.

Reluctantly, we sailed on.

Chapter 22

There was a woman once. In a desert.

During one of our pilgrimages our boat was caught in a savage gale and blown far off course. As soon as we could, we landed and went ashore.

We entered a harbour town like other harbour towns we had visited: naked children chirping like crickets, tiny houses leaning against one another to keep from falling down, beggars leaning against the walls for the same reason, mangy dogs and buzzing flies and meat crawling with maggots in the market-place. Yellow-eyed goats who bleated at us and dark-eyed natives who darted suspicious glances in our direction. Yet there was one difference: beyond the town stretched a barren wilderness.

The others spent their time in the town. An impulse led me into the desert.

Where I found an oasis.

She fed me exotic fruit and bade me spit the seeds into the palm of her hand. She said she would plant them.

I ached; burned; reached for the woman. Who was not Íta.

I wonder if those seeds became trees. Do they still stand, reaching towards heaven?

After one of his voyages Brendán wrote to Íta,

> Somewhere off the coast, a swirl of silver clouds across a sapphire sky made me catch my breath. Such a small thing, a fleeting beauty that changed even as I watched, yet it is scribed upon my mind forever.

In her letter, Íta replied,

> The peak is the smallest part of a mountain. The stars are tiny pinpricks of light. Yet we know our mountains by their peaks, and without the stars the night would be a vast emptiness.

As cautious as ever in this one particular matter, Brendán always used the excuse of another voyage to write to Íta, which limited the number of letters they exchanged. He was painfully aware that nothing prevented him from visiting Cill Íde. Yet he did not make the short journey. Nor did she invite him.

'In the Year of Our Lord 523,' Brendán recorded in his journal, 'Pope Hormisdas died, and was succeeded as the bishop of Rome by Pope John. Two years later we in Ireland suffered a more personal loss. Brigid of Cill Dara died in the seventieth year of her life. She was laid to rest in the abbey she founded. At the insistence of her noble clan, her body was put into a casket made of gold and silver, studded with jewels, and placed under a suspended crown at the right side of the high altar.

'Among other notable deaths that year was the untimely death of Pope John, who was succeeded by Pope Felix the Fourth. Achieving the papacy was no guarantee of long life.'

Brendán often discussed death and dying with his brother monks. It was a subject of enduring interest. Most of them had experienced death in their immediate families, sometimes through violence. Brendán's most personal experience of dying had been the gentle fading away of Bishop Erc.

"Life is divided between light and shadow," he told his companions. "Even as the new blade of grass is springing upward it is growing towards death. Another will take its place on the earth. So it was ordered by the Creator. Should things be otherwise? Would one deny death to the old and keep the new from life?"

Eber laughed mirthlessly. "Wait until you're facing death yourself, Brother Brendán—or holding someone you love in your arms while they convulse and their bowels open. The stink alone is enough to teach you a different lesson."

The sea was always the enemy. Voyage after voyage, Ruan endured its proximity with clenched teeth. If they walked far enough inland to enable him to sleep at night without hearing the voice of the sea, he offered a silent prayer of thanksgiving.

When Brendán enthused, "Listen to the music of the waves! Is it not wonderful?" Ruan refused to lie. "I prefer silence. I think I might be happier deaf."

Brendán reproached him. "Hearing and eyesight are gifts from God, Ruan, sensory organs of the Divine. Be grateful for them and use them to their fullest for his sake."

Ruan shrugged. And smiled.

The smile had become habitual. The other monks thought he was a naturally happy man. He handled the rudder with the competence he employed in any endeavour but he took no pleasure from it.

The one assignment Ruan would have enjoyed—caring for the raven—was Brendán's alone. In pagan territories, Préachán was invaluable. The raven was a potent symbol to many tribes. Some feared the huge bird, others revered him, but either way, his affinity with Brendán provided the man and his companions with an invisible aura that kept them safe. There was no repetition of the incident that had almost killed the raven.

Brendán's most recent letter elicited an unexpected comment from Íta. "You mentioned your desire to visit both Rome and Athens. I commend your intentions, but suggest you study the language of the Greeks first. You will need more than a raven to win their respect."

A suggestion from Íta was a commandment to Brendán. The study of Greek was still limited in Ireland; as yet only Clon Ard was actually teaching the language.

I told myself it was childish to avoid Ninnidh after so many years. Besides, he might not be at Clon Ard any more. And even if he was, Ruan seemed to like him, so he couldn't be all bad.

When Brendán first saw Clon Ard he wished he had come sooner. The abbey of the High Meadow was everything he had wanted Ard Fert to be. Although it followed the same general design, the extensively carved stonework lifted Finnian's foundation into another realm entirely.

As Brendán approached the main doorway a priest emerged. Seeing a new arrival in monk's garb, the priest stepped forward with both hands outstretched. "Welcome in the Name of God, Brother."

Obviously Ninnidh didn't recognise me. I recognised him in spite of the changes time had wrought. I recalled him as a large man, but he was much smaller than my adult self. He had the pasty complexion of a person who rarely sees the sun. His thin lips were an unhealthy, fevered red, and no longer wet.

When I took his hands in mine I detected constant tiny tremors running from wrist to fingertip.

"Do you remember me?" Brendán asked.

Ninnidh peered at him nearsightedly, chewing on his lower lip as an animal chews on a wound. "Brendán!"

"The same," Brendán replied tonelessly. Waiting to see what came next.

Ninnidh stretched upward to sweep one arm around Brendán's shoulders. "It really is wonderful to see you here! I feared we might never meet again."

Brendán could hardly conceal his astonishment. "You wanted to meet me again?"

"I did of course. I always liked you, Brother Brendán, and I could never understand why you didn't like me. I've been hoping for a chance to rectify the situation before I died."

Brendán was speechless.

Before he could think of an appropriate response, Ninnidh had led him into the abbey and began introducing him to the monks. "This is Brother Brendán, an old and dear companion of mine; we studied together at Tearmónn Eirc. Of course he's better known now as Brendán the Navigator. You all have heard of his splendid missionary work."

A crowd formed around Brendán, asking the familiar questions. "Where did you go?" "Who did you meet?" "Were you ever in danger?" "How far has the Word of God spread in your opinion?"

And, "Were you ever frightened?"

At that moment I was only frightened of Ninnidh, who stood off to one side watching me with an expression on his face like that of a wolf watching a lamb. Or so I thought.

'The abbot of Clon Ard accepted me as a student to learn the language of the Greeks, and live with the brothers for the duration of my stay. I had to make adjustments, as one does when entering a new family. The rule was different at Clon Ard and so was the spirit of the abbey. At that time it was the largest monastic school in Ireland and beginning to attract students from as far away as Alba and the land of the Britons. I was thankful that my travels had enabled me to feel comfortable among strangers.'

Comfortable except for the presence of Ninnidh.

Brendán planned to spend twelve months at Clon Ard, combining intense study with a strict monastic regimen. The language of the Athenians was difficult; it had nothing in common with Latin, even its alphabet. After the first couple of weeks he said to another monk, "I can understand why my friend Ruan gave up on learning Greek."

Ninnidh overheard the remark and thrust himself into the conversation. "I've always wondered why Ruan didn't return to us. We missed him, he was very gifted. Did he enter another monastery?"

"He was one of the first monks at Ard Fert," Brendán replied coolly. "Now he handles the rudder on my voyages."

Ninnidh gave a wistful sigh. "How I wish I were stronger. I would pray to be allowed to sail with you."

Brendán waited until he had an opportunity to speak to Ninnidh alone. "We've never liked each other, so stop pretending a friendship that doesn't exist," he said, sounding exasperated. "Are you so desperate to impress the others that you need the glow from my lamp?"

Ninnidh looked hurt. "I always wanted you to like me, Brendán."

"I find that hard to believe. You used to stare past me as if I were a pimple on your nose."

"I was afraid to approach you."

"Afraid of *me*?" Brendán almost laughed, but something in the other man's voice stopped him. "I was only a child, how could you be afraid of me?"

"Not of you, but of what you represented. It was my dearest dream to follow in Bishop Erc's footsteps and carry his crosier someday. Then you came along and all his attention went to you. The bishop thought you were an angel from heaven."

"He didn't," Brendán protested. "And I wasn't."

Ninnidh gave a wry smile. "Perhaps not, but that's the impression I had. I knew the bishop very well; if I attempted to befriend you he would have suspected my motives."

"Yet you did everything else to get closer to him."

"Was I that obvious? I was only trying to keep him mindful that we were related by blood. Our fathers' fathers were brothers, but they went to war over some stolen cattle and never feasted together again. Nor did their families ever trust one another. When I was accepted at Tearmónn Eirc I took it as a sign that I might be allowed to heal the breach. But . . ." Ninnidh closed his eyes. Gave a weary shake of his head.

His hands were trembling badly.

I had misunderstood both the man and his motives. Children see the surface. The ability to see what lies beneath the surface comes—if it comes at all—much later.

When Ninnidh offered to tutor Brendán, the younger man accepted. "I have been privileged to visit both Rome and Athens on behalf of our abbot," Ninnidh said, "which has given me a linguistic opportunity few men enjoy."

It was in keeping with his character that he had wormed his way into a position of influence with the abbot. I had started to think I might like Ninnidh, but for a brief time I hated him again. My feelings didn't bother him because he didn't know about them, they only slowed down my ability to learn.

"Bishop Erc taught us the wrong Latin," Ninnidh told Brendán. "Church Latin with an Irish accent was inadequate preparation for the effusion of language I encountered in Rome. There are many versions of Latin, from the stiff formal diction used by ecclesiastical scholars down to the profane cries of the fish sellers in the marketplace. Whatever its source, the hard consonants and abrupt vowels grated on my ears at first. It was like having stones thrown against my head.

"Ah, Brendán, how I longed for the vivid speech of our native tongue; for phrases that caper around a subject without touching it, yet convey a world of meaning. As you know, every tribe has its own version of Irish and every class of society adds its own flavour.

"With time I realised the same was true in Rome. The only real difference was that the better educated had a wide range of vocabulary which the lower classes lacked. Thus the poor were impoverished in more ways than one.

"Besides, Latin is not without its charms. What it lacks in nuance it makes up for in precision. By using Latin it is possible to be absolutely clear—something which does not always happen in Irish.

"Patrick's imperfect understanding of the language was what caused him so much trouble in writing his 'Confession.' One could see that he was desperately trying to make himself understood but his Latin often failed him. By the time I have finished with you, Brendán, your Latin will be good enough for you to converse with a senator, and you should be able to read a page of Greek text as well."

It was no idle boast. Ninnidh made me work harder than I had ever worked in my life.

God bless him.

In his journal Brendán wrote, 'At Clon Ard a priest called Ninnidh, whom I knew from Tearmónn Eirc, offered to be my tutor. In spite of poor health he was of great help to me. Three times a day I prayed on my knees for Ninnidh's complete recovery. When he pronounced me able for Rome and Athens, I returned to Ard Fert to gather a crew.'

Ruan was the first man he asked.

His friend responded warily. "We've never sailed so far before. Could we not travel overland instead?"

"Have you done much travelling on foot, Ruan? I can tell you from experience that sailing is better. The sea is wide open. There are no borders, no boundaries, no tribelands. Just . . ." Brendán struggled for a word. "Just *outward*." His face lit with a glow his friend knew well.

Ruan shrugged. "I'll get ready," he said.

They set sail on a bright spring morning: nine strong monks and a crippled raven. Their boat was well provisioned for the first leg of the journey. A large crowd gathered on the shore to bid them farewell. The bishop of Altraighe-Caille blessed the boat and placed a vial of holy water in the prow. The abbot of Ard Fert blessed the monks and Préachán as well, exchanging a wink with Brendán.

Brige hugged her brother before he climbed into the boat. "Be safe," she whispered in his ear.

Fursu, the newest monk and youngest member of the crew, scrambled aboard with stars in his eyes. "I've followed your advice, Navigator," he told Brendán.

There was not a cloud in the sky. A gentle wind was enough to propel the boat with no effort on the part of the rowers. They talked among themselves and enjoyed the changing scenery of the coastline.

Préachán, attached to his perch with soft leather thongs for safety's sake, made occasional comments.

There is pleasure and there is joy. They are not the same and one does not necessarily bestow the other, but as we began our journey I felt both. I could hear the sun singing.

Young Fursu was wildly excited. He had to be warned repeatedly about digging his oars into the water too hard. The others laughed: the warm, understanding laughter of comrades.

There was never a merrier crew. Those who think religious orders consist of sombre folk are mistaken. Living with a constant awareness of God lightens the heart. I was no longer a boy, or even a young man, but my spirit had not aged. I was still struck with wonder by the sudden gift of being alive.

As the boat neared the harbour below the mouth of the River Lee, Brendán told his crew, "The wind's rising fast, so we'll seek shelter there for the night. In the morning we can visit the community Brother Abbot established before he came to Ard Fert."

The monks prepared to alter their course slightly. Ruan had promised he would give Fursu a turn at the rudder, and this seemed a good time to teach him the rudiments of steering. He stood up and beckoned the young man to take his place.

Brendán was busy with the sail and did not see what happened next. There was a shout and an alarmed squawk from Préachán; no one could say which came first.

When Brendán turned towards the stern he saw Fursu standing there alone. "He . . ." The young man gesticulated wildly. "I . . . he!"

The nearest monks jumped to their feet and peered down into the water. Brendán hurried to joined them. For a moment they saw Ruan's head above the waves. Then he was gone.

Cerball flung off his robe and leaped into the sea. No one asked if he could swim, though it was unlikely. The other monks watched, sick with fear, as he flailed the waves, rolled into a ball and disappeared, resurfaced gasping for air, dived down again.

Came up alone.

Brendán threw Cerball a rope, but he would not get back in the boat. He held on to the lifeline long enough to draw several deep breaths and gather his strength, then returned to the search.

"Pray!" Brendán exhorted his crew.

The wind strengthened. The waves grew larger. Just when Brendán was afraid he had lost both of them, Cerball reappeared with one arm crooked around Ruan's neck.

Several monks almost fell overboard themselves in their anxiety to haul the two men into the boat.

Fursu kept sobbing, "We were only changing places. Ruan stepped aside for me and the boat rocked just then and . . . and . . . and . . . we were only changing places!"

They laid Ruan in the bottom of the boat. His swarthy skin was bluish white; there was a little foam at the corners of his mouth. His heavy eyelids were at half mast. Brendán crouched beside the body of his friend and leaned close to his face, trying to peer through the dead eyes into the dying brain.

When he pressed his ear to his friend's chest he did not hear the drumbeat of life.

In the Celtic Church, the place of dying is called the Place of Resurrection. It marks the transition point between worlds and is a holy site, the gateway where mortal life gives way to immortality.

Which was Ruan's gateway—the sea, or the boat?

The sorrowing monks prayed over their lost brother before putting into the harbour for the night. There would be no visiting in the morning. Brendán announced they were turning back to take Ruan home for burial. He would be the first in the crypt at Ard Fert.

While the others slept, Brendán kept watch. *For such a dark lad, Ruan had such a bright smile.*

When they sailed into the bay of Tra Lí their boat was observed from afar. A crowd met them at the shore. A crowd that fell silent as the dead man was respectfully carried from the boat. Dubán, an old man now, was summoned together with his wife, and Brendán told them of their son's death as gently as he could. His words could scarcely be heard over Fursu's disconsolate sobbing.

Gowrán put an arm around the young monk's shoulders and led him away.

Brendán struggled to keep his grief in check, knowing that if he gave way the other monks would not be able to bear it. He waited until after the funeral; until Ruan had been laid to rest in a new robe of bleached linen with his crucifix in his hands. When the crypt was closed, Brendán fled to Brige.

His sister folded her arms around him. "Weep," she said. And he did.

After the last tear had been wrung out of him he said, "Poor Fursu will blame himself all his life, but it wasn't his fault. It was mine. I knew Ruan hated the sea, I should never have let him go with me. If I had really thought about it—really thought about *him* . . .

"The real cruelty of death isn't the loss of life, Brige. As Christians we believe the soul is immortal. The pain comes from realising you never told someone how much you loved them until it was too late.

"I should have told Bishop Erc, but I was young then. Darting here, darting there, harder to catch than a minnow in a waterfall. I was so busy being me I didn't give much thought to other people. After Erc died, I realised my mistake, yet I didn't apply the lesson to anyone else. Now Ruan's gone too. It all happens so fast. . . ."

There were more tears after all. Brige held him and stroked his hair until at last he fell asleep, exhausted, with his head in her lap. She sat in the twilight, waiting for Bishop Molua to return to his house and take Brendán to Ard Fert.

Some of my crew claimed a giant serpent with writhing coils and flaming eyes erupted from the sea. Others insisted a gryphon swooped down from the sky with gaping beak and outstretched talons. I did not see the monster until it was upon us. Everything happened so quickly, I only had a fleeting impression of vast, leathery wings and the head of a lion.

Terror has many faces.

The monks cried aloud, begging God for mercy.

We were Christians. In our boat we carried no weapons, nothing dedicated to the destruction of life. The shadow of

the monster blackened out the light as if the sun had set. We had bladed implements for preparing food and cutting wood, but in our distress we could not find them. We were helpless.

"Good Lord, deliver us!" I cried in the darkness.

Only my ears told me what happened next.

There was a scream, a loud rustling noise, then a harsh cawing sound, followed by another and very different scream. A mighty struggle took place just above us. Turbulence roiled the air as we—all except Colmán—cowered in the bottom of the boat. We pulled up our hoods and tried to make ourselves as small as we could.

We were not merely small, we were insignificant. What was happening had nothing to do with us, I realised. Other forces were at work. Wars are waged for many reasons between many antagonists, and the sounds are always appalling: the rending of flesh and the crunching of bone; the long slimy slither of intestines ripped from a body cavity.

When silence came the monks remained too frightened to move. Colmán was still standing, though like the rest of us he had covered his head. Now he threw back the hood. He said in a relieved voice, "Arise, brothers. The danger has passed. See for yourselves."

We got to our feet and went to the sides of the boat. Huge chunks of bloody flesh were floating on the water. A frightful stench arose as if the meat had been rotting for a long time. My crew stared in fascination. Later some of them would claim the flesh was covered with scales. Others insisted it had patches of fur.

But that was not what I saw. Averting my eyes from the disgusting spectacle in the sea, I raised them in gratitude towards Heaven. Thus I alone witnessed the black raven's feather drift lazily downward to settle, victorious, in the bottom of the boat.

We sailed on.

CHAPTER 23

'After the death of Brother Ruan,' Brendán wrote in his journal, 'I abandoned my plan to visit Rome and Athens.' *That was the penance I assigned myself.*

'With God's help I built several chapels on Corca Dhuibhne and founded another monastery on one of the islands that lay beyond the end of the peninsula. A number of people lived on the largest of these islands, *An Blascaod Mór*, the Great Blasket, so the monks and I built a church for them as well.'

Being out on the islands was as close as Brendán would allow himself to being at sea again.

Ruan's death forced me to think about dying as I had never done before. The young believe themselves immortal, but I was older now.

He found Fionn-barr where he often was: on his knees in the chapel at Ard Fert. "Brother Abbot, as my spiritual confidante you're the only person I can talk to about this. The resurrection was Christ's victory over the grave, but . . ."

"Yes, Brother Brendán?" Fionn-barr urged.

"What about the rest of us? I used to talk a lot of fanciful nonsense about death and dying—until Ruan died. Then I discovered those words were no comfort to me. The blunt fact is, death is final. The man I knew has been destroyed. All that he was is lost."

Fionn-barr laid a steadying hand on his arm. "I'm a bit older than you and I've had more time to think about such things. Instead of being interesting, they begin to be urgent. Listen to me, Brendán. Everything that lives, dies. There are no exceptions. We are born to die and whatever happens along the way is extra. Death seems to be the whole point of life. So it must have a purpose." He fixed a stern gaze on the younger man. "*Why* do we die?"

Brendán slumped deeper into his misery. "That's what I keep asking myself. Why?"

"But you already know the answer."

Brendán looked up in surprise. "Me?"

"You've said it often enough. 'All of life is a school.' Where did you hear that?"

"I'm not sure. It just came to me one day."

I wasn't about to say what he wanted to hear. I have some humility.

"Whatever the source, you spoke truly. I knew it the first time I heard you, just as I know when a harper strikes the right chord. If all of life is a school then death is just another lesson, Brendán."

We build ourselves stone by stone, as one builds an oratory. Friends and foes alike contribute useful material. Some of it we have to dig out for ourselves. The hardest lessons become the foundation of the man.

The monastic movement in Ireland was going from strength to strength. Brendán's follower Fionán founded a community on the pinnacles of a submerged mountain rising from the Western Sea, almost a day's sailing from Altraighe-Caille. He dedicated the site to the archangel Michael and called it *Sceilg Mhichil*—Michael's Crag.

A boat landing was prepared at the base and more than six hundred steps cut into the shaley sandstone. Near the north summit Fionán built a cluster of beehive huts, round on the outside but square on the inside, and a stone oratory in the shape of a boat. The monks who lived on Sceilg Mhichil would subsist on fish, seabirds and their eggs, and a few vegetables grown in crevices in the rock by mixing seaweed with bird droppings to form soil.

They would be anchorites: recluses for God.

Applicants were interviewed at Ard Fert before being accepted. Considering the hardships of the life and the inaccessibility of the location, there were a surprising number of them. Monks courageous enough to join Fionán far out in the ocean had one overriding purpose: to prepare themselves for the final journey to God.

Like Brendán, they were men who had absorbed the beliefs of a much older faith and adapted them to create their own version of Christianity. Where better to practice such a religion, they thought, than in one of the Thin Places? According to Celtic belief, Thin Places were areas where two disparate worlds touched, such as land and sea, or mountain and sky. In Thin Places the boundaries between this world and the next were almost non-existent.

Sceilg Mhichil, halfway between earth and heaven, was the exemplar.

Brendán was making his way back to Ard Fert from a meeting with Bishop Molua when he saw a figure on the path ahead of him, a figure that seemed familiar. He trotted to catch up. "Colmán? Can that possibly be you?"

The man turned around.

His face was more freckled than ever, but the red hair was grizzled with grey—what hair remained. His head was shaved from ear to ear in a monk's tonsure.

"Brendán?" he asked tentatively.

"Have I changed so much?"

"Have I?"

Both men laughed.

Brendán escorted Colmán into the monastery and insisted upon washing his feet and giving him a bowl of wine and some bread before they settled down to talk.

"After our meeting I thought about things you'd said," Colmán related. "Not often, but often enough. My life went on; I fought more battles—won some, lost some—and killed a few men. I began to wonder if they were sins on my soul; if I had a soul. So I went in search of a priest. We talked and I thought about things he said. Not often, but enough. First thing I knew I was being baptised."

"So you joined a band of people who would accept just anybody?"

Colmán grinned. The grin was still crooked. "You have a good memory, you. I've been a Christian for seven or eight years now and I've never regretted it. For once I can be certain I'm on the winning side."

"In the fight to save our souls from the devil, victory's not assured until the last moment," Brendán said.

"That's why I decided to enter a monastery: no king demands that a monk to take up the sword. Besides, I thought there would be fewer worldly temptations.

"I've always liked women; a lot. Once I told a woman that she had eyes like two pearls. The chief of my clan had some pearls he'd acquired in trade; they were grey and lustrous and so were this woman's eyes. Then something sparkled in them and I realised her eyes were not opaque at all, but as deep as my heart."

Colmán drew a deep, slow breath. "She died," he said. "The

woman with the grey eyes. That's me done with women. I came to join the brothers on Sceilg Mhichil because they never see a woman. Or even the shadow of one."

Brendán leaned one elbow on the refectory table and studied his friend's face closely. "Suppose there really were no women on earth, not anywhere. How would you feel then?"

The response was immediate. "I wouldn't want to live."

"All right," said Brendán.

In his journal he wrote, 'I persuaded Brother Colmán to join us at Ard Fert instead of Sceilg Mhichil. He brought qualities which the other brothers lacked.'

Colmán was concerned about the condition of his body as well as his soul. With the abbot's permission, he devised a programme based on the training of warriors. He soon had the monks of Ard Fert fighting mock battles with wooden staffs; leaping and lunging with great enthusiasm and laughing like boys again. Brendán's erstwhile crewmen had grown sluggish by the time Colmán arrived, but he cured them.

Although he was faithful to his vows, inevitably a monk encountered women around the parish. Brendán noticed Colmán following them with his eyes. One in particular: a small but sturdy woman with chapped red hands.

Not every man is meant to be a monk. In different circumstances, I myself . . .

When he knew Molua was busy elsewhere in the parish, Brendán visited the bishop's house. Brige met him at the doorway and, as always, threw her arms around his neck. He returned her hug, then took a step backwards and tried to see his sister as another man might see her.

Small but sturdy. Chapped red hands. A warm armful of woman, but not young anymore.

We are none of us young any more.

"Have you ever regretted not marrying?" Brendán asked his sister.

She put her fists on her hips. "I've had the care of two demanding old men in my life," she replied more sharply than he expected. "What would I want with another one?"

"I thought you liked taking care of people."

"Did you ever ask me? Did anyone ever ask me?"

Brendán was taken aback. "But you seem so content as you are."

"What good would it do me to act otherwise? I could be as sour as vinegar but that wouldn't change anything."

When we were children a casual remark of my sister's had expanded my horizon. From the vantage point of empathy I reached out to her.

"If you could change things, what would you do differently?"

Brige did not answer at first. Even a hypothetical offer of power was unfamiliar to her.

Brendán waited.

"I would be a nun," she said softly.

"Because you want to, or because that's what Bishop Erc wanted for you?"

"I don't know what the bishop wanted and it doesn't matter now anyway. When I visit you at Ard Fert and hear the brothers singing . . . when I see the comradeship you share . . . when I feel the sense of peace within the monastery walls . . . my whole heart leaps with longing."

Chapter 24

"I've stayed in one place for longer than I can tolerate," Brendán finally admitted to the abbot. "God wants me to be moving again. Brother Colmán has suggested we found a monastery on the estuary of the River Shannon, in the tribeland of his mother."

Fionn-barr asked, "Are there any monasteries nearby?"

"None, he tells me."

"Then go with God's blessing."

"One thing more, Brother Abbot."

"Yes?"

"I would like to found a nunnery for my sister."

In his journal, Brendán recorded, 'Together with my sister, Brige, Brother Colmán, and several other monks,

I travelled from Ard Fert to found a monastery on *Inis Dadroum*, the Island of Two Backs, in the Shannon estuary. Afterwards we built the nunnery of *Annagh Down*, named for the Marsh of the Fort, by the shore of *Lough Corrib.* The bishop of the diocese performed the consecration, and six good women joined my sister to take their vows.'

During that time Brendán had watched Brige and Colmán closely, to detect any indication that he was making a mistake. In his imagination he could see the two of them married; could see himself as an elderly monk sitting on a little stool by their hearth while their children played around his feet and tugged on his robe.

But that would never be. *Brige was too old anyway. And from the beginning, I believe, God had other plans for her.*

Colmán recognised that too. A tiny lamp that had never really been lit went out. He threw his heart and soul into the monastic life and became the stalwart of Ard Fert.

Brendán wrote, 'In the Year of Our Lord 545, Ciarán, who had been trained at Clon Ard and at Magh Enna, founded the monastery of *Clon ma Nois* on the banks of the Shannon, beside the great road leading to Tara. The twin pillars of monasticism and literacy had become increasingly important in Ireland.

'The battle of *Cul-Dreimnhe* was fought because of a book. A widely-travelled monk known as Colm Cille had transcribed a manuscript without the knowledge of its author, who was very much alive and took umbrage. The author applied the matter to the high king, Diarmaid, for judgement. Diarmaid decided on behalf of the aggrieved author, stating, 'To every cow belongs its calf.'

'Colm Cille and his followers joined in battle against the king and his followers, with the usual bloody outcome but no definitive result.'

Once the monastic movement took hold in Ireland it spread like fire through dry brush. Ard Fert was filled to the brim; more accommodation was needed for the numbers who wanted to join the order.

I had thought pride and ambition were stifled in me but I was wrong. Or perhaps it was God who made the suggestion, to test my humility. If so, I failed.

Brother Abbot was surprised by the request. "You want to found another monastery and become its abbot, Brother Brendán? You had Ard Fert, yet you willingly relinquished the abbacy to me. Why start over again?"

Brendán possessed the rich vocabulary of the Gael and a working knowledge of Latin and Greek, yet he could not find words to describe the force which impelled him. The apparently random disorder of life that blew seeds across the earth and stars through the heavens.

He only knew that he was being driven. If not on sea, then on land.

Outward.

'In the Year of Our Lord 556, the monastery of Clon Fert, the Meadow of the Grave, was founded. The name was chosen because of an ancient tomb we were careful to leave undisturbed. The brothers included most of those who had been with me from the beginning. Although they had to travel a considerable distance to the new monastery, their departure left room for new brothers to enter Ard Fert.'

For a healthy man in dry weather, Clon Fert was fifteen days' brisk walk from Ard Fert but only three from Annagh Down. Brendán chose to build on an island in a bog, thus fulfilling Erc's requirements for a diseart, a deserted place. With the help of the nearest Christians, he and his monks erected a large earthwork bank to protect the monastery from floods and the depredations of wild animals. Timber and sandstone were used in construction, which combined features from both Ard Fert and Clon Ard. A church stood at the exact centre. Facing east.

During the years when I was founding monastic communities in Ireland I had never visited Cill Íde, though once or twice I had passed within a day's walk. A temptation avoided is a temptation denied. It made me stronger. We corresponded frequently and I was content—if not as blissfully content as Brige at Annagh Down. Naturally I invited Íta to the consecration of Clon Fert. I didn't think she would come.

Ninnidh was the first of the invited guests to arrive. He was carrying a magnificent gilded book satchel with him. "This is something I collected on my travels," he told Brendán, "and I want you to have it for your new monastery."

Brendán fumbled with the elaborately engraved silver clasp, which was set with beads of amber. "You've brought me a book? I'm impressed, Ninnidh."

"It's not just a book. This is a manuscript copy of *Conferences*, by John Cassian, in which Cassian examined various aspects of spirituality by putting discourses into the mouths of fifteen Egyptian priests. You will find it fascinating reading."

Brendán lifted the manuscript from the container, marvelling at the number of thick vellum pages. "I'm not familiar with John Cassian," he said.

Ninnidh looked pleased at the admission. "Cassian also wrote *Institutes*, which describes the organisation of a religious community. It's something you really should read if you ever have the opportunity.

"John Cassian was born half a century after Athanasius, of Scythian lineage. He entered a monastery in Bethlehem as a young man and later spent several years in Egypt studying with the 'desert Fathers'—hermits striving to emulate John the Baptist. That experience became the source of *Conferences*, in fact. After further studies in North Africa he moved to Rome and then to Provence, in Gaul. At Marseilles he founded both a monastery and a nunnery."

Brendán felt a quickly suppressed pang of envy. "A true wanderer for God," he murmured.

"Just so. Cassian taught that the Psalter was the most important text for a religious community. The hermitages around the

Mediterranean coast took their inspiration from Cassian, as did the monastery founded by Honoratus on the island of Lérins—the monastery where Patrick studied and became a deacon before his eventual return to Ireland."

"Bishop Erc never mentioned Cassian."

"He probably knew nothing about him," Ninnidh replied. "You and I, who have travelled, know more of the world, and I am happy to acquaint you with Cassian. You'll find you have much in common with him. He was a moderate man who eschewed extremism, which often put him at odds with the more fanatically inclined."

I took those words as I hope they were intended: as a compliment.

When the diocesan bishop arrived to consecrate the monastery, Brendán proudly showed him the book.

Over a hundred people assembled for the consecration; almost every Christian within a day's walk and regional clerics and chieftains in carts and on horseback. The event might almost have been mistaken for a fair. Flanked by his monks, the new abbot of Clon Fert stood in front of his new church. He bowed his head as the air rang with hymns of thanksgiving.

It was the most wonderful day of my life.

When the bishop began to speak, Brendán looked up. One face in the crowd stopped his heart. One guest who had quietly arrived and slipped in among the others without his noticing.

To everyone else Íta was an old woman. To Brendán she was unchanged. Noticing the expression on the abbot's unguarded face, Gowrán said softly, "You're right. She is beautiful."

It was the most wonderful day of my life.

There was no possibility of speaking with her alone; not for a while. But their eyes met.

I could hear the sun singing.

The consecration and attendant prayers and responses took up most of the morning. Afterwards the brothers served food to their guests. At the refectory table the abbot sat on the bishop's right. Ninnidh sat beside him. Brendán talked with each of them in turn; talked with his monks; talked with his guests. Talked with God in his head. *Thank you. Thank you. Thank you.*

For those who had travelled some distance to attend the consecration, the guesting house was prepared. Its occupants would include three nuns from Cill Íde.

After Compline, Brendán walked alone in the courtyard. It was the custom of the brothers to walk together there, two by two, but on this special evening the other monks left him to savour the moment by himself.

The suggestion had come from Gowrán.

Our new courtyard. Our new church and scriptorium and refectory. The first time for everything. I had founded other monasteries, but I knew in my heart Clon Fert was my last. This was my crowning achievement; I could rest. I had done what God wanted of me.

She tread so lightly he did not hear her approach until she was beside him.

He felt her in the pores of his skin.

"It was good of you to come," Brendán said without looking around.

She matched her steps to his. "How could I not?"

They walked a few steps in silence, folding their hands like people praying. Brendán said, "I tell the brothers that life is a school. It is. I've learned many lessons but not the lessons I expected to learn." Daringly he added, "I've been given many gifts but not the gift I desired."

"I've learned only one lesson, Braon-Finn," she replied evenly. "We are given what we need, not what we want."

They paced the perimeter of the courtyard in perfect step. Somewhere nearby a cricket chirped. A nightjar sounded its purring trill. Otherwise it was very quiet; the monastery seemed to be holding its breath. When they reached their starting point they made another circuit.

We did not talk, there was nothing we needed to say. Yet on that night I was more alive than ever in my life.

Before they parted, Íta brushed his forehead with her lips, a touch as light as a butterfly's. She kissed each of his eyes in turn. "Your blue eyes," she said.

I have known ecstasy.

The sea was calm, the waves little more than ripples. The sails were empty of wind. We drifted for a time. Our last landfall had been on a shore where the water was polluted. I had warned the monks against the water but some drank anyway, and were ill. I was content to wait until they felt better before pushing on.

Then Aedgal announced he saw an island some distance away. Those who could man their oars rowed towards it. As we approached land I told the brothers, "Three choirs live on that island. One is composed of boys, the second of youths, and the third of elders."

"How do you know?" asked Solám. "Have you been there before?"

"Never in my life," I told him truthfully.

The island was extraordinarily flat, like the top of a table. The air was very still. When we landed the boat we saw no trees, no bushes, nothing that would blow in a wind. Yet everywhere on the ground were huge clumps of white and purple fruit, plump and tempting to the eye.

Three choirs constantly moved from place to place among the clumps of fruit. One choir was composed of boys, one of youths on the brink of manhood, and one of old men.

The brothers turned to me in astonishment.

"How did you know about this?" Crosán asked.

I had no answer.

The choir of boys, who were dressed in white robes, stopped and chanted in sweet, childish voices, "The saints will go from strength to strength and see the God of gods in Zion."

No sooner did they finish this verse than the youths, who were attired in blue robes, took it up. The air was echoing with their words when the elders began the same chant. It was repeated over and over again in this fashion.

We listened in wonder. The music was incredibly beautiful but the singers paid no attention to us. I was not sure they could even see us.

We had landed in mid-morning; the choirs sang until a bell rang for Prime. Then they all dropped to their knees and prayed, as we did ourselves. Afterwards the singers came towards us and embraced us warmly, welcoming us to their island. They brought basins of water to bathe our feet and pitchers of fruit juice to slake our thirst. While we refreshed ourselves they began singing again. Their voices were so pure none of us had the audacity to join in—except for the youngest of the three latecomers who had demanded to join us.

When the choir of youths chanted, "May God be merciful to us . . ." and followed it through to the end of the psalm, he sang with them. His voice blended so perfectly we could not distinguish it from theirs.

At Terce the psalms were "Out of the depths," and "Behold how good," and "Praise the Lord O Jerusalem."

For vespers the choirs chanted, "A hymn is due to thee O God, in Zion," and "Bless the Lord, O my soul, O Lord my God," and "Praise the Lord, children."

To all of this we listened with a sense of profound peace and joy. But only the latecomer sang.

Instead of sunset, a cloud of extraordinary brightness

covered the island, shimmering with a hundred rainbows. We lay down on the soft grass amid the delicious fruit, and slept and ate and slept again. "This cannot be Paradise," said Tarlách, though he sounded unsure.

The next day was the same. The three choirs chanted the psalms for the canonical hours while my crew and I rested and restored our strength. Then the chief elder, who had never identified himself or his companions by name, began the prayers for the Lord's Communion. In this we gladly partook.

When the sacrifice was over, two youths gathered a basket of purple fruit and carried it to our boat. "Accept this fruit from the Island of Strong Men," they said. "Give us our brother to live with us in happiness and virtue, and go forth yourselves in peace."

My crew exchanged glances. "Your brother?" queried Mernoc. "What do you mean?"

They went to the third latecomer. One put a loving arm around his shoulders; the other took him gently by the hand.

He turned towards me with a quizzical expression. "I do not understand, Brother Abbot. If, as you prophesied, this is God's reward for a deed of great merit, there must be some mistake. I am a simple man; I have never performed a memorable deed."

"God does not make mistakes," I told him. "At some time in your life you have done something that seemed trivial to you but was great in the eyes of God. You may never know what it was, but God knows. God always knows.

"Embrace your former companions and go with those who summon you now. It was a good hour when your mother conceived you, and a good hour when you were born to enter such a community."

When he had embraced all of my crew in turn I said, "My son, be mindful of the great favour God has conferred upon you. Go and pray for us who have not yet earned such joy."

And we sailed on.

CHAPTER 25

Long before gods had names her ancestors had worshipped Those Who Are Sacred. Sky Fire, Birthing Woman, and Sweet Water.

As the scion of an ancient royal line, she had been educated. Ignorance is of no value. She could scribe her name in the sand with a rouged fingertip. She could recite the names of the Great Cities from Ur and Babylon to Nineveh and Tyre. With her own dark eyes she had seen Aleppo and Alexandria and even the ruins of exotic Algiers, destroyed by the Vandals.

Once her tribe had possessed great riches. Gone now. Looted, stolen, carried away on horses and camels and in the hot clutching hands of sweaty men. She too had been transported on horses and camels, like the treasure she was.

Now her only treasure was a small soapstone image of Birthing Woman. She thought the carved figure very beautiful. Immense mounded belly, heavy breasts swollen with milk. Life, bounteous and indestructible.

When she was young and beautiful her name had been murmured in Antioch; songs in her praise had been sung in Damascus.

The woman kept the soapstone carving inside her gown, between her breasts. She was ashamed that she had become so thin. "When our men ruled, our women were plump," she whispered to herself. Speaking in the tongue of her vanished tribe gave her comfort.

So did caressing Birthing Woman. Or naming the Great Cities aloud to be certain she never forgot. She always began with Çatal Hüyük, the Ancient Mound in the center of the plain beyond the Taurus Mountains, where the first ancestors had built spacious apartments of mud brick and tilled the richest grain fields under the sun.

Until the winds of change blew.

The winds of change nothing can resist.

Çatal Hüyük was very long ago and very far away. The gods of war and acquisition had dispersed her people across Anatolia and beyond. They had put down roots wherever they could, and over the centuries other names had become part of their history.

Persia.

Syria.

Arabia.

And the wind blew and blew and the dust rose and swallowed towns that were supposed to last forever, and some men became kings and their children became slaves and everything changed. Prophets extolled new gods and the gods demanded bloody sacrifices and everything changed.

In an unstable world a beautiful woman could survive—if she was very clever.

Her father had sent the soapstone carving to her from his deathbed. The statue was her only inheritance, but it was enough. In the night she had fled from the tent of the last man who thought he owned her. She took only the tiny goddess and a bag of seeds, and let the wind blow her where it would. When she came to a patch of earth that called out for her seeds she planted them.

There was a town in the far distance. A poor and hopeless town. Nervously at first, the elders of the town approached her. Because she was creating a green heart for a barren land they thought she was holy. They knelt before her and listened to her jabberings in an unknown tongue and thought they heard truth.

When she was an old woman she sat in the shade and listened to the music of the wind blowing through her trees.

In the Year of Our Lord 560,' Brendán wrote in his journal, 'the abbess of Cill Íde died peacefully in her sleep.'

How can a mortal continue living after the immortals are dead? Erc. Brigid. Íta. Where has she gone? Has she abandoned me, is her soul fleeing through the spaces between the stars?

Brendán could not share his grief with anyone. He wrote a letter to Fionn-barr at Ard Fert and never sent it. He had thought Colmán's strenuous exercises were beneath his dignity as abbot, but he resumed them. Throwing his body around as if he were a young man, trying to exhaust himself so he could sleep at night.

Sleep and not dream.

There was only one outlet for his unspent love. Brendán prayed with an urgency he had never known before. He prayed for his sister and each of his monks, for sunny days and rainbows after rain. He prayed for the people he had met on his travels—for Malo on the long-eared horse, and the woman in the desert, and Paul the hermit, whose hair had grown to cover his body, and a dark-skinned man on an unfamiliar shore who had welcomed him with a smile. He prayed for the bishop of Rome and the bishop of Byzantium and the abbot of Ard Fert. He prayed for birds and animals and the fish in the sea as fervently as he prayed for human beings.

His friends grew concerned about him.

"Brother Abbot looks strangely hollow," Aedgal remarked, "as if the life's been sucked out of him."

Moenniu said, "Of course he's hollow, he hardly takes a bite of food. I keep urging him to, but . . ."

"That isn't the problem at all," Tarlách interjected. "I know what's wrong with him, it's the dreadful weather."

"According to Brother Abbot," said Liber, "the weather is never dreadful, it's always a gift from God. I think he has a sickness in his chest, myself."

"It's in his stomach," Eber averred. "That's why he has dark circles under his eyes."

Gowrán shook his head. "Don't any of you recognize grief when you see it?"

Fursu spoke up. "You mean he's still mourning Brother Ruan? But that was years ago! And not my fault anyway," the monk added under his breath.

Colmán listened to the conversation without comment, then sought out Brendán. He found him in the cell the abbot had built for himself; a small bare room furnished with two stools, a table, and a sleeping pallet. One of Brigid's crosses hung on the wall.

Brendán was sitting on one of the stools, holding his head in his hands. He looked up as the monk entered.

"The brothers are worried about you," Colmán said bluntly.

"I'm all right."

"You don't look all right. Brother Gowrán thinks you're grieving. Are you?"

Brendán heaved a sigh and got to his feet. "The personal feelings of your abbot should not be refectory conversation."

"That's dog dung and you know it. This is me you're talking to, Brendán."

"Brother Abbot!"

"Brendán," Colmán reiterated. For a moment the warrior he had been looked out of his grey eyes. Brendán sat down again.

"We've walked together through sun and rain," Colmán reminded him. "We've shared food and fire, told lies and admitted truth. You keep your knife in the scabbard I gave you. Do you think of that when you cut the bread?"

"Sometimes."

"Then think about this too. You've made everyone here a part of your life. If you're sorrowing, we have a right to share your sorrow and try to help you."

I had once told Fionn-barr I didn't want to be responsible for anyone else. At the time, I meant it. One of my many mistakes.

I was deeply touched that these men I had come to love felt responsible for me.

"Colmán—*not Brother Colmán, not then*—please believe me; nothing short of a miracle could help. Be patient. I'll be all right."

"I did the best I could," Colmán reported to the other monks. "He didn't deny he's suffering, but he told me nothing about the cause."

"The man's entitled to his privacy," said Gowrán.

For their sakes, Brendán made an effort to be his old self. It was difficult at first. The sun rose and the grain ripened; the sun set and the leaves fell.

And eventually the abbot of Clon Fert was able to laugh again.

He was laughing over a remark of Anfudán's when one of the newer monks tugged at the sleeve of his robe. "Brother Abbot, you have a visitor. He says he's the abbot of Ard Fert."

'My kinsman Fionn-barr came to me full of excitement,' Brendán recorded in his journal. 'I listened to his story.'

I made him tell it twice. 'Afterwards he went to the guesting house for a much deserved rest, and I retired to my cell.'

What is heaven, Sister Íta?"

"Heaven is a memory, Braon-Finn."

Was she right? Is heaven not an aspiration, but a memory?

Is the Garden a lost reality? Is it still out there somewhere?

The Isles of the Blest. Paradise.

Alone in his cell, Brendán spread the wings of his soul.

And flew.

There would be one last voyage.

Clon Fert was inland; the boat would have to be built on the coast. Brendán carefully selected the monks he wished to take with him, then set out for Ard Fert.

I was the abbot of Clon Fert; so I would live and so I would die. I named Brother Sechnall, the oldest and wisest of the monks, to hold authority in my absence. If I failed to return the abbacy would be his.

No one had ever built a boat to sail to Paradise before. When Brendán reached Altraighe-Caille and told his old friends, the fisherman, what he proposed to do, they were intrigued. Endless questions. What seas would they cross? What might the weather be like? How large a crew, what provisions, what reinforcements for the hull, what size the sail—the only thing on which everyone agreed was they would need at least two sails.

In the early, heady excitement of Mernoc's discovery, Fionn-barr had been certain that Brendán would want to sail to Paradise and had been eager to go with him. Reality had set in on his return from Clon Fert to Ard Fert. He reminded himself that he was older than Brendán, who was old enough. But thanks to Colmán's regimen Brendán was as fit as the former warrior.

Fionn-barr felt every one of his years. They added up to a weary body with definite limits.

"When you set sail I shall be with you in spirit," he told Brendán, "but my son can go with you in the flesh."

'Mernoc, son of Fionn-Barr, joined our crew,' Brendán wrote, 'and we commenced building a craft to take us to Paradise.'

Currachs and coracles and dugout canoes each had their purpose, but Brendán's voyage by its very nature required innovative design.

From long experience of the sea I created a picture in my mind of the boat I wanted. It must be as supple as an eel, to withstand the battering of the waves, and as graceful as a swan, to be pleasing in the sight of God.

Many days were spent beside the bay in deep discussion. The fishermen worked with the monks until a design was agreed upon. The boat would be long and narrow, with prow and stern curved upwards like those of a currach. Brendán was adamant that oak and ash be used for the frame.

Oak was the king of trees and I was born of a kingly line. Ash was the tree of health and we would need all possible health. We were none of us young.

Fionn-barr, the abbot of Ard Fert, knew people who knew people. In due course, wagonloads of timber arrived on the shores of Tra Lí.

The boat was constructed upside down. Two sturdy gunwales were carved from the heartwood of oak, then turned over so the frame—a latticework of thin laths of flexible white ash, lashed together with leather thongs—could be affixed. The frame would be covered by three layers of tightly stretched oxhide with two chambers between. These air chambers would help prevent the boat from being holed and keep its occupants further away from the icy sea.

Sewing oxhides together for a sea voyage of unknown duration presented difficulties. As Brendán well knew, long exposure to salt water rotted leather thongs. A woman of the Altraighe suggested spinning heavy thread from flax. Monks from Ard Fert were recruited to the task. They were rewarded with torn and bleeding hands, but managed to create a material of amazing strength.

I shuttled back and forth between the shore where the hull was growing at the hands of the fishermen and the monastery where the monks laboured to make rope and sails. My urgency communicated itself to everyone. "Why are you in such a hurry?" Fionn-barr wanted to know.

Even if he was an abbot, I could not tell him.

For much of my life I had been following someone else's dream for me. I was desperate to pursue my own dream.

While the men stitched the hides onto the frame, the women boiled countless pots of wool grease to create a waterproof seal for the leather. Then the entire vessel, inside and out, was thickly coated.

"How's that going to smell in warm weather?" Tarlách said.

Liber advised, "Don't think about it."

Topmast, foremast, and oars were carved from ash, and benches fitted to accommodate six oarsmen to a side. When the two square sails were fully employed there should be little need for oarsmen, but eight men would be required to handle the ropes controlling the sails.

"She'll fly," Dianách observed with a trace of jealousy in his voice.

A small shelter was devised in the stern so the brothers could take turns sleeping. Deer hides were sewn together to make a cover for lashing across the prow, to help keep out water in a high sea.

Compared to the boats I had sailed on my previous voyages, the new craft was luxurious indeed.

At sea the monks would wear their customary hooded robes,

but with sheaths on their belts so every man could carry a knife. Their Psalters were securely tucked into book satchels. Provisions included dried deer meat and smoked fish, the roots of sea holly to prevent scurvy, bags of grain and edible seeds, butter and beeswax candles and extra rope and plenty of hides for mending the boat.

Planning for the unexpected is impossible; we planned for the predictable. It was amazing how much we were able to fit into the boat. I was reminded of the miracle of loaves and fishes.

What miracles might we see on our way to Paradise?

'Late in the summer,' Brendán wrote, 'we finally set sail.'

I was an old man being allotted enough years to fulfil God's purpose.

Only an old man would dare undertake such a voyage; the young have too much to live for.

'The weather was kind at first; God gave us a chance to accustom ourselves to the boat. In bad weather we would have to shorten sail and prepare for constant bailing, but while we cruised pleasantly along under a radiant sun our spirits were high.'

Once the monks were out of sight of land their excited chatter dwindled to a murmur, then faded into silence.

The subtle silence which contains the singing of all things.

Brendán was relying on Mernoc to guide them to the islands marking the gateway to Paradise. Fionn-barr's son had given a detailed description of the islands. They were far out in the Western Sea, he said, but he was certain he could find them again.

Brendán and his crew sailed along the coast for several days and saw a number of islands, but none that answered to Mernoc's description.

Only then did I begin to question Mernoc's story. Perhaps I had been too eager to believe him for my own reasons.

If he was on an ordinary fishing trip when he found them, why had he gone out so far in the first place? The Altraighe were coastal fishermen.

One question led to another in my mind. What had caused the long estrangement between himself and his father? I did not really know

Mernoc; what if he was inclined to lie in order to aggrandise himself? Such storytelling was not unknown among the Gael.

Might our expedition be based upon some wild tale of Mernoc's, and his father's desperate but understandable eagerness to believe him?

But what about the fragrant cloak?

Brendán would not confront Mernoc in the presence of the monks. The only man who could answer those questions was Fionn-barr, at Ard Fert.

Brendán debated with himself about turning back but decided against it. God had brought them this far, for whatever reason. Faith would take them the rest of the way.

It was a lot to ask of faith, even mine. Yet part of me longed to have one last great adventure. And a larger part of me cherished a dream I could not forsake.

'Having committed to the voyage, we sailed on,' Brendán wrote in his journal.

He made a point of talking to Mernoc as often as he could, trying to sound out the man. Fionn-barr's son was almost as fair-haired as his father and had a narrow face with a pointed chin. It might have been an honest face.

"Tell me again about the islands you found," Brendán urged.

"There were three of them close together, covered with flowers. When I went ashore, at first I thought they were Paradise. Only later did I observe that they formed a formation like the head of a spear, with the tip to the west. At sunset the spear pointed along a broad golden road leading over the sea."

The story sounded plausible enough; anyone living on the west coast of Ireland had seen the golden path of the sunset many times.

The human yearning to believe is very strong.

Aboard the boat Brendán had a larger crew than ever before; a diverse lot of personalities. They came from various backgrounds; from chieftainly families and slaves taken in war; from farmers and fishermen and artisans. All had one thing in common. They were Irish and liked to talk.

While they were counting out the portions of food for the day, Fursu said wistfully, "I wish we had brought some soft fruits. My mother picked them for me when I was a little boy and I ate them by the handful. I don't know why I stopped."

Liber replied, "Children think the way of life they know is the only way. Then as they grow up, they rebel against it like the chick rebels against the egg. They try to crack the old way apart and make everything new. But I can tell you this, young man: when you're my age, you will long to return to the life you rejected in your youth."

"I don't want to go back that far. Just to the day when Ruan fell overboard, so I could do things differently."

"Regret is no good, lad."

"It serves a purpose," said Fursu. "It's God's way of punishing us."

Cerball noticed Brendán leaning on the gunwale of the boat, gazing down at the water. The other monks were engaged in conversation but Brendán was alone. Brendán seemed to prefer being alone, which was puzzling.

Solám asked Gowrán, "Do you suppose Brother Abbot is lonely?"

Gowrán looked towards the man in question. "Brendán, lonely? I don't think so. He's not a lonely person by nature, only a solitary one. I'm like that. The only time I'm lonely is when I'm in a crowd. That's when I feel separate from others."

Solám later confided to Moenniu, "Brother Abbot is lonely but he won't admit it."

"How can one be lonely who always has God at his elbow?" the other monk inquired.

After an interminable time at sea, when we had almost given up all hope, Iasconius appeared again. Aedgal was

the first to observe the great barnacled back rising out of the water. We heard a strange, unearthly song echo through the sea. Soon the giant fish was joined by others; his whole family, it seemed. They disported themselves around the boat, diving down and rising up, splashing the waves with their immense tails as if they were truly glad to see us.

Next a great flock of seabirds arrived. Some came down to the water to feed; others circled above Iasconius and his kin, calling to us in raucous voices that were also songs.

"Look!" cried Anfudán. "There are gulls among them. We must be nearing land."

At these words Iasconius half lifted his huge bulk out of the water. I could see his tiny round eye, almost hidden below a drooping brow. The eye looked at me with amusement.

How inconsequential I felt beneath that gaze. From that moment and for the rest of my life, I became as humble as God wanted me to be.

When Crosán said, "Look, he wants us to follow him," I thought he was making one of his jokes.

It was true. Iasconius swam ahead of us like a pilot boat, leaving a wake we could follow. The wind was minimal but my crew took up their oars with renewed energy and we set off after our friend. His clan and their retinue of birds joined us in the procession.

Man and boat and fish and bird and wind and wave.

As a child I had pestered Bishop Erc with endless questions. The one which upset him most had been this: "You say man is made in God's image. There are countless men, like blades of grass, and every blade of grass is unique to itself. So is God countless? And various?"

Now I knew the answer. Yes.

Yet there is only one.

Eventually all things merge into One.

CHAPTER 26

The large boat continued to sail along the Irish coast. When they could not find Mernoc's gateway they did not know which direction to take. "We shall put our trust in God," Brendán decided, "and head outwards. Perhaps that's what he wanted all along."

Grumbling broke out among the crew. It began with Tarlách. "Fionn-barr's son has failed us and possibly put our lives at risk. We should throw him overboard and let him swim home."

Brendán said, "If you made an honest mistake would you want to be thrown overboard?"

"How do we know it was an honest mistake?"

"How do we know it wasn't?"

During this exchange Mernoc pulled his hood over his head and sat as low as he could on the rowing bench.

Brendán sat down beside him. "I'm not going to ask if you really saw the gateway, Mernoc. Your father believed you and I believed you; that's why we're here, and why we shall go on. Believing is as important as what one believes in. Faith itself has weight and value."

Mernoc peered out from under his hood. "I don't understand, Brother Brendán."

"I'm sure you don't. That's why you're here: to learn."

At Brendán's behest, the monks sang. Rich monastic voices ringing towards the heavens, praising the Lord and imploring him to have mercy on them. When the wind was right, their music carried a long way.

They could not spend all their time singing. They were afloat on the Western Sea, the reputedly endless expanse that marked the rim of the world. The weather was rarely benign and often brutal. Great waves towered over the gunwales and drenched the monks with icy salt water. They bailed almost as much as they rowed.

When Brendán announced they would make their first landfall on an unfamiliar strand and take on fresh water, the monks were relieved.

After our great journey I heard it claimed that we had fasted for forty days before we set sail. We were monks, not fools; we could not have managed the boat after forty continual days of fasting.

I also heard it claimed that our voyage lasted for seven years. That too was impossible, though I could not be sure of its exact duration. On the sea one loses a sense of time. We were aware of day and night but had no bells to ring the canonical hours. When the sky was clear at night I consulted the map of the stars, and sometimes discovered we had been sailing in an immense circle for many days. We put ashore in a number of places where nothing of interest happened, so no incident stamped itself on my brain.

All I know is that we were away for a very long time.

'Our final destination was the earthly paradise of which the Bible tells,' Brendán wrote in his journal, 'where the trees are heavy with fruit and the sun always shines. We kept that image in our hearts through all our vicissitudes.'

Except for Solám and Fursu, we were not young men, and we were sorely tested. The long voyage had its effect on each of us. Plump Moenniu grew lean and sinewy. Anfudán learned to be less hasty, more restrained. Cerball replaced dangerous bravado with thoughtful caution.

And when weariness blurred the Navigator's vision, Fursu read the map of the stars for me.

'Towards the end of our journey the weather was savage. Bitter cold, fluctuating winds, mist and drizzle and rain; often all at once.'

Had any of my crew implored me to turn around and head for home I would have tried. To the everlasting credit of the brothers, they kept their nerve.

'When we were joined by the clan of Iasconius, we took it as a sign that deliverance was close at hand. Instead of the perfume of Paradise, however, we soon encountered an immense bank of fog.'

We could sense the bodies of the great fishes near us in the water. Their haunting music gave us comfort.

The wind had fallen off. The sodden sails hung limply. Brendán had the unsettling feeling that life ran in a circle and he had returned to a familiar moment in time. He looked towards the prow, half expecting to see Préachán there.

A hand tugged at Brendán's sleeve. "Do you know what this fog is, Brother Abbot?"

"I do not, Brother Gowrán."

"I believe it encircles the land we have been seeking all this weary while."

Gowrán believed. His faith had shape and weight.

"Take up your oars," Brendán called to the monks, "and row as you have never rowed before!"

With Gowrán, I chose to believe that Paradise lay ahead of us. My companions were good men in spite of their human weaknesses. They deserved Paradise. Whether I deserved it or not was another question. As we glided forward into the gloom, I had hope. Hope that the one dream I cherished in the depths of my heart would be waiting for me on that blessed shore.

Iasconius did not desert them. More of his clan joined the party, circling the boat until Brendán feared they might collide with one of the gentle giants in the fog. At his command, the rowers rested their oars.

"What do we do now?" Fursu wondered.

"Let's go on," said Dianách. Colmán agreed.

"Wait," Brendán told them. "Have you not yet learned patience? If we have to sit here all day, we shall not endanger our friends."

They waited.

One of the swimmers—a creature much smaller than Iasconius—leapt out of the water right beside the boat, clearly visible to the astonished monks. Up and up he went, his gleaming body painting a graceful arc on the air.

Like a symbol in a language we did not know.

He dived back into the sea with hardly a splash.

And the fog began to thin.

"Take up your oars," said Brendán. "But be careful to advance slowly."

The fog shredded; the unmistakeable outline of land appeared in the distance. Brendán began to chant, "The Lord is my shepherd . . ." The paean of gratitude was taken up by the monks. With all their might, they rowed towards the distant shore.

Aedgal shaded his eyes with his hand. When he saw a rocky beach strewn with boulders, he exclaimed, "There's our landing place, waiting for us!"

As soon as they were near enough, the more agile men clambered over the gunwales and splashed through the shallows.

Shouting. They did not know what words they cried. It was enough to be alive in that moment; in that place.

With the last of their strength they dragged the boat ashore.

Sechnall looked around. "Paradise," he said in a dazed voice. He sat down abruptly and put his head between his knees to keep from fainting.

The beach was overlooked by a low ridge crowned with scrubby trees. On the beach was an abundance of driftwood; some of it above tide line and dry enough to burn. Brendán ordered the brothers to collect enough wood to build a fire. "We need to gather our strength again before we do anything else."

Leaving the huddle of men on the beach, Colmán walked up the ridge. The stand of little trees along the crest had been twisted into bizarre shapes by the wind. They smelled almost but not quite like the pines he knew. Beyond them lay a rugged landscape composed of rocky ledges thrusting out of dense forest.

"We're here," Colmán said aloud. To assure himself it was true.

His voice was a stranger to the silence it shattered.

The answer was a cry unlike any he had ever heard. From somewhere in that rugged landscape came an inhuman scream of defiance.

Colmán swiftly drew his knife from his belt.

"Come back down here," Brendán shouted to him.

"But there's a . . ."

"Come back here! We need to stay together."

Reluctantly, Colmán returned to the beach. Moenniu was saying to Brendán, "If this is Paradise we should be safe."

Brendán gave him a sharp look.

If this is Paradise . . .

The tiny fire was blazing to life. The crackle and snap was familiar, and comforting. So were the voices of gulls scolding the invaders. But Brendán could not hear the belling of the silver-horned stags; not on this shore. The sound was different.

The smell of the air was different.

The strings of seaweed lying on the sand were different, and the sand itself was a different colour.

Even the light . . .

Paradise.

They did not spend their first night on the beach but made a camp on the ridge; the high ground. Colmán stood the first watch with his knife in his hand. Brendán observed the knife but said nothing.

In the morning the sun rose, singing, out of the sea.

Sunrise. Right here.

Brendán recorded in his journal, 'To commemorate our landing we searched for an appropriate stone. Upon its face we carved the ogham symbol for friendship, and the fish for Jesus Christ.'

Leaving Cerball and Tarlách to guard the boat—a precaution Gowrán scoffed at—the monks turned their backs to the east and explored for almost half a day without coming to the western shore of the island. They searched out stones to carve and leave as signposts so they could find their way back.

Ogham is a handy skill.

Machutus, who was fond of wine, was overjoyed to find grapevines growing wild. "If this were not Paradise it could be called the Island of Grapes!"

The seemingly limitless forest was interrupted by streams and lakes abounding with cranes, swans, geese, and ducks of every size and description. In the trees were sparrows and linnets and finches and a score of unfamiliar varieties in all the colours of the rainbow. Brendán observed glossy blackbirds with scarlet patches on their wings and large speckled thrushes with red breasts; he saw four different types of hawk and a vast flight of pigeons that blackened the sky.

Of course it was Paradise. There was nothing comparable in all the world.

When half a day had passed, they headed back towards the boat for the night. Cerball listened in open-mouthed envy to the sights they described.

Tarlách was less impressed. "If this is Paradise," he said, "why didn't you see any other people? You can't tell me we're the only men who ever made it to Heaven."

"The answer is simple enough," Gowrán assured him. "Paradise must be large enough to hold every good person who will ever be born."

The following morning they launched the boat and sailed further down the coast, then went ashore and continued exploring. This time they caught a reassuring glimpse of human beings peering at them from behind trees; bronze-skinned, black-haired, with features unlike those of the Celts.

In his travels, Brendán had met people of other colours. In a soft voice and with many inviting gestures he tried to persuade the bronze people to come out in the open, but they ran away. "Obviously Paradise contains people of every race," he said to the monks. "We should meet some of our own soon."

'For forty days we wandered this magnificent wilderness,' wrote the abbot of Clon Fert. 'We made camp on the banks of a wide river whose waters bore thousands of river-hyacinths. In a different place on a different morning we awoke to the cooing of a thousand doves. We experienced every season in swift succession, moving between the heat of summer and bitterest winter.'

In fact we built more than one drystone shelter against the climate. As might be expected, Tarlách constantly complained about the weather.

'No matter where we roved, we saw the strange and wonderful. But in spite of our most patient efforts we were unable to converse satisfactorily with the inhabitants. They were shy at first but not hostile; they merely seemed astonished by us. We gave them gifts of the little we had.'

Eventually Brendán discovered a few sounds and signs which some of the bronze people appeared to understand. He and Gowrán attempted to talk to an elderly woman with sad, liquid eyes. She laughed at everything they said. At last they gave up in defeat.

Gowrán remarked, "She must have misunderstood. When we asked her where we could find God she said . . ."

"I know what she said. 'Everywhere.' "

"Can it be that simple, Brother Abbot? It sounds almost pagan."

Brendán nodded wordlessly.

"How are we to find him, then?" Gowrán wanted to know. "If he is here—and I have no doubt that he is—why doesn't he appear to us?"

My gift is intuition. Intuition had led me to accept Tarlách as an important part of the whole; without him we might still be wandering in . . .

In the abbey of Clon Fert, Brendán laid down his quill and rubbed his burning eyes.

Almost time for Vespers, thank God.

A monk exhaling the odour of boiled eels spoke at his shoulder. "No matter how carefully you choose your words, Brother Abbot, whoever copies your manuscript may change a few of them. And the next copier may change more. It has been my observation that people often think they can improve on someone else's writing."

Brendán shoved his stool back before the monk could read what he had just written, and looked up. "Is that what you do, Brother Tarlách? Change the Gospel of the Lord in order to improve it?"

"Never! I was merely saying what I know to be true of mankind in general."

"Why would anyone make a copy of my journal?" Brendán inquired.

"I seem to recall you promised to send one to Gildas."

The abbot shook his head with rueful amusement. "You

forget what you should remember, and remember what I'd as soon forget."

"Does that include your promises? I would have thought better of you," Tarlách said reproachfully.

"What I've written has meaning only for me, but a copy will be made for Gildas." Noting the suddenly wary expression on his friend's face, Brendán added, "I'll assign it to one of the other brothers, I wouldn't want to add to your work. First I have a little more to do on the manuscript. Not now, however. Will you walk with me to the chapel, Brother?"

Chapter 27

"Will you walk with me, Brother?" Brendán had said to Tarlách that day; that radiant summer day when Paradise was in full bloom around them. Side by side they strolled away from the other monks. Once they were out of earshot Brendán said bluntly, "Do you believe this is Heaven?"

Tarlách rubbed his nose with his sleeve.

"Tell me the truth," Brendán urged.

"I don't believe it."

"All right," said Brendán.

"And I don't think you do either, or you wouldn't have asked me that question. We've come all this way for nothing, haven't we?"

All this way for nothing.

Brendán's smile mingled sadness with serenity. "On the contrary, Brother Tarlách, during our voyage we've received everything we need. Perhaps not what we want, but what we need. We shall go home much richer than we left."

When I told my companions we were returning to Ireland each man responded in his own way. Young Fursu was the most reluctant; he would have gone on sailing to the ends of the earth if we let him. Those who were closer to my age pretended disappointment. But I saw the gladness in their eyes.

Brendán wrote, 'On our return journey there were none of the unpleasant incidents we had endured before. The weather was cold but clear for the most part, and the wind sped us on our way. We spent a peaceful Christmas and Epiphany with the community of Ailbe. Some of the brothers wanted to stay longer but Ailbe was too wise to agree. "You have your own place," he told us.

'I never appreciated Ireland until I sailed away. My voyages were always composed of two parts, and returning home was the better half. The brothers agreed with me. Upon entering the bay of Tra Lí we lowered our sails, shipped our oars, and knelt in the boat to offer prayers of thanksgiving.'

The miracles I had seen were mine to see. A different person might have seen something else, but I must look out of the eyes God gave me.

And I walk in the radiance of God.

Not every day, alas, and not as fully as I wish. There are still times when I worry, brood, desire, despair. The burdens of humanity remain with me, yet I lessen them by visiting the sacred place which is partly within my own soul.

I live in the here and now, wearing this skin, walking this earth, yet I am also living in eternity, where I shall be forever. Even after the sun and moon fall down.

With the passage of time my spirit becomes ever more lightly tethered to my body. For brief moments I can almost touch the incomprehensible yet perfect pattern that underlies Creation.

Humans are not true creators. We cannot make something out of nothing as God did in the beginning. We only can imagine that which already exists in some form. Because we live in a patriarchal society we envision God as an all-powerful father. We think of him as wrathful and jealous and compassionate because we are familiar with those emotions. We imagine Heaven as Earth Perfected.

We get everything wrong.

At night my sweet God talks to me. Sometimes, with an old man's foolishness, I think it is the cry of seagulls, but there are no seagulls at Clon Fert. Surely I of all men know the authentic voice of God. Have I not heard it singing a thousand times? In the sun and the sea, in the wind and the waves. The old woman was right. God is everywhere.

The good brothers worry about me. They consider my age an infirmity. They do not understand that the flesh is being abraded from the spirit, setting it free. As Fionn-barr said, death is the whole point of life. And life, from beginning to end, with all its fleeting beauty and certain pain, is an education.

An education is always intended to prepare one for what comes next.

We had spent the day sailing before the storm, watching for a place where we could put ashore. We began to fear we might have to spend the night on open water. Shortly before sunset Aedgal called our attention to a stark black rock rising from the sea like an accusatory finger.

As we drew nearer we could make out the figure of a man crouched at the base of the rock. He was half in and half out of the water, being cruelly attacked by the pounding waves and even the rags he wore. The wind lashed his face with his shredded cloak but he made no effort to protect himself.

Over the gale we could hear his shrieks of pain.

"An unfortunate survivor of shipwreck," Solám declared.

We bent to the oars and made all speed to offer assistance. When we reached the rock there was no landing place but we edged as close as we dared. The condition of the poor stranded creature was dreadful to behold. His emaciation was evident through his tattered clothing. He must be near death from starvation.

In the language of Rome I called to him, "Reach out your hand and we will bring you into our boat."

He raised his head and looked straight at me. I have never seen such agony on a human face. His sunken eyes were pools of pain. "You cannot help me," he said in the same language. "Go away and leave me to my fate."

"Never!" I leaned as far as I could towards him. "Extend your hand."

Instead he made a weak downward gesture, calling my attention to his body. For the first time I noticed heavy iron chains around his torso and ankles, holding him affixed to the stone. Incredibly, the chains appeared to have rusted in place.

Satisfied that I realised his predicament, he dropped his head onto his breast again and sagged against the chains.

The waves were rising. The boat shuddered with their force. If we remained where we were for much longer, our vessel would be dashed to pieces against the rock.

"We have tools that can break your shackles," I called desperately. "You have only to reach for them, but you must hurry!"

Hearing my words, he lifted his head one more time. His face was smeared with his own blood. When he spoke his voice seemed to come from very far away, some lightless cavern of the human soul. "You do not understand," the suffering man said. "I am he who was called Judas Iscariot."

Brother Machutus gasped aloud. "That cannot be!"

Yet I had no doubt. I was looking into those eyes.

"What you see here is not punishment," said the captive, "but the ineffable mercy of the Lord. This is the escape I am allowed from sunrise to sunset on every Sabbath during the seasons of Christmas and Easter. This is a veritable paradise compared to the tortures I suffer otherwise. For the rest of eternity I writhe in the blazing bowels of Hell, being smelted like lead in a pot."

Across the bitter sea, across the agony of centuries, I gazed at that face. That pitiful face.

The ineffable mercy of the Lord.

Tears rolled down my cheeks.

"I can tell that you have a kind heart," said the man called Judas, "and there is something you can do for me. Intercede with the Lord Jesus on my behalf. Ask that I be granted one additional day on this rock each year, in honour of our meeting."

We bowed our heads and began to pray.

When I looked up again he was gone. The rusted chains hung loose.

Brendán's lips moved silently as he scribed the final words on the vellum. 'After we landed our battered boat on the strand of Tra Lí for the last time, I went alone to Diadche. God spoke to me on the mountain.

'God. Not a, or the.

'God. Who is All.'

The fate of the tragic individual chained to the rock is the exception to my rule of relating incidents when I remembered them. It is right to conclude with him; he is never far from my thoughts. I suspect that God's purpose in all my voyaging was to arrange our meeting.

The lesson of Judas is this: the punishment will be in proportion to the sin.

The message of Christ is this: every sin can be forgiven.

The bounteous land we found was not Paradise, nor did it hold the dream I have cherished for so long. All right. Through the ineffable mercy of Our Lord I know that Paradise still lies ahead of me. On the other side of the dark.

But I am afraid of the dark.

Historical Note

On the sixteenth of May in the Year of Our Lord 576, Brendán died in the abbey of Annagh Down, where the nuns had been caring for him in his extreme old age. A royal chariot transported his body back to Clon Fert for burial.

During the sixth century, more than three thousand students, many of them from Britain and the European continent, attended the great monastic colleges of Ireland, including Clon Ard in Meath and Clon Fert in Galway. In institutions like these the flame of literacy was kept alive through the Dark Ages.